Cruel Boss: Dark Mafia Romance

Alice Knight

Published by Alice Knight, 2024.

This is a work of fiction. Similarities to real people, places, or events are entirely coincidental.

CRUEL BOSS: DARK MAFIA ROMANCE

First edition. January 14, 2024.

Written by Alice Knight.

Also by Alice Knight

Table of Contents

When first-year resident Daisy Taylor gets involved in the criminal world after a terrible encounter at a park shooting, she must do everything she can to outsmart the mafia don: Alessandro Bosio. Determined to free from his clutches, Daisy must use every trick up her sleeve. **But can she resist the explosive attraction between them long enough to escape?**

Alessandro Bosio may be the most feared mafia don in Las Vegas, but as a single father to his six-year-old son, he has a weakness that his enemies would not hesitate to target.

After his wife was killed by a rival mafia organization, he made it his top priority to find the man responsible and to protect his son at all costs. Getting romantically involved is not in his plans - especially not with the doctor he's holding hostage to save his son's life after a gunshot wound... But there's just something irresistibly powerful about Daisy, even if her fiery personality annoys him to no end.

Leave it to Alessandro to kidnap a doctor; leave it to Daisy to capture a criminal's heart.

CHAPTER 1

A LESSANDRO
"Look daddy!"

"Wow, bud. That's awesome!" I didn't even need to look up from my phone to know that that was my son's voice. I think something happens to you when you become a parent, it's like your ears are programmed to pick out the exact tone of voice of your child instantly. There could be a tornado, an explosion, ten other screaming kids in the sandbox, and I could still pick Ty's voice out perfectly clear as if we were sitting in silence. I could tell by the pitch in his voice when he called for me whether he was tired or hungry or just wanted to play or if something was really wrong. That's the one that would be burned in my mind forever.

Perhaps it was some superhuman skill you got when you became a parent, but I had a hunch it was more related to how hyper vigilant I had become around him in the months since his mother had been gone. Just thinking about Talia's murder sent rage pulsing through my veins, and the fact that we hadn't caught the guy yet just made it all the more excruciating. It had been six months. Six damn months since I came home from a business trip to a voicemail that said I needed to come to the hospital immediately. Six months since Talia's mother cried in my arms in a filthy trauma center, recounting how she had found her daughter unconscious on our bedroom floor. Six months since my son had watched his mother be beaten nearly to death in our own home, since they had told me that the bruises

2

on her face had made her unrecognizable. Six months since the grief-stricken doctor had told me that there had been an awful mistake and Talia had died on the operating table. She could have survived her injuries, but something had gone wrong with the anesthesia and they hadn't been able to revive her.

I had been completely blindsided. They told me she was going to be okay—accidents like that aren't supposed to happen in the hospital. They were supposed to save people, they were supposed to save my wife. I was so blind with rage that I nearly killed the surgeon right there, slamming him against the wall with my hand at his throat. It wasn't until I heard Ty's voice floating through the chaos that I snapped back to reality. Every eye in the trauma center was on me, including the big blue eyes of my five-year-old, that matched his mother's exactly. If I did that, Ty would grow up without both of his parents. With Talia gone, Ty's well-being was solely in my hands, and I needed to put that first. With nearly every ounce of restraint in my body, I dropped the surgeon to the ground and walked towards Ty, scooping him up in my arms and holding him tightly against my chest.

My best friend Joe was also my lawyer, and in the following weeks, he settled things with the hospital quietly. I couldn't handle things the way I wanted because it had become such a public case. Records were sealed and I didn't even know the name of the doctor who had made the mistake. Because the local police knew my reputation, they kept a close on me, and if I even drove within a few miles of the hospital, I could expect to get stopped. They were tolerant because they knew I had been through a horrible tragedy, but they weren't taking any chances of me retaliating on the hospital.

This was why I hated dealing with the police. They only complicated matters and stood in the way of true justice being served. I had always kept them out of my business, mostly so they couldn't shut me down, but it hadn't been my choice this time. My mother-in-law had found Talia and called the police, and now I was bound by all of this political tape.

I had to resign myself to the fact that she wouldn't have even been in the hospital if it hadn't been for the men who attacked her in the first place. At least I could get my hands on those men. The only problem was, I had no idea who they were. I had heard rumors through the mafia world, but nothing concrete. I was close, though, and God help them when I did find them.

The last few months had been a nightmare trying to balance being there for Ty and searching for Talia's killers. I knew how badly my son needed me, but I couldn't rest until I could hold somebody accountable. Thank God we had Joe and Emily in our lives. Joe had been my best friend for years, and his wife Emily had been an absolute saint the last few months. She took care of Ty when I couldn't so that I didn't have to hire a nanny. Our lifestyle wasn't conventional by any means, but at least Ty had all kinds of people around him who loved him.

— ⟨∾⟩ —

Talia's mother was around occasionally, but I knew she blamed me for her daughter's death. How could she not? I should've been there, it was my job to protect her. She visited Ty when I was out of town on business most of the time, and it was probably better for both of us that way. She had never liked me all that much, and now in wake of what had happened, the wedge between us was even worse. Talia's father had worked under mine for years as a Capo, and our marriage had been a business transaction. It differed from other arranged marriages though, because we actually cared for each other. Talia was a perfect wife, and an even more incredible mother. She and I were great friends and got along amazingly well. We both understood our roles, and while I wouldn't say she had been the love of my life, I deeply cared for her. I missed her companionship every single day and sometimes, the weight of the guilt I felt for not saving her was crushing.

———— ⟨∾⟩ ————

I wiped the sweat off my brow and glanced up towards Ty. His shoulders were already getting red in the blistering Vegas sun and I realized I had forgotten to put any sunscreen on him. Damn it. This was the kind of thing I sucked at. I could take Ty on all kinds of adventures, teach him how to play sports, roughhouse—but it was the day-to-day things that he needed that just escaped my mind. Like the fact that I needed to plan twenty extra minutes to get him to school each morning just to wait in the drop-off line. Or that it wasn't a good idea to let him watch zombie movies with me and Joe because he'd wake up with nightmares. Or where we kept the children's Tylenol, and once I found the damn stuff how much did I give a six-year-old?

———— ⟨∾⟩ ————

"Five more minutes, Ty," I called, just as my phone started ringing. The name of a contact of mine in New York flashed on the screen. I'd been trying to get a hold of him for the last several days about a lead he had given me.

"Do we have to?" Ty whined.

I answered the phone quickly, not responding to Ty. "Marco?"

———— ⟨∾⟩ ————

"Alessandro, hey. Is this a good time?"

"Yeah man, what's up?" I shoved my fingers through my hair in anticipation. Marco worked with a crime family that pretty much ran the entire East Coast. If my guy had ties anywhere over there, he would know about it.

———— ⟋⟍ ————

"I'm not positive about any of this, so I don't want you to get your hopes up, but we might have a lead. I met with a supplier yesterday who spent some time out west. He was in Vegas a few months ago working with Los Chavos, a new group in La Eme, and some young kid was running his mouth about a job they did."

La Eme? This was a Mexican Mafia hit? That didn't seem right.

———— ⟋⟍ ————

"Our supplier was asking me about it because the kid was specifically bragging because they took out the wife of an Italian Don." The blood ran cold in my veins.

"You think I'm dealing with a street gang?" My voice was hoarse. I never had any issues with them before, but that story his supplier told was pretty specific. It had to be about Talia.

"I don't know, but I trust this guy, Alessandro. I don't think he's yanking us around." Marco's voice was even. "You need to watch your—"

I didn't get a chance to hear the rest of what he said because the park was filled with the shrill sounds of screams and panic and the pulsing of a machine gun.

———— ⟋⟍ ————

"Daddy!" Ty shrieked, looking around the playground for me frantically. I had only taken a step forward when I saw his little body jolt and the red of his blood seeping through his T-shirt. All the wind was sucked out of me like I had been shot myself. This couldn't be happening.

———— ⟋⟍ ————

The world seemed to slow down around me, and I felt like I was moving through cement to try to get to him. Panicked mothers and fathers were pushing their children out of the way and taking cover wherever they could. Others had been hit and the park quickly turned into pure madness. The shooting stopped as suddenly as it had begun and screeching tires peeled out from the front of the playground. I caught a quick glimpse of the car, but I was so focused on getting to my son that I could hardly retain any of it.

When I finally broke free of the crowd and got to Ty, a woman was leaning over him, putting pressure on his wound. She reached up with one hand to check his pulse.

"Come on buddy, stay with me," she whispered, pushing some of his blonde hair out of his eyes. I could hardly look at him lying there, my heart stabbed with pain, and I was almost frozen with fear. I should do something, but I didn't know what to do. My mind couldn't process what needed to happen. I couldn't do this, not again. I couldn't lose my son, too.

I fell to my knees next to her, and she noticed me for the first time.

"Is this your son?" the woman asked, glancing up at me. Her tone was even as she kept her hand on Ty's wound. I heard her words, but I couldn't seem to formulate any of my own, so I just nodded.

"I'm a doctor at St. Luke's. He's going to be okay, but I need you to call an ambulance. We need to get him to the hospital." Her lips turned into a soft, sympathetic smile, and for a brief moment, I believed this random woman in the park.

Her mention of the hospital jerked me back to reality. She wanted me to call an ambulance, but I couldn't do that. There wasn't a shot in hell I was going to take Ty back to the same hospital where my wife died. I didn't trust them in the slightest. I needed another plan, and fast.

———— ᚖᚖ ————

"No." I shook my head wildly. "No hospitals."

The woman's face twisted in confusion. "Are you crazy? We need to get him to a hospital so he doesn't bleed out. The bullet is still inside of him."

Fuck. She was right, I needed to do something and I could already hear police sirens. I needed to get Ty out of here safely before they got here and blocked my chance at retribution again. What was I going to do? If I didn't get Ty help soon, he could die, but I certainly couldn't wait around here or take him to the hospital. Then it hit me.

———— ᚖᚖ ————

"You said you're a doctor, right?" I asked, my voice cracking with emotion.

"Yes but—" she started.

Without thinking, I pulled my gun out of my waist band.

The woman's eyes widened. "What are you doing?"

"You're coming with us," I growled, keeping the gun pointed at her while I scooped Ty into my arms.

———— ᚖᚖ ————

"You can't do this." She glared, but moved compliantly as I ushered her towards my car.

"Shut up!" I tried to control my breathing and get ahold of myself. Ty's life depended on me. He stirred slightly in my arms.

"Dad..." His cry killed me, but it was a tremendous relief he was conscious again.

"It's okay, buddy. I've got you. Everything is going to be fine," I tried to soothe.

"We have to get him to a hospital, he's going to die." The woman glared at me.

I opened the door and laid Ty on the seat. "You're going to keep him alive, and if you don't..." I narrowed my eyes at her. "I'll kill you."

CHAPTER 2

DAISY

This was the exact reason I never ran in that park. Well, maybe not the exact reason, but only because I couldn't have dreamt up something like this happening in my wildest dreams.

"You know this is illegal, right?" I hissed at the man driving the car. He chuckled, locking eyes with me in the rearview mirror as he weaved in and out of traffic. I had no idea where we were going, and we were now in a part of the city I had never seen before. Judging by the man's reaction and the gun he still had trained on me, he knew exactly how illegal this was, and he just didn't care.

The little boy, Ty as his psychotic father had called him, groaned from the seat next to me. His bleeding had stopped for the most part, but he kept fading in and out of consciousness. That meant the bullet was probably lodged in an artery or something blocking his blood flow. "You know your son is going to die if we don't get the bullet out soon."

"Then get it out," he growled, narrowing his eyes at me in the mirror.

"In a moving car?" I shrieked. "You really are out of your mind. Especially with driving like yours."

He glared, glancing back at Ty. "We're almost there, just keep him stable."

I threw my arms in the air in exasperation. Did he think I was some kind of magician? I had no supplies, no medication, I was hardly wearing more than a sports bra from my run in the park. Who knew what kind of germs were in the back seat of this guy's car, and if he didn't stop jostling me around, I might vomit. This was hardly an ideal place to be trying to save his son.

"Damn it." The man banged the wheel, honking his horn at the stonewall of traffic. "There's a jam, you're going to have to do it here."

"I can't." I shook my head definitively. I had just barely graduated for crying out loud. I had only seen bullets removed, never actually done it myself. "I'm not even a real doctor!"

"What did you just say?" He spun around in his seat, his eyes like daggers.

"I'm just a first year resident. I graduated in December. I can't do this." My voice was tight with emotion, everything starting to catch up to me. I had been moving on pure adrenaline before, and it was quickly fading as the reality of my situation sunk in. I have been kidnapped by a crazed man who thought I could save his son. Surely he'd kill me now.

The man groaned in frustration, glancing back between Ty and me. His next move completely shocked me. He put the gun down, tears welling up in his eyes. "Please," he begged. "You are my only shot."

My breathing settled a little bit as I stared back at him. The look on his face was one of sheer heart break and desperation. Was I actually feeling sorry for this guy? The same one who refused to take his son to a hospital and forced me into his car at gun point? The same one who had been nothing but hideous to me despite my efforts to save his son?

Damn it, Daisy. I sighed, realizing what I was about to do. How do you get yourself in situations like this?

"I'm going to need something sharp, I have to make the opening bigger." I collected myself, pretending I was in my operating room calling out orders.

The man nodded, reaching into his pant pocket and tossing a pocket knife back to me. It landed in my lap with a thud and I jumped.

"Okay." I was bewildered. "Anything with alcohol?"

"There is a latch in the back of the passenger seat. Everything you need should be in there."

My eyes widened as I looked in the smooth leather seam of the passenger seat. Sure enough, there was a small latch and when I turned it the entire thing swung open like a door. "Oh," I gasped, as a bottle of vodka, some towels, and a makeshift first aid kit fell out.

I looked back at him in horror. Why would he need this kind of thing in his car?

"For emergencies," he said flatly, as if reading my mind.

"What kind of emergencies require you to have a hidden compartment of medical supplies in your car?" I immediately thought better of asking the question once it was out of my mouth, but I couldn't seem to bite my tongue.

He glared at me. "Less talking, more saving."

I didn't need to be told twice. I grabbed one of the towels, placing it under Ty's wound.

"He won't feel any of this, right?"

I shook my head. "Not when he's unconscious, but he keeps coming in and out so I'm going to have to do it fast."

The man nodded, continuing to try to get us around the traffic. I had no idea where we were going, but I didn't care as long as we stopped moving. Unfortunately, if I didn't get the bullet out, Ty might not make it to wherever we were headed.

I quickly grabbed the bottle of vodka and poured it over the wound to clean it out. Ty didn't move, so I grabbed another towel and blotted it away. Now that it was clean, I could see a little better what I was dealing with, but the bullet was still so deep inside I couldn't see anything but a tiny speck of it.

Rummaging through the makeshift first aid kit, I found a pair of tweezers. I pressed the blade of the man's knife to Ty's skin and winced as the cut elongated. Ty still didn't flinch, which was good. I poured more of the alcohol on the wound and finally could see the bullet. I pried it open with one hand, and grabbed the tweezers with the other, moving as gently as I could. Every few seconds the man looked back at what I was doing as if he was trying to keep tabs.

My hands were shaky as I put the tweezers inside of Ty's wound, and I tried to calm myself. I pressed them firmly against the bullet, getting as best of a grip as I could and tugging gently. Soon, it broke free and came out completely intact. I let out a huge breath of relief, and set the tools quickly down.

Now that the blockage was removed, blood started spurting out of the wound.

"What the fuck is going on?" the man hissed, frantically. Both anger and concern were dripping from his lips.

"It's just from the blockage. He's okay, the bullet came out cleanly."

I couldn't believe I'd actually done that. I was so proud of myself I could hardly stand it. Unfortunately, the man didn't feel the same way.

"Why is he bleeding so much?"

"The bullet was lodged in him blocking his blood pathways. Once it's gone, the blood can flow freely. We just need to stop the bleeding and..."

The man got out of the car and slammed his door abruptly. I hadn't noticed we stopped until now. The door to the backseat opened and he scooped Ty up, grabbing the towel out of my hands and pressing it to his wound. "Let's go." He barked.

"Where are we?" I asked, only to be completely ignored. I had just saved his son's life, you would think he would be a little more grateful.

"Here." He thrust the towel back at me. "Keep pressure on it."

I had to fight the urge to laugh. I was the professional here, now he was ordering me around? This guy really was something. Nevertheless, he was right, we needed to keep pressure on the wound and the two of us arguing wouldn't help Ty at all.

The man fumbled with his keys, eventually leading us into a warehouse type building. He burst through the door, and a few men looked up from the table they were sitting at.

"Jesus, Alessandro, what is going on?" One of them rushed towards us abruptly.

"Drive-by at the park." The guy said flatly. Apparently his name was Alessandro. He sat Ty down on the couch, taking the towel from me again and holding it to the wound in his son's abdomen.

"Ty was hit?" The other guy's face turned white.

Alessandro nodded. "Once in the stomach. I think he's stable now though."

"What the fuck is all this blood from then?" another guy said, joining us by the couch.

"The bullet was blocking his blood flow," I jumped in to explain. "When I took it out, all of the backed-up blood was free so it just seems like he's bleeding a lot. He's going to be okay, really."

They all stared at me in stunned silence as if for the first time noticing my presence.

"Who is she?" The first guy we had seen nodded his head towards me.

"She's a doctor," Alessandro said. "She volunteered to help Ty."

I let out a sharp laugh. This guy either lived in some kind of alternate universe that only revolved around him or he was on some really good drugs. "Volunteered? More like you forced me into your car at gunpoint."

His friend rubbed the bridge of his nose. "Jesus, Alessandro. Please tell me she's kidding."

Alessandro didn't answer.

"Alessandro!" the guy barked again.

Alessandro threw his hands in the air in exasperation. "Well, what did you expect me to do, Joe? It wasn't like I could take him to the hospital. It was Los Chavos, I know it."

I frowned in confusion. He knew who did the drive-by? Who in the world was Los Chavos?

"La Eme?" the other friend snarled.

"Enough," Joe hissed. "We're not talking about this in front of her."

All of a sudden, Ty's body jolted. He started coughing and a few drops of blood appeared on his lip.

Damn it. The bullet must have hit something else.

"Help him!" Alessandro barked, tears springing to his eyes.

I bit my lip, trying to figure out what to do. Taking out the bullet had been easy, I could do things like that. This was totally different. He needed x-rays and an ultrasound and a tube in his chest. I couldn't do any of that, especially not here.

"Please let me call the ambulance," I begged. "They'll take care of him, I promise."

"No." Alessandro whipped out his gun again, pressing it to my temple and cocking it back. "You're going to do it."

I squeezed my eyes shut, a small tear escaping. Holy shit. He was going to kill me. This was where I was going to die, on the floor of this dirty warehouse, gross and sweaty from my run. What would my family say? Who was I kidding, they probably wouldn't even know what happened to me.

"Alessandro, you have to get a hold of yourself." Joe tried to calm him down. My breathing became shallow with my nerves. "Give me the gun."

"Not until she helps Ty." His menacing eyes were glued to me. I was too terrified to even look at him.

I took a deep breath, holding my hands up. "Okay. He needs a chest tube. The bullet probably pierced one of his organs and we need to get the blood out."

"Do it," Alessandro growled.

I looked around the room frantically for anything I could use. There was a straw on the table, it was flimsy and completely unsanitary but it would get the job done until I could convince Alessandro to get Ty to a hospital.

"I need the vodka and the first aid kit from the car."

"Get her what she needs," Alessandro directed the other guy. He took off for the door to get my supplies.

I moved towards Ty, pushing Alessandro out of the way. To my surprise, he didn't put up much of a fuss. I was so nervous I had to consciously stop my body from trembling. I shouldn't be doing this. We needed to get Ty to a hospital, not be putting some makeshift tube in his chest. But with Alessandro's gun pressed to my head, I didn't see much of a choice.

Alessandro's friend handed me the supplies from the car, and I poured the alcohol over the straw, hoping to kill off any germs that were on it. I felt around on his chest and abdomen, trying to figure out where the pressure was. I could feel it right in the center of his chest just below his rib cage. It wasn't the worst-case scenario, but it certainly wasn't the best either. Judging by the location, the bullet could've pierced his lungs or at least grazed one. I made a small incision over the area and blood started to come out quickly. I poured more alcohol over the incision and quickly worked the straw in between the folds. I had put a chest tube in countless times, but never like this. When I got it inserted about halfway in, I set it in place, holding my breath and hoping it would start drawing out the blood.

Everyone in the room watched on edge. Come on, Ty. Please.

At first I thought my eyes were playing tricks on me, but a small drop appeared at the top of the drain and then several more. A steady trickle started to come out and the pressure in Ty's chest deflated and he seemed to settle down.

Alessandro looked up at me. "He's okay?"

"For now." I nodded. "But this isn't going to hold forever. He's going to need a real chest tube, and medication, and somebody to monitor him. You really need to take him to the hospital."

"You have supplies to do all of that at the hospital?" Alessandro arched an eyebrow at me.

I nodded enthusiastically. Maybe I was finally getting to him. Suddenly, he turned to Joe.

"Take her to the hospital so she can get the supplies she needs, and bring her back here."

Joe nodded.

My eyes widened in horror. "Are you crazy? You can't do this. This is kidnapping, it's child endangerment. Your son needs a doctor."

Alessandro stood up, stalking towards me quickly. He stopped only inches from me, so close I could feel anger radiating off of him. "I've had about enough of that smart mouth of yours. He has a doctor. And if you want to live, I suggest you do what I say. Go to your precious hospital, get the supplies you need, and come back here and fix Ty. If anything happens to him, or you so much as utter a word of this to anyone at the hospital, I will put so much lead in you that you'll sink to the bottom of the Hoover dam. Are we clear?"

I sucked in a sharp breath, so terrified I couldn't speak. Who was this man?

He gripped my bicep tightly. "I said, are we clear?"

I nodded wildly, trembling with fear. I was in way over my head here.

CHAPTER 3

D AISY
　　My hands trembled the entire time that Joe drove me towards the hospital. I was so nervous I couldn't even speak, despite all the questions swirling in my mind. Joe fixed his stone-cold stare on the road, barely glancing over at me and getting me no relief whatsoever.

It didn't take a genius to know that whoever these guys were, they were involved in some pretty shady stuff. Alessandro carried a gun when he went to the park with this son, and he kept a gunshot wound kit hidden in his car "for emergencies". They had a warehouse in the middle of nowhere, and no one batted much of an eye when they found out that he had forced me to come with him. And now, he was using me to rob a hospital, which I was pretty sure could constitute as a felony. If I got caught, I wouldn't just be kissing my career goodbye, but staring down hard time as well. I had no idea what they were involved in, but I knew enough to know I wanted nothing to do with it. I had to figure a way out of here the first chance I got.

"Breathe," Joe instructed, glancing at me with a small smirk.

"What?" I asked in confusion, letting out a breath I hadn't realized I was holding.

"You keep holding your breath because you're so nervous. You're going to make yourself pass out," he said, handing me a bottle of water. "And if you don't get your nerves under control, the people at the hospital are going to see right through you."

"Maybe I want to tip them off," I grumbled. Joe's idea wasn't all that bad. If I passed out in the hospital, they would have to keep me there and check me out. It would at least buy me some time to figure out a better plan.

"I wouldn't do that if I were you. Alessandro doesn't make empty threats. If you lollygag around here and something happens to Ty, you'll regret it. And I'm guessing a pretty little thing like you wouldn't last 24 hours under Alessandro's torture. Trust me, princess, it's in your best interest to do exactly as he says."

A pit grew in my stomach, nearly causing me to throw up. Torture? "What kind of people are you?" I nearly whispered.

"The less you know the better. Especially if you have any wild ideas that Alessandro will let you go. If you know too much, there's no chance of that." Joe whipped into a parking spot in front of the emergency department. My heart was hammering so hard in my chest that I was pretty sure I could hear it out loud.

"How do you want to play this? Tell them I'm your boyfriend? Cousin? How well do you know these people?"

Tears welled up in my eyes. "Can't I just go and get you the supplies and then you let me go? I'll get you everything you guys need for Ty. Please, just let me go," I begged frantically. Alessandro was a monster, but maybe I could reason with Joe.

"You know I can't do that princess." He almost looked sympathetic. "Besides, I guarantee you Alessandro has men looking up every single detail about you right now. You wouldn't be free for long even if I did let you go."

Realization washed over me. There was no way out except to play his game and hope for the best. "He's going to kill me even if I save Ty, isn't he?"

Joe clenched his jaw. "Let's just get through this." His avoidance of my question was anything but reassuring.

I sucked in a sharp breath trying to psych myself up for this. To go in there, lie to my coworkers, and steal thousands of dollars worth of medical supplies. The only saving grace I had was that I knew how badly Ty needed it. I had taken an oath to help those in need, and though this was completely unconventional, maybe if I thought about it in that way, I could get through this.

I opened the car door, choking down my fears and determined to do what I had to do. Joe followed close behind me. I wasn't even two steps in the door before I ran into Dr. Bauer, my boss.

"Daisy! Thank God! I've been trying to get a hold of you all morning. There was a shooting at the park, we have eight victims. They need you in trauma immediately."

I winced at the mention of the shooting. I hadn't really even thought about there being other victims. I bit my lip gingerly. "I'm so sorry Dr. Bauer, I can't. I'm just here to get a few things out of my locker. I'm not in today."

He looked at me in disbelief. "What do you mean you can't? I know you're not in today, but it's all hands on deck."

I sighed heavily, trying desperately to think of a good enough excuse to give him. Before I even knew what was happening, Joe butted in.

"Dr. Bauer?" Joe stuck his hand out. "I'm Daisy's cousin, Joe. We had a death in the family and have to go out of town immediately. That's why she can't come in today." I nearly scoffed at the way he called me Daisy like he had known me my entire life. I had only met the guy an hour ago, but I had to admit he was a good actor.

"Oh I'm so sorry to hear that." Dr. Bauer frowned. "Daisy, take all the time you need."

"Thank you, Dr. Bauer." I smiled sheepishly. "I'm just going to get a few things out of my locker."

"Of course." He hurried off down the hall, leaving Joe and I standing there alone. Joe smirked, obviously pleased with himself.

I rolled my eyes at him. "You're a pretty good liar."

Joe chuckled. "I'm a defense attorney, I lie for a living. What can I say?"

"Wait here," I instructed, hurrying down the hall. I wanted to spend the least amount of time here as possible. I hated the thought of lying to Dr. Bauer like that, and everything about this just made me feel dirty.

I ducked into the supply closet and started stuffing things in my bag. I knew a few of the things I would need, but then I just started grabbing things randomly, just in case. This would be the easy part. Ty needed medication. Something for the pain and antibiotics to make sure it didn't get infected. I tossed in some sedatives and lidocaine just in case, also. It was going to be much more difficult to smuggle those out of here. I hoped he hadn't lost so much blood that he would need a transfusion, and that there wasn't much internal damage. It wasn't like I could sneak an ultrasound machine out of here. He seemed to be stable, but there was always a chance.

I tiptoed over to the pharmacy, not wanting to draw much attention to myself. Everyone seemed to be wrapped up in the chaos of the shooting, so I was able to get there virtually undetected.

The pharmacy tech was staring brightly at me when I got to the window though. "Hi Daisy, need something for one of the shooting victims?" She smiled brightly.

"Um, yes." I nodded. "Dr. Bauer wants to order a 35 count of oral amoxicillin and 18 of oxycodone."

She frowned. "He wants pills? That's odd, he's been ordering IV drips for most of his patients."

"It's a patient that's discharging. He wants to send him home on the medication."

"That makes sense." She nodded. "Let me just pull up my system..."

I glanced back at Joe while I waited for her to get on the computer. He winked at me as if he had something up his sleeve.

"Of course! The busiest day of the month and our systems are down." She huffed. "Why don't you just write the name of the patient here and I'll log it as soon as I can get the system back up and running?"

"Okay." I nodded, taking the pen from her and quickly making up a fake name. Had Joe really compromised the entire hospital pharmacy system? Who the hell were these guys and what were they capable of? The thought sent shivers through my body.

"Have a good day!" the pharmacy tech said as I hurried away.

I tucked the pills into my bag with the rest of the supplies and joined Joe at the front of the hospital.

"Ready to go?" he asked.

"Yes, let's get out of here."

Joe slung his arm around me. "We make a pretty good team, Mads."

I winced, squirming out from under him. "Don't call me that."

"Feisty," he chuckled. "You just might survive Alessandro Bosio yet."

CHAPTER 4

A LESSANDRO
    Daisy Marie Taylor. Twenty-six years old. Born and raised in St. Louis, Missouri. In a few months, she'd graduate medical school and she already had her Residency lined up at St. Luke's. Her father owned a pediatric practice in St. Louis, and both of her older brothers worked there. She volunteered at a local animal shelter, could run a marathon in four hours and twenty-three minutes, and she nearly drowned in her backyard pool when she was seven. Those were just some of the highlights; the file Q had amassed about her was overflowing with information, most of it interesting if not completely useless. I didn't really need to know that she worked at an orphanage in Africa, but reading all of this had certainly distracted me from the reality of the situation, and made her all the more intriguing.

I thumbed through a few of the pictures he had printed off for me, stopping on one in particular of her in a long black dress. She had her hair done up in curls, at a wedding of some sort. She was stunning, and I couldn't believe I hadn't noticed until now. Soft pink lips, honey colored hair and light brown eyes that looked like they could see down into the depths of your soul. Her smile was so big and bright it was almost blinding. Towering tan legs I could almost feel wrapped around my waist. I sure hoped she was a good doctor, it would be a shame to have to kill a woman that looked like that.

"Are you sure about this, Alessandro? We could take him to another hospital, it doesn't have to be—" Q ran his fingers through his hair. He obviously didn't agree with the way I was handling things, but it wasn't his kid and this wasn't his mafia group.

"We're not going to the hospital," I snapped definitively, halting any attempts he made to question me. "He'll be much more comfortable here anyway. And I can control the situation." There would be no fatal mistakes this time. And if there were, Daisy would be dead before her body even hit the floor.

"Right." Q let out a sharp laugh. "And what do you plan to do with the girl once all this is over? It's not like we can just let her go."

Q had a point. She would know too much about our operation, and about the attack. I couldn't let her go free, at least not without a high level of security on her at all times making sure she didn't go to the police. It would be costly, but it would be worth it to keep Ty safe. "Depends." I shrugged, not committing to anything yet.

"On?" Q pressed.

I glared at him, irritated that he wouldn't just let this go. "On whatever I fucking decide, Q. Just drop it."

Q narrowed his eyes as if there was more that he wanted to say, but he thought better of it.

Ty stirred slightly beside me. We had moved him over to the house while Joe and Daisy were gone, and he was already more comfortable. I could already tell he was doing better, some of the color returning to his cheeks, but I still wished they would hurry. He woke up briefly, even speaking to me before falling back asleep. It had mostly just been to tell me how bad his chest hurt and how thirsty he was, but it had been a tremendous relief just to hear his little voice. He didn't deserve any of this, and while I may not have pulled the trigger, it was my fault he was lying here with a hole in his abdomen. I could only imagine what Talia would say if she was here, and none of it was good. She had begged me for years to get out of the business for the sake of our family, and now it had gotten her killed and almost done the same to Ty.

When we had first gotten married, Talia understood what our marriage meant and accepted what our life would be like. It wasn't until after Ty was born that she started to have a change of heart. She wanted out. She wanted us to be a family far away from the violence and danger of the mafia, claiming it was no place to raise a child. I couldn't blame her, something changed inside of me when Ty was born too. The second I held him in my arms, my entire world became about protecting him and giving him the best life possible. Talia and I just had different ideas of what that was. I felt like there wasn't a safer place in the world for our son than one where he was surrounded by hundreds of men who loved him and would die for him. Today had been like a knife to my gut, and for a brief second I had considered that Talia may have been right. What if I wasn't cut out for this? What kind of Don couldn't even keep his own wife and son safe? How was I supposed to reassure the men and families in my ranks?

It was fleeting, though. I knew I was good at this shit. I had only been in charge for six years, and had already nearly transformed our family, and Talia's. The problem was, the better you were at this job, the more danger you attracted. Everyone wanted a piece of you, everyone was gunning for you. I still wholeheartedly believed that Ty was safest here. I just needed to find some way to fix this.

I had always been good at fixing things, taking care of the problems, but the only way I knew how to do that was to use more violence. I was all Ty had left now, so I couldn't make any rash decisions. Once I knew he was healthy and safe, I could start working on a plan of revenge.

I heard the front door to the house open and snapped Daisy's file shut on the coffee table. I could already hear her objections to my research on her and that wasn't a discussion I felt like having with her right now.

"You moved him?" She wasn't even two steps through the front door before she was harping on me. Jesus Christ, this girl was exhausting.

I narrowed my eyes at her. "Yes. I thought he'd be more comfortable here."

"He might not be stable enough to move yet, you could've ruptured the tube." Damn, I hadn't even thought about that.

"Well, if the tube came out of place, wouldn't that mean you didn't put it in securely enough?" Instead of admitting she was right, I lashed out.

She groaned, rolling those deep brown eyes at me. "Actually, no—"

"Enough," Joe snapped. "He's here now, so let's do what we have to do."

Daisy nodded, scurrying towards Ty. Why was she so inclined to do what Joe said and not me? Maybe she needed a reminder of who was in charge around here.

I opened my mouth to speak and let her have it, but was silenced by the sound of Ty's voice.

"Daddy?" He turned his head in all directions looking for me.

I knelt down next to Daisy. "I'm right here, bud. How are you feeling?"

"My chest hurts." He winced, tears bubbling in his eyes.

"I bet it does. I can help with that." Daisy smiled, pushing the hair out of his eyes and immediately morphing into Dr. Taylor instead of the feisty brat she normally was. I hung back as she got to work.

"You were at the park." Ty recognized her. His breathing was labored but he was more alert now than he had been before.

"That's right I was. And you were really brave. I definitely would have cried." Daisy gave him a million-dollar smile, getting some of her supplies ready.

"Crying is for babies. That's what daddy says." Ty cracked a smile.

Daisy rolled her eyes, as if she was already expecting me to be so callous. I hadn't actually meant it the way he had taken it, but now I looked and felt like an idiot. I had only said it to him a few times when he was having a fit about not getting his way, not about anything like getting hurt. Definitely not about getting shot.

"Well, I think you're brave regardless. I need to take this out of your chest and replace it so that it doesn't hurt so much, is that okay?"

"Is it going to hurt?" Ty asked, frowning in fear.

"It might a little bit," Daisy said sympathetically. "But we're going to do it really quick. And your dad is going to hold your hand the whole time and you can squeeze as hard as you want."

Ty cracked a small smile. "What if I squeeze so hard I break his fingers?"

"Even better." Daisy winked.

I felt a small smile creep across my face. She was really good with him, even if they were having fun at my expense.

"Okay." She nodded at me, and I moved up towards his head, taking his hand. I usually wasn't one to take orders, but something about the way she was giving them made me spring to action.

She rubbed a little bit of cream around the incision and put her fingertips at the base of the drain. "Ty, I'm going to give you a quick shot and then all you need to do is take a deep breath in and count backwards from 10. Think you can do that?"

Ty nodded.

"Great." She smiled. "You tell me when you're ready."

Ty hesitated for a second before finally giving her the go ahead. "Okay."

Daisy started immediately, giving him a shot next to the incision and rubbing it vigorously. After a few seconds she pulled the straw from the incision and Ty cried out.

"You're okay, Ty. Remember to count. Ten... nine..." she instructed, continuing to work on him.

"Eight." His voice was shaky and I could tell he was on the verge of tears.

I squeezed his hand in reassurance and started to count with him. "Seven... six...five...four..."

She moved quickly, her hands working confidently and inserting a real tube into where the straw had been. Ty squeezed my hand so hard his little body was shaking. Tears threatened to fall from his eyes, but he was being so tough.

"You're doing great, buddy," I coached. "Almost done."

"One more big breath in for me," Daisy said. I was in awe of how good she was with him. It was like they had been friends forever, and her presence was even starting to calm me down.

Ty did as she said. "Good. Three... two... and one." We all finished the last numbers together.

Daisy smiled wide, snapping her gloves off. "All done!"

"That's it?" Ty and I both said at the same time.

She nodded enthusiastically. "That's the hard part. Now I have some medicine for you to take that's going to make you feel a lot better."

I clenched my jaw in suspicion, and Daisy caught it immediately. "It's just something for the pain, and an antibiotic to fight off infection."

I nodded. "Hear that buddy? You're going to be feeling better in no time!"

"But you're going to need to rest. Lots of video games and movies for the next few weeks. Doctor's orders." She smiled, fastening some bandages around the drain to hold it in place.

"Why don't we get started on that now?" Joe smirked, coming into the room and turning the TV on. He plopped down on the couch next to Ty causing Ty to giggle.

"What? She said doctor's orders." He chuckled.

It wasn't even worth it. Ty was happy, and if Joe was with him keeping him occupied, I could get to work on finding out who was behind the attack.

I turned to Daisy. "I don't even know what to say besides thank you. I don't know what I would've done if something happened to him."

She looked surprised I even knew the words thank you. "He's going to need antibiotics twice a day for the next two weeks. I wouldn't give him the pain pills unless he absolutely needs it. It's a lot for his body to take."

I nodded, committing her instructions to memory.

"I need to get going now," she said sheepishly.

"Going?" I arched an eyebrow. "You're not going anywhere. At least until I figure out what to do with you."

"What are you talking about? You said if I saved him you'd let me go."

"What I said was if you saved him, I wouldn't kill you," I clarified.

Her face turned white as the reality of her situation sunk in. I really should just let her go, she had no business being here. Ty was stable now, and keeping her here would only get me into trouble. She didn't strike me as the type to run to the police, and I could always put one of our rookies on her to make sure she didn't. Why did I want her to stay? What the fuck was wrong with me? It was like I could see a train about to crash, but I could do nothing to stop it.

"Alessandro, please..." she stuttered.

"Q, can you show Daisy to a room upstairs?" I ignored her, as Q nodded.

"Alessandro, you can't do this!" she insisted, growing more and more infuriated by the second.

I smirked, with a sharp laugh. "Daisy, if you haven't figured it out by now, I can do just about anything I want. I appreciate what you did for Ty, but you can imagine that I can't just let you go now. I can't take the chance of you running to the police or telling someone what happened today."

"You're insane. Actually insane." She threw her hands in the air. "I swear to God I won't tell anyone anything. Please just let me go home."

A placating smile tugged at my lips. "I wish I could trust that, I really do. But I can't take that chance. I have to take precautions to protect my family."

"So what? You're going to keep me here forever?" she hissed, her eyes burning into mine with pure fire.

I shrugged, not having thought that far ahead. "Q, take her upstairs please."

"You're an asshole." She glared as Q grabbed her arm and led her towards the staircase.

It was peculiar that she wasn't afraid of me. I had held a gun to her head and kidnapped her this afternoon, but she was still as feisty and argumentative as ever. I wouldn't even let Talia get away with speaking to me the way that Daisy was, but something about her tenacity drew me in.

"She's right, you know," Joe chided. "Keeping her here is a dumb idea."

"I didn't ask."

Joe rolled his eyes, chuckling at me as I watched Q cart her up the stairs. He knew as well as I did I didn't need to keep her here. This wasn't about keeping her quiet, it wasn't about safety, it wasn't even about Ty. No, keeping Daisy was for my own benefit, and something told me I was going to enjoy every second of it.

CHAPTER 5

D AISY
     Just who exactly did Alessandro Bosio think he was? He couldn't keep me caged up here like some sort of animal. This was absurd, not to mention completely against the law. Call me crazy, but I didn't think that Alessandro had much regard for following the law anyways. He didn't have much regard for anything. The man walked around in some self-absorbed bubble having no clue that anyone existed outside of his own world. He was infuriating, and the worst part was, he seemed to see nothing wrong with the way he acted.

Did he honestly expect me to stay here? I had played along with his stupid game, putting my job and my freedom in jeopardy in the process, but now I had a life I had to get back to. If I didn't show up for work tomorrow... Shit. No one would notice. Joe had made sure of that when he told my boss that we had a death in the family. They had been planning for this from the very beginning, and I had been oblivious to it. No one would even know to look for me. My mom would know something was up if I didn't call in the next few days. I had to laugh about how she had been vehemently against me going somewhere like New York City or LA when I was choosing the hospital for my clinicals because it was so dangerous. Las Vegas had been a compromise, but little did she know... I talked to her last night, so it would be at least three days before she got concerned, and that was a long time to be trapped here with Alessandro. I could only imagine the things he could do to me in that amount of time. Joe's words about torture echoed in my mind.

The thought made my mouth go dry. The truth was, I knew next to nothing about Alessandro and what I did know was pretty terrifying. I didn't even know people like Alessandro existed in real life. He was the kind of thing nightmares were made of, and I had no idea what he was actually capable of. My anger at him slowly started to transform into fear as I realized the gravity of the situation. What kind of person carried a gun in his waistband when he went to the park with his son? Had a band of cronies hanging around ready and waiting to carry out his every whim? Collected a file of information on random people he had just met? What kind of man refused to call the authorities when his son was gunned down? A criminal. A felon. A monster.

I didn't want to wait around to find out what exactly Alessandro was, I had to find a way out of here, and fast. I rushed to the window, forcing it open. It took a lot of strength but I finally got it up and peeked my head outside. I was on the second story, but if I put the bedsheets together, I might be able to shimmy my way down. Alessandro's property was surrounded by trees so thick that I couldn't even wrap my mind around where we were. I couldn't see a road, or even a skyrise which was unusual for Las Vegas. With my luck, I would get lost out there and wind up right back on Alessandro's front steps. And even if I did manage to get away, he probably had more than enough information to track me down.

I steadied myself against the window sill, weighing my options. I could stay here and suffer through whatever Alessandro had planned or I could make a break for it and hope for the best. Why did it feel like choosing between the lesser of two evils?

"I wouldn't do that if I were you..." Alessandro's voice sent chills down my spine as I turned slowly to face him.

Alessandro was the quintessential bad boy. Despite his paralyzingly intimidating looks, I could see right through his charade. His dark eyes held all kinds of secrets that I wasn't sure I wanted to know. He hid behind a harsh attitude and colorful artwork on his forearms. I was willing to bet if you took that one size too small dress shirt off, he would have a chiseled chest full of tattoos as well. I could already see the swell of his muscles bulging underneath his shirt, and if I wasn't infuriatingly mad at what he was doing to me, I might have actually been turned on.

"Do what?" I gave him my best innocent smile. If it was games he wanted, it was games he would get. I had dealt with cocky, outspoken men my entire life, and if he thought he could get to me, he had another thing coming. Albeit the gun and violence were a little new to me, but I could handle him all the same. I had a feeling that the arrogance was something deeper in Alessandro and that was the part that made me uneasy. I had no idea what he was capable of, but I had already seen that he was willing to do whatever it took to get what he wanted.

He let out a sharp laugh, stepping towards me. He didn't stop until we were only inches apart. "Do you think I'm stupid, Daisy? I know you were thinking about running."

I bit my lip, trying to compose myself. Was I really that easy to see through? "I wasn't thinking of running."

Alessandro gave me a knowing smirk. "Good. Because you wouldn't make it to the road without a bullet in your head."

"What do you want from me?" I whispered, clenching my jaw. I kept my voice even, showing him no hint of what I was actually feeling inside. I wouldn't give him the satisfaction of knowing how badly he had shaken me.

"I came up here to offer you a proposition. And I guess an apology." He stared at his hands, as if this was difficult for him.

"An apology?" Was he serious? That was the last thing I had been expecting. Honestly, I was surprised he even knew the word. Our bodies still teetered only inches from each other.

"Yes." He gritted his teeth, a begrudging glare on his face. I was willing to bet Joe was making him do this. "It has come to my attention that I haven't been as friendly to you as I could have, especially since you saved Ty's life. And if you took it that way, I'm sorry." He nearly choked over the words.

A sharp laugh escaped my lips.

"Something funny to you?" He arched an eyebrow at me.

"That's not how you apologize to someone." I crossed my arms over my chest, refusing to back down. Butterflies fluttered in my stomach, but on the outside, Alessandro would have no idea how uneasy he made me.

"Excuse me?" His face twisted in disgust.

"You can't say you're sorry for the way I took something. An apology is about taking responsibility for something you did and all you did was pass off the blame to me."

Alessandro rolled his eyes with enough drama to be worthy of an Oscar. "You know, I'm the one with the upper hand here. I would be careful how you speak to me from now on."

"Really? Because I'm pretty sure I'm the one with the medical degree here. You need me to make sure Ty recovers." I smirked.

Alessandro's fingers found their way to my chin and he lifted it up so I was forced to look in his eyes, his touch immediately disarming me. He leaned in, his lips hovering dangerously close to mine. "We need each other, doll."

Every rational part of me knew I should back away and run as fast as I could. Alessandro Bosio was bad news in every possible way. But instead, I stood still as a statue, letting his fingers rest on my neck. He could either pull me in for a kiss, or squeeze the life out of me right then. Both possibilities brought a tingling sensation to my skin.

His eyes locked with mine for a moment, and a knowing smile crept across his rosy lips. He knew exactly how flustered he was making me right now. It seemed neither one of us was as good of an actor as we thought. A strange sensation washed through Alessandro's eyes, and he backed away suddenly, ripping his touch away. Why was I disappointed?

"You don't have a medical degree yet. And the second you do, you'll be drowning in about $200,000 in debt. Which brings me to the other reason I came up here." He was back to business. For a second, I wondered how he knew that. Oh right, his background check.

"The proposition." I pressed my lips together, remembering what he had said earlier.

Alessandro nodded. "You're right when you say that I need you to make sure Ty recovers well."

"You don't need me, you need someone. A home nurse or something if you still refuse to take him—"

He cut me off abruptly. "I don't want anyone else, Daisy. I want you."

I swallowed a growing lump in my throat, detecting a hidden meaning behind his words. By the look on his face, he realized it too, and quickly tried to cover his tracks. "Look, I'm not good at this shit. I appreciate what you've done for him so far. Not even just removing the bullet, but the way you were with him. You really put him at ease." He paced back and forth, flustered by his own admission. I had to hide my amusement at the way he stumbled over any kind of thank you or admission that someone other than him had done a good job. "He's comfortable with you and if I have to get someone else in here, it'll be starting from the beginning. You and I both know wasting time isn't in his best interest. I have a very successful business, Daisy, and if you agree to help me out, I will make sure your debt disappears and you have your pick of positions at St. Luke's when you graduate."

I was stunned at his offer, almost speechless. "You have that kind of pull at St. Luke's but you won't take your son there?" Something about that didn't feel right.

Alessandro clenched his jaw and let out a deep sigh. "St. Luke's and I have a history. Trust me, they'll do whatever I want."

I pursed my lips, considering what he said. His offer was incredible, almost too good to be true. In fact, it probably was too good to be true. Alessandro hadn't specified what he meant by helping him out. I was literally making a deal with the devil here, without any idea of what I was getting myself into.

"What exactly does this entail?" I proceeded cautiously.

"I want you to move in here and take care of Ty while he's recovering."

I scrunched my nose, taking offense to what he had said. "I'm not a nanny, Alessandro."

"I realize that, Daisy." He rolled his eyes again. "That's why I'm willing to compensate you as much more than that. I need somebody who understands what's going on with him and has a medical background. At least while he's recovering. I realize you have to be at the hospital a few days a week for your clinicals, but I can arrange my schedule to be here when you are not so this doesn't mess with you getting your degree."

I sucked in a sharp breath. This was all a lot to take in. The idea of having all of my loans paid for was too attractive to ignore though. I had been adamant about putting myself through medical school as a way of proving myself to my parents. And it wasn't like Alessandro was paying me for sex, or as some sort of escort. I would actually be using my degree, a live-in nurse was a legitimate job.

What was wrong with me? Was I actually considering this? The man had kidnapped me and held me here against my will, I shouldn't be agreeing to do anything for him. Not to mention what I already did for him was illegal. This was a terrible idea. The more time I spent around Alessandro, the more danger I was putting myself in. At best, the things he was involved in were more dangerous and illegal. At worst, they could get me killed.

"And what if I don't agree to your offer?" I asked.

Alessandro stiffened, clearly having expected me to jump at the offer without any hesitation. "If you don't want to, you can leave here tonight and we'll go our separate ways. But I will have constant eyes on you to be sure you're not going to the police about anything that happened today. And you can forget about getting a position at St. Luke's after you graduate."

My eyes widened. "Are you serious? How did you compromising turn into blackmailing me?"

"I told you, my top priority is the safety of my son, and I will stop at nothing to make sure of that. You know my terms. When you've made your decision, I'll be downstairs." His face hardened, and he stalked out of the room, slamming the door behind him.

The noise made me jump. What had just happened? And more importantly, what was I going to do?

CHAPTER 6

A LESSANDRO
When I left Daisy, I was completely caught off guard by our interaction. I prided myself on being able to read people and control situations, but with her around, I was floundering. She had completely thrown me off my game, something no woman had ever managed to do before. Normally, my interactions went one of two ways. Either the girl was paralyzed with fear of me or she was falling all over herself trying to impress me. Either way, it was pretty easy to get them to do whatever the hell I wanted. I was used to being able to manipulate them for my own benefit, but Daisy was an enigma to me.

A sexy enigma at that. I hadn't been attracted to a woman like that in years, and I wasn't exactly sure how to feel about it. Daisy was breathtaking with her long dark blonde hair and deep chestnut eyes that swam with passion and desire. Those perfectly kissable lips and the way she bit softly on them trying to calm her nerves. Not even her baggy tank top and running shorts could hide the perfection that was her body. Tall, slender, and legs for days. I was already imagining what it would be like to run my hands along each of her curves. That was exactly what couldn't happen though. I couldn't afford a distraction, no matter how tempting it may be. And I could already tell it was going to seriously test my restraint if she decided to stick around. The sexual tension between us was enough to make me question whether this arrangement was a good idea at all.

I cleared my throat, trying to focus myself on the task at hand. Right now, my son needed his father, not some horny teenager.

"Where are we with the investigation?" I snarked, walking into the living room to find Ty fast asleep on the couch while Q and Joe were totally entranced by the new Smurfs movie.

They both sprang up, as if they had been caught. I fought the urge to roll my eyes, as we all walked into the kitchen and away from Ty. I always kept him as far away from my business as possible, except now that wasn't even safe for him.

"Q has a call in to Chief Howes to see if we can get our hands on some of the evidence. These guys knew exactly what they were doing. It was such a public place that it's almost impossible for us to investigate ourselves."

"Isn't that what I pay Howes for?" I growled. The guy had been on my payroll for the last five years, his job was to give me what I needed and keep his force off of my ass.

Joe sighed. "I don't think I need to remind you of all the red tape there is with this. It was a park in the middle of summer. There were hundreds of witnesses and three people were killed. We don't even know if someone was targeting us directly or if it was totally random."

I scoffed, rolling my eyes. A coincidence? Was he serious? "Bullshit. You know this was no coincidence. Someone knew Ty and I were going to be in that park."

Joe got a sullen look on his face, like he usually did when he thought I was overreacting. "I'm just saying we need to be careful about this. Let's see what Howes comes back with and we will explore other avenues in the meantime."

"You need to look into La Eme." I scowled, not appreciating being told what I needed to do. Joe was about the only person I'd let get away with it. "I was on the..." I winced, remembering how distracted I had been when Ty got shot. "Marco thinks that La Eme is who carried out the hit on Talia. I was talking to him when the shooting started. This has got to be them, too."

Joe and Q shared a worried glance. "La Eme? Alessandro, I know you want to find who is responsible but that seems like it's reaching a little bit. They're a street gang, we've never had any trouble with them before..."

"Just fucking look into, Joe. Jesus Christ." I ran my fingers through my hair in frustration. I wasn't reaching, we didn't have anything better to go on right now, anyways. Marco's tip was about the only thing that had been talked about on the circuit even remotely resembling what happened to Talia. The kid he talked to either did it, or knew who did.

"Okay." Joe sighed heavily. "But you have to promise me that you are going to let me handle this and you focus on Ty. He needs you right now."

I looked over into the living room at my sleeping son. For the first time in the last several hours, he looked at peace. Joe was right, Ty did need me, but I also needed to find the people responsible. I wouldn't sleep until I did. Someone was fucking with my family and if they thought I was going to take that lying down, they were seriously mistaken.

"Fine," I said, having no intentions of actually letting him handle this. I knew Joe and my men were perfectly capable of finding who was responsible and making him pay with every drop of blood in his body. It wasn't about that though—this was personal. I wanted whoever it was for myself.

"Is Daisy staying?" Q asked.

I shrugged. "She's thinking about it."

"For the record, I still don't think this is a good idea," Joe quipped. He was seriously testing my patience tonight.

"And I still don't care," I hissed. "Ty needs the best care he can get, and she's it."

Joe chuckled. "She's a med student with close to zero experience, Alessandro. The only reason she is still here is because she's smokin hot."

Without hesitation, I pulled my gun out of the back of my pants and pointed it squarely at Joe. "Would you two just get the fuck to work? You're on my last nerve."

Joe wasn't falling for it, and he started chuckling. "Okay, okay. Let's go, Q. I think we've had enough gunshot wounds for the day."

"Although now Alessandro has a naughty nurse to fix us in case he does shoot us," Q snickered, now joining in on the fun.

"Now!" I bellowed, my mood souring by the second. They were my best friends, closer to me than my own brother, but I was in no mood to joke around. I could've lost my son today, and that was no laughing matter.

"Daddy?" Ty called from the living room. Damn it, my ranting had woken him up.

I shoved my gun back into my waist band so he wouldn't see. Joe and Q followed me into the living room. "I'm right here, bud."

He was sitting up slightly, already looking worlds better.

"How you feelin, munchkin?" Joe smiled, ruffling Ty's hair.

"Hungry." Ty grinned, eating up the attention.

"That's my guy." Joe laughed. "I'll bring Em by to see you tomorrow, think you might be up for that?"

Ty nodded enthusiastically. He adored Joe's wife, even more so since his mother had been gone.

"Good deal." Joe ruffled his hair once more and turned back to me. "I'll be at the office for the next few hours, but call me if you need anything. You want me to have Emily bring something over for dinner?"

"Nah, we'll be fine. Thank you though." My irritation at him was slowly fading. "I'm going to get us some dinner and we'll settle in for a movie. Let me know what you find."

"Always." Joe fake saluted me in a teasing way and the two of them headed out of the house.

"How does a hamburger sound buddy?" I said, sitting down next to him.

"And fries?" He arched an eyebrow at me suspiciously.

"I think I can manage that. Why don't you lie back down and I'll go make us some?"

"Deal." Ty nodded, snuggling back down into the couch. I pulled his blanket over him before heading into the kitchen.

I didn't have a lot in my cooking arsenal, but burgers were my specialty. The last time I had made them had been for Talia's birthday. Both of our families had come over, and despite she and I having a gruesome fight earlier in the day about getting Ty away from the mafia, we put on brave faces for the party. The memory stung worse tonight than ever before. Talia was gone and Ty had been shot today.

I tried to distract myself, but as soon as I did, thoughts of Daisy crept into my mind. The longer it took her to decide, the more irritated I became. I had made her a pretty irresistible offer. She should have jumped at the chance, like a normal person would have. I was quickly coming to the realization that Daisy was far from normal. She was like nothing I had ever encountered before. She had this small-town confidence about her that the big city hadn't yet squashed, and it was as refreshing as it was infuriating. She wasn't scared of me in the slightest, and although Joe had been right about her lack of real experience, she had saved Ty's life today. He had taken to her immediately, and she worked on him like she had been doing it all of her life.

I was mad at myself for being so drawn to her. I made sure no one had the kind of power over me to make me lose control, and for a brief moment upstairs, I had. The spark that surged through me when our skin touched had rocked me to my core, and I could feel myself getting hard just thinking of the flare of her lips. The most perfect rosy red lips I had ever seen. Chills spread throughout my body imagining them wrapping around my length. Fuck.

"Ahem." Someone cleared their throat behind me and I turned to see Daisy standing on the other side of the island. My breath hitched as I silently thanked God there was something between us so she couldn't see how hard I was.

"Hi," she said sheepishly, breaking the silence.

"Hey," I said nonchalantly, trying to act like I hadn't just been fantasizing about her.

"I'll...stay. I'll take your deal," she stuttered, clearly trying to hide her emotions as well. Was it possible I had the same effect on her that she was having on me?

"Great." I gave her a tight-lipped smile, not wanting her to see my enthusiasm.

"But I have a few conditions." She bit her lip, looking up at me through those damn eyelashes.

My brow furrowed. Normally I was the one giving people conditions, not the other way around. "Which are?"

"My work at the hospital has to come first. I worked too hard to slack on it now."

"Of course," I assured her. "I can work around your schedule to make sure one of us is with Ty at all times."

"Which brings me to my next condition." A slight smile crept on her lips.

I motioned for her to continue. This ought to be good.

"If you're serious about this, I need you to promise me that you're going to do what I say when it comes to Ty's care. You're paying me because I know what I'm doing, you can't be arguing with me every step of the way." Her gaze was sharp.

A protest was on the tip of my tongue, but I realized she was right. As difficult as it would be, I was going to have to concede to her.

I let out a heavy sigh. That was certainly going to take some getting used to. "Anything else?"

"Yes, actually."

I rolled my eyes, of course there was.

"I don't know what you do, what kind of world you live in where abducting someone is okay, but that's not the way this is going to be. If I'm staying, I want to come and go as I please."

Oh, she could cum as she pleased alright.

Dammit, Alessandro. Focus.

"Today didn't play out how I wanted it to by any means, but I was desperate. You can come and go as you want, but safety is my top priority. When you're out with Ty, I will have one of my security team with you at all times. And if I get any indication that you're in danger, I'll send somebody to the hospital with you. That's not negotiable."

She pursed her lips as if planning her next move. I could tell she wanted to ask me more about what I did, but the potential scared her. That would have to wait for now.

"Are you hungry?" I said, taking away her opportunity to ask. "I'm making burgers for Ty and I and I can easily add another."

She gave me a funny look. "Ty can't eat that. A chest tube is pretty major surgery, he's going to need to be on a liquid diet the next few days."

"You've got to be kidding me. The kid is sitting up and..."

She arched her eyebrow at me as if to remind me we had just talked about this.

"Fine. Then you have no choice, hope you're not vegetarian." I chuckled, handing her the plate I had made for Ty. "He's not going to be happy with his new nurse, you know."

Daisy rolled her eyes. "You know I'm not a nurse right? The education and training are completely different. I'm his new doctor."

Even better, I'd let Dr. Daisy examine me any day.

I kept this last thought to myself, winking and grabbing some fruit out of the freezer to make Ty a smoothie instead.

Oh yeah, staying away from Daisy was going to be a lot harder than I thought.

CHAPTER 7

DAISY
I was completely out of my mind. Had I fallen and hit my head or something? Did I have some kind of mind-altering brain tumor? I had seen that several times, people making rash decisions that were completely unlike them and then finding out that there was a tumor growing in their brain affecting their decision-making ability. That had to be what was going on with me. Otherwise, I never would have agreed to what I did yesterday.

When I woke up this morning, I almost thought I had dreamt yesterday. The shooting, Alessandro kidnapping me, me stupidly agreeing to work for Alessandro and help him take care of Ty. It wasn't until I opened my eyes, realizing I was in a room that wasn't my own, that I knew that this had really happened and the sinking feeling set in.

I knew next to nothing about Alessandro. He was mysterious and dangerous and I was pretty sure he was into some shady shit. I couldn't say for sure, but the dots were all there just waiting for me to connect them. I was already in over my head, and then I had gone and agreed to continue to work for him. What had I possibly been thinking?

I knew what I had been thinking. I had been thinking that leaving medical school with a cushy job and no debt sounded pretty good. I had been thinking that this was my chance to finally prove myself, to prove that I was just as good at medicine as my brothers and I didn't need them, or my father, to pave the way for me. I was thinking that Alessandro Bosio wouldn't exactly be the worst thing I could spend my days looking at.

The problem was, he made me a deal I couldn't refuse, and he knew that. He had backed me into a corner that I had no hope of getting out of. He was even more manipulative than I gave him credit for, and I had fallen right into his trap. I had spent my life being ordered around and overshadowed by the men in my life and in an attempt to change that, I had found my way right into the arms of a man just as overbearing and sexist as my own father. Life was cruel in that way sometimes.

I sat in front of the hospital trying to get up the courage to go inside, as if I hadn't stolen thousands of dollars in supplies and medication yesterday. If anyone found out about that, I could lose everything. All of this with Alessandro would be for nothing, and I would be done before I even began. I wouldn't get to prove anything to anyone, I wouldn't get to carry out my passion, something I had been dreaming about since I was a little girl, I wouldn't even graduate. I could already see the look on my father's face. He already thought I was biting off more than I could chew, that I should settle for being a nurse or PA, not an actual doctor. If I got kicked out of medical school, I would only prove his point.

When I couldn't stall any longer, I grabbed my purse and headed inside. My heart skipped a beat when I stepped into the emergency department, halfway expecting the security to tackle me and haul me off to jail. I started to relax a little bit when that didn't happen, but I was still anxious and jittery. I remembered what Joe had said yesterday about them being able to detect I was nervous by my breathing and tried to slow it down.

"Daisy?" Dr. Bauer frowned. "I wasn't expecting to see you so soon. How are you doing?"

I stared back at him in confusion at first. What was he talking about? Then I remembered the story Joe had told him, that we had a relative pass away.

"I'm doing okay, thanks, Dr. Bauer. Ready to be back at work." I gave him my most convincing smile.

"Glad to hear it, you let me know if you need some more time." He smiled sympathetically. I hated lying to him, but I couldn't exactly come clean now. "The pharmacy technician was looking for you this morning but I told her you were out."

The blood in my veins froze. She must have known I made it all up.

"And there are a few patients in ER I would like for you to see this morning. Why don't you get settled and come find me?" he said, walking towards the lobby.

"Sounds great." I gave him a tight-lipped smile and ducked into the staff lounge, quickly throwing my things in my locker.

Dr. Bauer was able to keep me busy for most of the day, and I did my best to keep my mind off of everything. Time flew by, and before I knew it it was almost time for me to go home. Well, not home exactly. I had to go back to Alessandro's. And just like that, the pit of nerves was back in my stomach.

I let out a huge breath as I sat down in the lounge. It was the only time I sat all day, not even taking a lunch break. The hospital had been slammed, many of the victims from the shooting yesterday were still here. It made me feel even worse about what I was doing, when there were people here suffering, and Alessandro was insisting on private care for Ty who was nowhere near the worst off.

"Daisy! I'm glad I found you!" Quinn, the pharmacy technician, smiled brightly.

"Hey Quinn." I smiled nervously. "Dr. Bauer said you were looking for me, I'm sorry I didn't make it over there yet. We've been crazy today."

"No worries, I just wanted to double check on the name of the patient that those meds were for yesterday. I looked for her once the system was back, but couldn't find her." She frowned, opening up her locker and grabbing some things out.

"Oh, that's strange," I lied. It wasn't strange at all. I had literally made the name up off the top of my head. This was a nightmare. "I'm rushing out right now and won't be back until Thursday, but I can come by then and fix it for you."

"That'd be perfect." She smiled. "See you then!"

I hurried out of the lounge and made my way to the parking garage. At least I bought myself some time to try to figure this out.

I got to my car, contemplating running away for a minute. I could leave all of this behind me right now, move to Mexico, dye my hair and get a new name. But I'd have to give up my dream, and Alessandro would probably find me anyway. I had way too much at stake right now. I had to suffer through.

I stopped by my apartment to grab a few essentials. The rest would be sold or taken care of by the movers Alessandro hired. I made my way towards his house and pulled into the entrance. I punched in the code Alessandro had given me and drove my car down the windy, tree-lined driveway. His place really was amazing, nestled quietly back among the trees with a beautiful little pond in the back. It was like a dream for a little boy to grow up here.

Before I was even out of my car, Q was standing next to it.

"Hey Daisy, let me help you with that." He grinned, taking my suitcase out of my hands.

"Uh, thanks..." I said, a little surprised at his kindness. Yesterday, he had pretty much hauled me up the stairs and threw me into a locked room. I much preferred this version.

I followed him inside and cringed immediately at the disaster that the house had somehow turned into. It had been nice and neat this morning, but somehow over the course of the day it turned into an absolute pigsty. There was laundry strung out all over the place and all kinds of dirty dishes. Joe was sprawled out in the recliner and Ty was sitting up on the couch playing some sort of video game. It was like some sort of frat house.

"Ty, I need it now!" Alessandro called from somewhere in the house.

Ty looked down at his shirt, pulling it over his head and tossed it over his shoulder. "Here dad."

As a dirty T-shirt came flying through the air, Alessandro caught it right before it hit me. "Hey!" he snapped, pointing a finger at Ty. "What have I told you about throwing things in the house?"

Ty groaned, rolling his eyes. "Sorry."

"Don't say sorry to me, you almost got Daisy," Alessandro scolded.

"Daisy!" Ty exclaimed. "You came back."

"How are you feeling, buddy?" I smiled, setting my bag down and walking over to sit on the couch next to him.

"Good. My dad won't let me play basketball with uncle Joe though." He glared back towards Alessandro.

I chuckled a little bit. "Sounds like he's taking good care of you then."

"It's time to lie back down anyways, Ty," Alessandro said, coming over. "You've been sitting up playing for a while."

"Ah, come on, dad!" Joe mocked, grinning at Alessandro.

"Yeah, come on dad!" Ty echoed.

"One more game. But that's it." Alessandro arched an eyebrow at them. They both grinned excitedly and started another round.

"Sorry." Alessandro let out a heavy sigh. "Between laundry and trying to keep him quiet, I haven't had time to start dinner. Are you hungry?"

I had to stifle a laugh. He sounded like such a househusband, completely out of his element. He wasn't quite as scary or domineering with the dish rag over his shoulder.

"I'll tell you what, I'll get started on dinner if you want to finish up the laundry. It looks like Ty is occupied for a little while."

"At least Joe is good for something." Alessandro winked. "Thank you. It's been a long time since I've been responsible for all of this."

That much was apparent. Ty's mom probably hadn't left very long ago. I couldn't help but wonder what happened between her and Alessandro. From what I could tell, she wasn't involved in Ty's life at all anymore.

"No problem." I smiled, and headed into the kitchen.

Alessandro didn't have a ton to work with, but he had enough that I was able to throw together some chicken enchiladas and get them in the oven. I got some yogurt and applesauce ready for Ty and took it out to him. Joe and Q had left, and I could tell that Ty was exhausted. He was trying to act tough because he wanted to play with them, but he was still in pain and really tired. Once he ate, he fell right asleep on the couch.

When he was asleep, I went into the kitchen and checked on the enchiladas. Almost immediately, Alessandro joined me.

"It smells absolutely incredible in here. What did you make?" he asked, pulling a bottle of wine off the shelf.

He gestured towards me, and I nodded.

"Enchiladas," I answered, pulling them out of the oven. "I hope you like Mexican food."

"Love it." He grinned, handing me a glass of wine.

"Thank you." I smiled, taking a huge gulp and letting out a sigh. I could already feel myself relaxing after the crazy day I had had.

"Tough day at work?" Alessandro said, picking up on my mood. He was good at reading people, I had to give him that.

"Just busy." I gave him a tight-lipped smile, not wanting to get into the specifics. "Nothing I can't handle."

Alessandro's eyebrow furrowed. "What happened?"

"It's really nothing, Alessandro." I grabbed a few plates out of the cabinet and started dishing up the enchiladas.

Alessandro grabbed my wrist, preventing me from moving. "I don't like being lied to, Daisy. Is someone at St. Luke's giving you a hard time?"

"And I don't like being manhandled." I jerked my arm out of his grasp. "No one is giving me a hard time. When I took the medicine for Ty, I had to come up with a fake name to give the pharmacist. Joe did something to the computers so she couldn't look right then, but when she went to put it in later obviously she couldn't find the person. I just have to figure something else out."

Alessandro scratched his chin. "What name did you give her?"

"Why does that..." I started to question.

Before it was even out of my mouth, Alessandro cut me off sharply. "What name, Daisy?"

"I just made something up. Janet Collins, I think." I shrugged. I had no idea why he was making such a big deal out of this.

Alessandro nodded. "I'll make sure Janet Collins is in the hospital system by 6 AM tomorrow."

"You can do that?" I stared at him in disbelief. I guess it shouldn't surprise me, but packing a hospital database was kind of a big deal. Joe had made the system go down, but changing it was a whole different level of interference. Was Alessandro actually capable of that?

Alessandro smirked, as if my question was stupid. "Of course I can. Don't worry about it anymore. Now can we eat? I'm starved."

I opened my mouth to speak, but nothing came out. Alessandro had once again rendered me speechless. I was both impressed and scared that he had those kinds of capabilities. The only thing more paralyzing than thinking about the havoc he could wreak was feeling how drawn to him I was becoming. I hadn't expected us to eat together. Last night when he made dinner, we both went our separate ways.

Apparently tonight was going to be different.

"Sure." I hesitated, handing him a plate. The more time I spent with Alessandro the greater risk I ran of falling prey to him. Falling for his tricks and into his dangerous web. Alessandro was no good for me, no matter the magnetic energy between us. I knew he felt it too and that only exacerbated things. I needed to stay focused on why I was here, and get out before I trapped myself.

"Ty seems like he's doing much better," Alessandro said, leading me out to the patio. The sun was setting and the view of it over the lake was absolutely breathtaking.

"Mhm," I agreed, taking a bite out of the steaming plate. Skipping lunch had left me completely famished. "He looks exhausted though. I think he was excited to hang out with Joe and acted like he felt better than he did."

Alessandro frowned. "You do?"

I nodded. "He's improving quickly, but he still really needs his rest. Sometimes the mind heals faster than the body and we get ahead of ourselves."

"I'll keep that in mind." Alessandro smiled widely, laughing to himself.

"Why are you looking at me like that?" I laughed nervously.

"No reason." He smirked. "I just really love listening to you talk about medicine. I can see how passionate you are about helping people."

A rush of heat blanketed my cheeks under his intense stare. I suddenly felt completely vulnerable in front of him. "Thank you."

"So you'll be able to be with Ty tomorrow, right? I have a few meetings but won't be gone all day." Alessandro continued eating, hardly pausing to speak. He was almost inhaling the meal.

"Yes." I nodded. "I don't have to be back at the hospital until Thursday."

"Thank you again for agreeing to this. I know it's a little unconventional." Alessandro let out a nervous laugh, trying to disguise his emotion. "I just... I want to make sure everything with his recovery goes according to plan. I'd die if I lost him."

"He's going to be just fine." I gave him a reassuring smile and reached out, putting my hand on top of his. I didn't even realize what I was doing until it had been done. It was something we had been taught in medical school when trying to comfort patients. I took my hand back inconspicuously, but the look on Alessandro's face told me that the moment of connection we shared hadn't been lost on him.

"Just don't kidnap me again," I teased.

"I'll do my best." Alessandro chuckled. "Like I told you before, giving up control isn't my strong suit. In fact, all my life has been about gaining control. As much as humanly possible. I thrive in control."

"Is that why things didn't work out with Ty's mom?" I pressed, feeling like we were finally making some progress.

Instead of answering me, Alessandro stiffened right up and his entire demeanor changed.

"Ty's mom didn't leave, she's dead," he said flatly, grabbing his plate and standing up.

Nausea hit me like a ton of bricks. There was no way I could have known, but I still felt awful. "Alessandro, I..." I didn't even know what to say.

"I'm going to take Ty upstairs and go to bed. Thanks again for dinner. I'll leave instructions for Ty tomorrow."

Alessandro left me alone on the patio before I could even get my bearings. So much was starting to make sense, and my heart absolutely broke for them.

I needed to find some way to make this better for them, and some way to apologize to Alessandro for being so insensitive.

CHAPTER 8

ALESSANDRO
I could see Joe's mouth moving, but the words coming out sounded like a foreign language. Staying awake was a stretch for me right now, so paying attention was damn near impossible. Not to mention a certain blonde nurse that kept dancing through my mind and pulling my thoughts elsewhere. I was constantly wondering what they were doing while I was away, which was completely new for me. I had always been good at compartmentalizing, and until recently, never crossed my work and home lives.

It had been about a week since I snapped at her about Talia, and I hadn't slept well since. I spent my days avoiding being alone with her at all costs, and my nights tossing and turning, replaying how the conversation had gone in my head. Apparently, this was what guilt could do to a man. Eventually, I knew I was going to have to explain myself to her, or at least that's what Joe recommended, because we certainly couldn't continue on the way we had been living. Her tiptoeing around me like she was afraid to speak, and me growing more and more irritated with the entire situation. Daisy was spicy and outspoken, and as much as her forwardness got under my skin, I didn't like the side of her that seemed scared to offend me. And I needed to stop the awkwardness before it got so bad that she left. Everyone had immediately taken to her, especially Ty who thought she walked on water. He had already had so much disruption in his little world that I couldn't bear the thought of being the cause of any more. I knew I owed her an explanation for my behavior the other night, and since, but I didn't even know where to begin.

I don't know why it was so hard for me to talk about Talia. It had been months now. It wasn't like I could keep it a secret forever. It was a fact of life for Ty and me now. His mother, my wife and friend, was murdered. It wasn't at my hand, but it might as well have been. My work had gotten her killed, I hadn't been around to protect her, and I still hadn't been able to exterminate the vermin responsible. Maybe that was why I didn't like talking about it, because I had to admit defeat.

Daisy would think I was a monster, and I liked what we had going. Up until the other night, there was banter and attraction between us, and I was feeling lighter than I had in years even. Everything about her was intriguing to me. A few times, we had eaten dinner together and talked about things that didn't revolve around Ty. I felt like I already knew her on a deep level, and the best part was, I didn't know these things because I had looked them up. I knew them because she told me. But I knew the moment I told her what happened to Talia, and how it had been my fault, that she would run for the hills. Maybe that was for the best, though. She was in danger just by being around me, danger I had knowingly and selfishly put her in.

For the first time in my life, the secrets I was keeping were eating me from the inside. I felt compelled to tell Daisy, to tell her everything. My business, what I did, how Ty had watched from under the bed as his mother was nearly beaten to death. How I had been expected to marry Talia, but never truly romantically loved her. How the doctors at her beloved St. Luke's hospital had let my wife lie out on the table bleeding to death. How I had been battling my grief and guilt the last several months by pushing it to the side, only allowing it to grow. How many times I had considered leaving, and how that thought had only made me feel more like a failure. How dark and cold our house had been over the last several months, and the small hint of light that had been brought back to it just by having Daisy there the last week. She'd think I was insane. Any person in their right mind would. And the more she knew about the mafia, and my job within it, the more danger she was in. What moron had brought her into all of this? Oh right, me.

Everything with Daisy was easy. The way we had fallen into a pattern with taking care of Ty had me thinking things that could get me in serious trouble. Maybe I just needed to fuck her out of my system and get past all this foolishness. Or, maybe, this had the potential to be something else. Something more.

"What do you think, Alessandro?" Q asked, turning to me.

Oh shit. I had been zoning out for so long that I didn't even remember what we had been talking about. I looked to him and Joe for some kind of clue, but they had nothing.

Thankfully, I remembered discussing something about how we were going to approach Los Chavos. That had to be right. Joe and Q and I had been talking about it this morning, and then we brought the rest of my top men in. "I don't want to do anything until we have a firm plan."

Joe about shit a brick as soon as the words were out of my mouth, and I knew I had said the wrong thing. "What?" I shrugged, trying to play it off.

Joe shared a worried glance with Q. "Why don't you guys give us a second?" he said, dismissing the rest of the men.

Once they were out of the room, I immediately jumped on the defensive. "I just don't think it's a good idea to go in blind."

Joe let out a sharp laugh, narrowing his eyes at me. "Neither do I. That's why we just spent the last hour formulating one."

Fuck, an hour? I needed to get a hold of myself, so I could take down the man responsible for all of this.

I rubbed my temples. "Look, I'm sorry. I haven't been sleeping well, I'm a little distracted."

"You think?" Q chuckled, folding his arms over his chest.

"I'm worried about Ty," I continued to defend. "I don't like leaving him..."

"Bullshit," Joe cut me off abruptly, a scowl on his face. "Ty is doing fine, you're worried about Daisy and I'm telling you right now..."

"I don't need to hear it," I snarked. "I get it."

"No man, you don't get it. Your head belongs here, not at home with your flavor of the week. You go home, and you fix this shit with Daisy, or you cut her loose, because all of our lives are in danger if you're not on your game."

"Jesus, Joe." I clenched my jaw. "You make me sound like a complete dick."

"I'm your best friend, Alessandro. I'm the only one not afraid to fucking say it to your face." He rolled his eyes, chuckling. "Just get your shit together before this thing blows up."

"Everything is under control." I glared. "Now why don't you two morons do what I pay you to do and bring me a Chavo?"

"On it Boss." Q smiled eagerly.

Joe, who was more irritated than normal today, rolled his eyes again. "Can you remind your guys to be more discrete this time? I'm tired of cleaning up unnecessary messes."

Q frowned, taking offense to his comment. The last time his man had grabbed someone, they were sloppy and cocky about it. Joe ended up having to smooth everything over with the police, and it hadn't been easy. I'm not sure what he ended up promising his contact, but I know he had to do a bunch of pro bono legal work for a few weeks.

"I think I'm going to go home and check on Ty," I said, standing up and stretching.

Joe immediately started chuckling, and it hit me the wrong way. I glared, slugging him in the shoulder. "Do you have something you want to say?"

"Not a word." He chuckled, rubbing the sore spot on his arm.

"Good," I growled, grabbing my jacket and heading for the door. I didn't want to admit it, but he was right. I needed to settle things with Daisy one way or another so I could focus on destroying these guys. I'd talk to her tonight and hopefully convince her to stay. Not just for Ty's sake but my own.

"Hello?" I called, walking into the house from the garage. Everything was in tiptop shape, as it always was on the days that Daisy was home with Ty. That first day, I almost thought I walked into the wrong house. Everything was sparkling clean and put away and the smell of marinara sauce was wafting through the hallways. It almost seemed like a giant cloud had been lifted off of the house. I had had to do a double take when I walked into the kitchen and saw Ty sitting on the counter next to the stove and Daisy with her back to me, stirring something on top of it. For the first time in almost a year, our house felt like a home and it almost made me emotional to think about how much I wanted that for Ty.

Tonight, it was quiet, but as clean and wonderful smelling as ever. I hadn't realized Daisy was a cook when I asked her to move in with us, but I certainly wasn't complaining. She was a magician in the kitchen, and Ty was thrilled when she finally said he could start eating solid foods. That night, she had cooked lemon chicken piccata and I watched in amazement as Ty wolfed down a huge stack of broccoli. Usually, I couldn't get him to touch anything green with a 10-foot pole. In just a short time, she was already making a huge impact on him. I couldn't let her go.

I was surprised to find the kitchen empty, because the last few nights, that's where I would find them when I got home. Ty would help Daisy cook, and even do some of the dishes. He was like a different kid. I could hear faint laughter out on the patio through the glass door, and like a fly to the light, I was drawn to it.

Daisy sat at the edge of the pool dawning a sheer, lacey cover up. Underneath, I could see the outline of a skimpy black bikini and the small tease was enough to send me into overdrive. It was getting hard to deny my attraction to her under normal circumstances, and even harder when she sat dangling her painted pink toes into the water, a sparkling smile on her lips, not a clue how gorgeous she really was. Biting my lip, I stifled a moan as I imagined ripping the delicate fabric right off of her. And if Ty hadn't noticed me at that exact moment, I very well may have.

"Daddy!" Ty shrieked, nearly toppling over the surfboard he was floating on.

Daisy whipped her head around, startled by my sudden appearance.

"Hey buddy!" I smiled, waving animatedly at Ty. It was good to see him active again. Daisy had prescribed some serious rest over the last week and even though he was improving, it was hard to see him like that. I was used to him running wild and jumping off the walls.

Not wanting to get my suit pants wet, I pulled a lounge chair up to the edge of the pool and sat down next to Daisy. "Sorry, I didn't mean to scare you."

She smiled. "It's okay, I just wasn't expecting you home so soon."

"I snuck out a little early. I was actually hoping we could talk." I was never good at small talk, and after I had spent the week avoiding her, I owed it to her to cut right to the chase.

Daisy arched her eyebrow skeptically. "Okay..."

"The other night, when you brought up Ty's mom..." I started, wringing my hands together. "I wanted to tell you I'm sorry."

A small smile spread across Daisy's face, easing the tension. "Alessandro Bosio, apologizing? I never thought I would see the day."

"Very funny," I chuckled. "If you keep interrupting me, you still might not."

Daisy made a zipper motion across her lips and grinned.

"Anyway, it just caught me off guard, and I reacted poorly, snapping at you and then avoiding you all week. I haven't talked about Talia to many people, but I should have told you from the beginning. She was murdered and I feel responsible for it." It amazed me how easy the words came, like Daisy triggered some kind of word vomit reaction in me. I could already feel my mind clouding with emotion from even saying Talia's name.

Her eyes softened as she sensed my emotion, and she reached up and grabbed my hand sympathetically. "Alessandro, you certainly don't owe me an explanation, let alone an apology. I shouldn't have brought it up. I'm sure it's hard for you to talk about and I never imagined... I'm the one who should be sorry. I never should have pried, it's not my business."

"But I do owe you an explanation," I disagreed. "It kind of is your business if you decide to continue with us. I haven't been completely honest with you, and I know I'm asking a lot of you so I don't think that's very fair."

Daisy hesitated. "What do you mean?"

"My job... the work that I do is... it's dangerous. And sometimes people I care about get hurt. Like Talia and Ty."

"Alessandro, I know where you're going with this." She stopped me.

"You do?" I frowned in confusion.

"I don't know the specifics of what you do, but I kind of figured it wasn't a normal office job when you kidnapped me and forced me to do surgery on your son in the backseat of a car." She gave me a small smirk. "I knew it was dangerous to get involved with you when I agreed to this. I'm here because I want to be." She paused, giving me a tempting smirk. "For Ty."

Fuck, did this girl have any idea what she did to me? Of course she did, and she was enjoying it. Somehow, our relationship had reversed, and she was gaining the upper hand. The scariest part though, was that I didn't even care.

"I know it must be hard to talk about, but if you ever need to," she squeezed my hand, looking up at me with a longing in her eyes, "I'm here."

"Thank you. Why don't you let me make up for being such an asshole the last few days by letting me handle dinner?" I suggested, fully aware that I needed to put a little distance between Daisy and I before I did something I would regret later.

"You cook?" She feigned shock, eyeing me teasingly.

"I can work a phone, and if you know the right people, that's practically the same thing nowadays." I chuckled, shrugging.

"Far from it." She dissolved into laughter and I found myself smiling at the beauty of the sound. She was never more beautiful than when she was laughing. That sparkling smile, the soft glittering of her eyelashes, the way her whole body seemed to get in on it. It was mesmerizing, holding my attention in a vice grip. "I appreciate the offer, but I'm going to have to take a rain check. I have dinner plans tonight."

"Oh," I said, trying to hide my shock and disappointment. Dinner plans? Who the fuck was she seeing? Did she have a boyfriend? I would know about that, wouldn't I? Rage and jealousy started pulsing through my body. I didn't even know the guy, but I wanted to pound his face in at the thought of him spending the evening with Daisy. This served me right, I treated her like shit all week instead of making my move, and now she was seeing somebody else. I had no right to be pissed off about this, but it didn't stop me from feeling that way.

"No problem." I gritted my teeth, standing up with my hands on my hips and calling for Ty. "Come on, buddy. Time to go inside."

"Ten more minutes!" he whined, working his way to the center of the pool.

"No, now," I called. "Daisy has a date and I have to get some work done." I tried to keep my breathing even so she wouldn't pick up on my anger.

"Alessandro, it's not..." She stood up, a deep frown on her face.

"You don't have to go to the hospital tomorrow, right? I have some things I need to take care of at work."

"No, but..."

I cut her off sharply again, knowing the longer this went on, the worse I was going to feel. "Good. Have a good time tonight."

Daisy's confusion turned into a glare, and I could tell she had some choice words for me. "You know, you can't..."

"Bye Daisy!" Ty climbed out of the pool, this time being the one to cut her off.

The anger melted off of her face in a split second and she gave him a big smile before kissing his forehead. "Bye buddy."

I turned in frustration and headed towards the house. Why could I never seem to get it right with her?

CHAPTER 9

D AISY
I was already completely out of sorts by the time I got to the restaurant. Alessandro literally had the patience of a five-year-old. Actually, I take that back. Ty had much more patience than Alessandro. I wasn't going on a date, my brother was in town, and if he had given me two seconds to speak without him jumping to conclusions, I would have explained that. Part of me wanted to continue to let him think it was a date as a penance for rushing to judgment. I liked seeing the look of simmering jealousy in his eyes. He deserved a little bit of discomfort since he liked to inflict it on everyone else so much.

The man was infuriatingly gorgeous and even when he was acting like a pompous asshole, my mind began to wonder. There was so much more underneath his skin, but he was as hard as a rock—in more ways than one. Tonight, when he apologized and told me a little bit about his wife, I saw the very first glimpse of a crack in his tough exterior since I had met him.

Alessandro was a tough guy to read. One minute he was flirting with me, the next he was angry. He had me spinning around so much I didn't even realize which way was up.

I almost burst out laughing when he told me his job was dangerous, like I didn't already know. I wasn't sure if it was when he pulled a gun on me in the middle of a crowded park or his calm and collectedness in the face of sheer terror that was my first hint, but

I knew Alessandro was used to danger. He had to be some kind of hit man or gang member. Normal people just didn't function the way he did. He constantly had a gun in his waistband, odd work hours, a group of cronies that hung around like flies, and what was up with that abandoned warehouse he took me to? Like I was supposed to believe regular business happened in a place like that? No, I was well aware everything about Alessandro Bosio exuded danger, and still for some godforsaken reason I had chosen to stay.

Dinner hadn't gone much better. I loved my brother, but he was a lot like our father. I spent two hours defending my decisions to be here and to be becoming a doctor. My entire family thought I should give this whole thing up and come home. With my training, it wouldn't take much time at all to become a nurse, so why was I wasting my time here? They didn't understand, and I was beginning to realize no amount of my reasoning would make them.

When I told him I had taken a job in home care, he nearly had a heart attack. I regretted it the second it was out of my mouth, but I tended to ramble when I was angry. Jake tried to say I had no way to pay for the education I was getting and I should be working for a while to save up. It didn't matter to any of them that this was what I wanted, or that I was graduating in a few short months, all they cared about was that I came home and took my place at my father's practice as a nurse of PA. Never anything more than that. It was like I was a magnet for egotistical and controlling men.

By the time I got back to Alessandro's, I was beyond irritated with my brother, and the few drinks I had had were hitting me like a brick wall. I needed a hot shower, and a good night of sleep. Why did men have to be so damn infuriating?

The house was quiet and I figured everybody was asleep. I tiptoed up the stairs and shut the door to my bedroom quietly. My bed looked so inviting, but I knew if I sat down I wouldn't get back up, and I needed to shower and brush my teeth.

The bathroom in my guest suite was almost as big as my entire apartment. In fact, the shower itself might be. There were three shower heads, one from above and one from each side that made you feel like you were getting a massage each time. The walls and floor were all tiled with stone, making it feel so natural and beautiful. I could press a button and the whole thing would fill up with steam that smelled like lavender fields. It was even better than going to the spa.

I started to peel off my clothes and toss them into the corner and let the water warm up for a minute. My mind was preoccupied, going back through the events of the night and wondering how soon it would be before I got a call from my father with his latest attempt at getting me to come home.

It was exhausting and defeating when the people you loved most didn't believe in your dreams. I knew I was doing the right thing, but I couldn't help but feel like I was letting them down. It wasn't fair of them to make me feel that way, and I ping-ponged back-and-forth between feeling disappointed in myself and angry with them.

I opened the door, ready to step inside when a furry creature in the corner of the shower caught my eye. A spider the size of a grapefruit sat back on its haunches, trying to stay out of the water spray.

"Aaaaaaaaah!" A shrill half cry, half scream escaped my mouth as I clambered away, desperately flailing for a towel. I backed myself into a corner, as far away as I could possibly get from the monster as it stood there taunting me. Spiders didn't normally scare me, but I had never seen one quite so big. It was at least 6 inches long. I sat frozen, afraid to even move.

All of a sudden, the bathroom door burst open and Alessandro stood in the doorway shirtless, looking like he had seen a ghost. "What? What's wrong?" he asked breathlessly.

"There..." I couldn't even put a sentence together. "In the shower..."

Alessandro moved cautiously, peering around the edge of the shower door. After a few seconds, he burst into deep laughter. "Are you serious? You screamed like that because of a spider? I thought someone was being murdered." I didn't find his smirk amusing in the slightest.

"That thing could easily murder me," I sputtered, trying to catch my breath. "Have you seen the size of it?"

"That thing..." he made a funny face, mocking me, "is a camel spider. It's not even venomous."

"I don't care. I still want it out." I was skeptical of Alessandro's assessment. It sure looked poisonous to me.

"Okay, princess." He smirked again, running his fingers through his hair. His eyes widened as they fell on my body, roaming every inch of it. Was I imagining things or was his breathing more shallow than normal? Did my fear turn him on? What was... Oh shit. For the first time, I was realizing I had grabbed a hand towel instead of a body towel in my haste to cover up. I was standing in front of Alessandro practically naked. The look on his face told me he was loving every second of it. I, on the other hand, felt extremely exposed.

Alessandro picked up on my embarrassment and having a rare gentlemanly moment, grabbed my robe off of the hook and tossed it to me. "I'll take care of the spider. You can use my shower in the meantime."

I grabbed the robe from him and hurried out of the bathroom. Not wanting any more awkward encounters with anyone, I ducked into Alessandro's bedroom and shut the door tightly behind me. I stood against it, catching my breath and surveying the room. This was the first time I was seeing it and it looked so... so harsh. Almost like no one even lived here. The walls were painted a deep gray and he had the shades pulled down tightly at the windows. I could only imagine how incredible his view was from this part of the house and it was a shame to keep it hidden. The bed was gigantic, almost as big as two king sized beds, and was neatly made. There wasn't a single thing on the floor and not a stitch of decoration in the entire thing. I couldn't imagine a woman ever living in this space. He probably changed it after Talia died and now it was a reflection of how he felt inside.

I spotted a set of doors on the other end of the room and assumed it was the bathroom. If I thought mine was amazing, Alessandro's bathroom was the Taj Mahal. His shower was twice the size of mine with 5 shower heads and a clawfoot jetted bathtub sat in the corner next to a window. I imagined sitting in the tub, enjoying the view and bubbles over a glass of wine and couldn't think of anything better. Alessandro's cologne hung in the air, filling up my lungs and warming me from the inside. Oh wait, that warming sensation I felt was the heated tiles underneath my feet. Those things really existed?

Wanting to avoid another spider incident, I checked the shower immediately and then turned on the water. I didn't see anything, but couldn't shake the feeling of creepy crawlies all over me. So much for a long hot shower. I dried off quickly, slipping my robe on and heading back out into Alessandro's room.

He was sitting on his bed with his laptop in his hands, still completely shirtless and as sexy as ever. I stared at him for a second before he noticed me, taking in each bulging muscle and painted piece of artwork on his body. It was hard not to be mesmerized.

There was a heavy mutual attraction between Alessandro and I, but so far neither of us wanted to admit it. I figured my staring was only fair after the show I had accidentally given him earlier in the evening.

"That was fast." He smiled, looking up and catching my gaze.

I cleared my throat, walking towards him. "Yeah, I couldn't get the spider out of my head so it wasn't quite as enjoyable as I had hoped. Did you kill it?"

"Your spider friend has been relocated and won't be bothering you anymore." He gave me a sympathetic smile. I didn't like the sound of relocation as much as dead, but I certainly wasn't going to be the one to handle it.

"And you're sure it wasn't poisonous?" I arched an eyebrow at him as I sat down on the bed, pulling my robe even tighter around my body. I couldn't afford another wardrobe malfunction around him right now. If he made a move, I don't think I would be able to deny him.

"Positive. We get camel spiders all the time. All they'll do is give you a nasty bite."

"I'd like to avoid that too, if possible."

"Not into pain?"

"Not in that way, no." I chuckled.

Alessandro had a surprised grin on his face, reading into my words.

Oh god, I hadn't meant it like that. Shit. "I didn't mean..."

"It's okay. I know what you meant." He set his computer to the side. "How was your date?"

I rolled my eyes. Great, here we go. Asshole Alessandro about to rear his ugly head.

"For your information, it wasn't a date," I growled, fuming. "My brother was in town and I went to dinner with him. But even if it was, you have no right to act like that to me. You're the one who has been walking around here all week avoiding me like the plague, and then you act like I..."

Before I even knew what was happening, Alessandro's lips were on mine, kissing hungrily. For a brief second I considered pulling away, but fighting the sexual tension between us was futile. As I leaned into his kiss, Alessandro took that as permission to go deeper. His fingers tangled in my hair, pulling me in closer to him as his tongue explored every inch of my mouth. He alternated between nipping and sucking on my lip, sending sensations through my body that I had never experienced in my entire life.

His kiss was debilitating, holding my body hostage in a sweet embrace that I couldn't get out of if I wanted to. Until now, I had no idea how badly I needed this, to kiss him, to feel him. How badly I just needed him. Every second we had been together, we had been teetering on the edge of this moment and now that it was here, we were diving in head first.

Alessandro leaned me back gently on the bed, hovering over me with a seductive smirk on his face. "I acted that way because I was jealous. I couldn't stand the thought of another man doing what I wanted to do to you."

His lips found the ridge of my collar bone and he dragged his tongue along it painfully slow. The tiny movement sent goosebumps over my skin and my body writhing with shivers. He continued down my chest, peppering my skin with kisses until he reached the V of my robe. "Tell me there's no one else, Daisy." His voice was husky and low.

"There's no one else," I whispered, never even considering the consequences of giving him what he wanted. I could deal with the consequences tomorrow, but tonight, I was going to enjoy Alessandro.

My response ignited something in him as he ripped at the tie of my robe, holding my arms in place as it fell open, putting me on display for him. Alessandro pinned my arms above my head, kissing my lips briefly before working his way down my body. First my chin, then biting gently at my neck, then to my collar bone, to my chest and finally stopping when his face was nestled between my breasts. He dragged his tongue along the sensitive skin and then pulled back slightly, blowing cool air against it and causing my body to convulse at the sensation. I jerked against his restraint of my arms, but he held me firmly in place.

"Alessandro..." I cried out, unable to control myself.

A grin formed at the corner of his mouth. "I want you Daisy."

"I want you, too." My voice was frantic, almost desperate.

"Are you sure? Are you sure you want to be a part of my world? Because if we do this, I don't know if I'll be able to let you go." His eyes were locked on mine, daring me to answer.

I didn't have a single hesitation. "Yes, I'm sure."

CHAPTER 10

ALESSANDRO
Yes, I'm sure.

Daisy had given me the golden key to her body with those few simple words. I moved as if I was an explorer, checking out uncharted territory, and if she let me, I was going to stake my claim on every inch of her. My fingers trailed down her sides, landing on her thigh and hip bones. It was like my hands were made to hold her, her body fitting into them like a glove.

She was sensational. Dangerous curves taunting me at every turn, and fuck, those noises she was making were so damn hot. I studied all of her in sheer appreciation of her beauty. Why the hell had I waited so long for this?

"Alessandro..." The moans that were escaping her lips were needy, but I fully intended to take my time. I had imagined this moment for days, and now that it was here, I planned on savoring it.

"Patience, Daisy." I pressed my lips to her ear, whispering against it.

She clamped her mouth shut, trying to stifle the pleasure I had induced. The way her body responded to me drove me fucking wild, I almost enjoyed pressing her buttons to see just how far I could push her to the brink before she toppled over.

Pinning her hands above her head, I had her at my full mercy, just how I liked it. My lips connected with hers, and I slipped my tongue between them exploring her sweet mouth. I sucked on her bottom lip, and dragged my teeth across it, eliciting just enough pain to make her moan against me. She was loving every second of this.

I could feel her smile growing beneath me, and pulled away for just a teasing second.

"You are a fantastic kisser." Her husky voice was so damn sexy. "But I'd like to see what else you can do with that tongue."

I let out a sharp laugh, her comment catching me off guard.

"Whatever the lady wants." I grinned evilly, releasing her hands and disappearing between her legs.

Daisy bent her legs, resting her ankle on my shoulder and running her tantalizing fingers through my hair as I got to work. She tasted like a small slice of heaven, so sweet and luscious that I was getting as much enjoyment out of this as she was.

"Oh God, Alessandro." She shivered as the stubble of my 5 o'clock shadow rubbed her inner thigh, as I sucked and nipped at her sensitive skin. I could feel her right on the edge, reveling in the facial expressions of pure pleasure she was making. I kept her teetering on the edge for a few more agonizing minutes before plunging my tongue inside of her and giving her the sweet release she was desperate for.

She moaned, arching her back as she exploded with passion, hardly able to catch her breath.

I took pride in delivering mind-blowing orgasms to women, and I had to say, this was one of my best. Watching Daisy's body convulse with pleasure made me rock hard and left me wanting to do it all over again.

I kissed her ankle as she removed it from my shoulder, finally coming down from her high and propping herself up. Before I knew what was happening, Daisy turned the tables on me, taking control and pushing me back onto the bed.

"That was pretty good." She smirked, dragging her nails down my chest and leaving tiny red lines in her wake. "But let me show you how it's done."

Oh, fuck yeah.

Daisy returned the teasing I had given her earlier, kissing and touching me everywhere but where I desperately wanted her to. Each time her head dipped down, I expected to feel those rosy lips wrapped around me, and each time they didn't, I grew fucking wild with anticipation.

She was playing with me, and she enjoyed it. The sultry look in her eyes told me she knew exactly what she was doing to me and while giving up this control was new to me, I wasn't hating it.

By the time her sweet lips grazed my cock, I was coming apart at the fucking seams. I had never craved a woman like I did Daisy, and the thought of that both thrilled and terrified me.

All I could focus on was the pure ecstasy I was feeling as she flicked her tongue against me before plunging me deep inside her throat. She felt so good I was dizzy, and as much as I wanted her to continue, I needed to be inside of her more.

"Fuck, Daisy." I hissed in pleasure, gripping her hair and tilting her head back so our eyes met. "This feels amazing, but I can't wait. I have to have you."

I grabbed her hips, hoisting her up so she was straddling me. She pressed her lips to mine and lowered herself on top of me, taking my direction, but still remaining in control.

"Fuck!" I growled again, when her body closed around me. She was so tight, so sexy.

Daisy's hips pulsed up and down as she rocked against me. It felt amazing, and the view was even better. Her bouncing breasts teasing me with every movement. When she finally dipped low enough, I caught one between my lips, flicking my tongue against the nipple.

"Alessandro..." My name came off of her lips in a whine. So fucking needy. And I intended to give her everything she wanted.

I was so hard I knew I wasn't going to last much longer, and nipped at her breast before pulling out. Daisy yelped, sucking in a sharp breath at the sensation.

I smirked and flipped her over onto her back. So my little temptress liked a little pain, good to know.

Daisy's big doe eyes locked on mine as I slipped my hand to the nape of her neck. She had had her fun, but now I was back in charge.

"Lift your leg," I instructed, guiding her as I gently extended it. I didn't have time for gentle though.

I secured it on my shoulder and then did the same with her other leg, so they were both suspended in the air. I wanted a clear view of her face as she screamed my name in pleasure.

"So fucking hot," I snarled, reaching quickly for the condom and tearing into it.

"I want it hard." She smirked, taunting me. The girl had no idea what she had coming.

"Yes, ma'am." I chuckled, slipping the condom on and then delivering a sharp slap to her perfectly round ass. If I gave it to her as hard as I could, I would break the poor thing in half, but that didn't mean I couldn't play a little rough.

She gasped when I plunged inside of her and began bucking my hips at a punishing pace, not even allowing her time to catch her breath. Her eyes widened as I moved in and out of her as smooth as honey, her fingernails digging into my back.

Fuck. I wasn't going to last long at all.

Daisy cried out, moaning and gasping as I gave her exactly what she asked for. In mere seconds, she was writhing with orgasm again. One look at the expression on her face, and knowing that I caused it, sent me over the edge as well. I exploded inside of her, clutching her body to mine as we rode out the high together. It was the longest and most intense orgasm of my life.

When we finally collapsed onto the bed next to each other, we were both gasping for air, at a complete loss for words.

"That was..." she started, trailing off.

"Yeah." I let out a sharp laugh. There weren't enough words in the English language to describe how incredible that was.

I had been hyping this moment up in my mind almost since I had met Daisy, and it somehow had blown my expectations completely out of the water. Daisy certainly didn't disappoint.

And I was in serious trouble here.

CHAPTER 11

D AISY
I was still in ecstasy as I laid against Alessandro's bare chest, his arm wrapped around me tightly as his thumb stroked my shoulder. We had crossed a hard line tonight and I knew there was no going back, and a part of me was excited about that.

Alessandro was about more than I could handle. One minute, he was infuriating me, and the next he was making me feel things I didn't even know I could. He was more experienced than I was, knowing exactly how far to push me and when to pull back. He touched my body like he had been doing it all of his life, and I was even more surprised when he pulled me into him to lie together after we had finished.

I had expected a guy like Alessandro to kick me back to my bed once we were done, but he continued to surprise me in the best ways possible.

"I should probably get back to my room in case Ty wakes up." I pulled back slightly but Alessandro yanked me right back into his chest.

"Stay here." He smirked. "Ty knows he's not allowed in here without permission first."

I flinched just slightly at his words, wondering if that was because Alessandro had women in here like this often, but I did my best to bite back that insecurity.

"You know it's highly unprofessional to be sleeping with my boss."

He winced. "You're right, what the fuck are we going to do about that?" A smile started to tug at the corner of his lips and I got the sense he was joking. "I've got it! Daisy, you're fired."

I shot up next to him in bed, frowning. "Be serious, Alessandro."

He was laughing almost uncontrollably next to me. "Daisy, I am serious. We both know Ty doesn't need full-time care, and that my reasons for having you stay were selfish. You're right, you shouldn't be sleeping with your boss, but good thing I'm not him anymore."

I bit my lip, feeling completely torn. "But what about..."

Alessandro put his finger to my lips. "You held up your end of the deal and took care of Ty when he needed you. I'll still hold up mine and pay off your tuition."

"I was going to say what about Ty, not the money." My brow furrowed, a little offended he thought I was concerned about the money. "You're not going to pay my school loans if I'm not working for you. That doesn't sit right with me."

Alessandro rolled his eyes, putting his palm to my cheek. "Then think of it as an investment in your career. I'm paying for it because I think you'll be a brilliant doctor and I want some credit when you find a cure. See, my reasons are utterly selfish when it comes to you Daisy." His finger trailed down my cheek until his thumb brushed gently against my lip. "I want to make my intentions with you very clear. I don't just sleep around with a bunch of women, this isn't a one-time thing for me. Now that I've had you, I can't bear to give you up. But I'll take this as slow as you'd like."

I opened my mouth to respond but nothing came out. I had so much on my mind but I couldn't quite put it into words. The idea of dating Alessandro was exhilarating. I had never imagined that him kidnapping me in a park one Sunday morning would result in that, but here we were. He was mysterious and demanding, but when he let his guard down he was passionate, and fiercely protective and I could see how much he loved Ty. My first assessment of him had been off base, but was that enough to jump into a relationship with him?

"You can't fire me, I already canceled the lease on my apartment." I let out a sharp laugh. Emotions were tough for me sometimes so instead of confronting them, I jumped right to logistics as to why it couldn't work.

"So?" Alessandro shrugged, scrunching his face up. "You have a room here."

I fought the urge to roll my eyes. "Uh... right. Because living with you is taking things slow."

Alessandro's face turned pensive as if he was pretending to think. "That's a good point. But you're down the hall so far it's as if you were in a separate apartment. Besides, who is going to kill the spiders if you move out?" He smirked as if he was throwing the ultimate trump card.

"That's a very good point." I laughed, settling back in a little bit.

"Look, I'm not asking you to marry me or anything, I just know you've felt this attraction between us too, and it's much more than physical. Although that's a nice perk." He chuckled. "I just want to see where this goes."

"Me too." I smiled, allowing myself to be open to what Alessandro was offering. He was right, agreeing to date him was less commitment than I had made when I agreed to be Ty's nurse. Giving it a shot couldn't hurt. I hadn't had much time to date since starting medical school; Alessandro piqued my interest in more ways than one. When he wasn't being an arrogant jerk, he was actually pretty charming, not to mention he was hot as sin. He had enough going for him for at least a first date.

"Good." He pressed a kiss to my forehead. "Now close those pretty eyes of yours. One of us has to work in the morning. And now that you've lost this job, you better hang on tight to your other." He smirked, enjoying teasing me.

"Just don't tell them that you fired me if they call for references." I smiled, joining in his fun.

"Oh, don't worry about that. I'll give you a glowing reference. Fantastic oral skills, very vocal, willing to try any position..."

"You forgot that I take direction well."

"Very well." Alessandro's arm snaked around me, pulling me on top of him. "And that stamina. Wow."

I shook my head, laughing. "I'll be sure to keep you in mind if I ever decide to apply for a job as a stripper."

"Now there's a job where you can sleep with your boss. As long as it's me, that is." He winked.

"Goodnight, Alessandro." I rolled my eyes, and turned over, snuggling into him.

"Goodnight Daisy."

ALESSANDRO

It was only a few hours after we had gone to sleep that Daisy slipped out of my room so she could get ready for work. She had to be at the hospital at 6 AM on these days, so I had gotten up to make her a cup of coffee, but quickly gone back to sleep after she left.

Ty would be heading back to school next week, so I had decided to let him sleep in, too. He had always been a good sleeper, which I thanked my lucky stars for. He really was doing so much better, and that was all credit to Daisy.

That girl certainly had my number. It was like one taste of those rosy red lips had me bending to her will and mercy. The more I was around her, the more I began to crave her. I had been since she got here, but seeing her naked body crouched in the corner in fear of the spider and needing me to save her had turned me on like no other.

Maybe it was my hero complex, but I could have almost kissed that spider for giving me my in. I loved the fact that she needed me. She was such a strong personality that she was rarely vulnerable enough to take the assistance of someone else. It had been just the confidence boost I needed, and I'll tell you what, kissing her had been one of the greatest decisions of my life.

I was still reeling from the night that we had had. It was the best fuck I had ever had, but it was more than that. I felt a connection with her that I had never felt in my life. She was special, and the fact that I was acting this way was concerning. When Talia passed away, I never imagined I would date anyone or find a mother for Ty, but Daisy had me considering all of that. It was early on, but those thoughts had already crossed my mind. It wasn't just me that I had to think about. Even dating someone meant I had to consider the ramifications for Ty. Daisy was a deadly combination, both empathetic and tenacious, mothering and sexy. I was in serious trouble.

"Where's Daisy?" Ty scowled, coming downstairs with a serious case of bed head.

"Hey Bud." I ruffled his hair as he slid onto the breakfast bar in the kitchen. "She's at work. How did you sleep?"

Ty groaned, throwing his head back dramatically and ignoring my question. "I thought she was going to be here. She's going to teach me how to play the piano."

"Wow." I arched an eyebrow. "That sounds pretty cool. I didn't know you wanted to do that." The piano had sat completely quiet since Talia had been gone. Most of the time, it was buried under a mountain of laundry because it was less painful if I didn't have to see it. Talia had music running through her veins and the sound of her musical talents could often be heard bouncing off our walls.

Ty shrugged. "Daisy said she can play the Batman song. I'm just going to watch." Talia had been in the middle of teaching Ty how to play when she died. I felt a sharp pain in my chest thinking of how excited he had been, and how he hadn't touched it since she'd been gone.

"How about some breakfast bud? Cereal? Toast?" I changed the subject.

"Daisy makes me pancakes," Ty said matter of factly.

I arched my eyebrow at him. "Every day?"

Ty nodded.

Well, damn. How could I compete with that?

"Tell you what, I can't make pancakes but how about Lucky Charms?" I rarely let him eat the sugary cereal so I figured he'd go for that.

Ty grinned enthusiastically.

I poured a bowl for him and sat down next to him to enjoy my coffee. Thoughts of last night still replayed in my mind and I was aching for her. Picturing her in those scrubs and wondering if she was thinking about me, still sore from last night. What the hell was wrong with me? I never lusted after a woman like this.

"What do you say we take Daisy something for lunch?" I suggested.

Ty's grin grew wide. "Yeah! Can we make her sushi? That's her favorite!"

I let out a sharp laugh. Make sushi? Yeah, right kid. "Did she tell you that was her favorite?" Now I was using my son to gain intel on her, that was a new low, but I was desperate to impress her.

Ty nodded. "She likes sushi and something called calamari that is like little teeny octopuses. Can you believe it dad? She eats octopus!! She told me one time she even caught one and ate it! Blehhh!"

"Disgusting." I chuckled. "You really like to spend time with her, don't you?"

Ty nodded wildly. "She's really fun, and really smart. Don't make her leave like my other nannies, okay dad?"

I burst out laughing. "Why would you say that?"

"Because they all start to like you, and then they have to leave." He narrowed his eyes at me.

I bit my lip to stifle my laughter because I could see how seriously he was taking this. "I'll do my best," I assured him. "But Daisy isn't exactly your nanny, she's like... a friend."

"Like a girlfriend?" He arched an eyebrow at me.

I nearly choked on my coffee. This kid was too smart for his own good. "Well, no. Not exactly, no," I stuttered, caught completely off guard by my 6-year-old.

"Do you want her to be?" A small smirk tugged at his lips. I immediately felt sorry for the women who would fall in love with him in the future. He was going to be a heartbreaker.

"I don't know, bud." I chuckled. "That's adult stuff. I'll tell you what, why don't you go change your clothes and we can stop and buy Daisy some sushi on the way."

Thankfully, he dropped the subject and scurried off up the stairs. It was way too soon to be discussing that with him. Daisy and I had slept together once, and even if I wanted more, I had agreed to take things slowly.

Although it seemed like she had already managed to position herself right in the heart of my little boy.

CHAPTER 12

D^{AISY} "Almost done." I squinted, looping the last stitch through and setting my utensils down. Derek gave me a goofy smile as he inspected his still finger.

"Looks good as new, Dr. Taylor. Even better than before." He grinned, waving his hand in the air. This was the third stitch job I had done on him in as many weeks. Derek was a carpenter with an affinity for being clumsy. Last week, it was a nail gun, the week before that a wet saw, and his latest injury was caused by a table saw. I hadn't actually seen any of his finished work, but with the amount of blood this guy lost in the workshop, I wasn't in any hurry to.

"I don't know about that." I smirked, snapping my gloves off and throwing them into the trash can. "Try to stay away from the table saw for a few weeks, okay? As much as I enjoy our time together, if you come in here again, I may just insist you find a new job."

"Well, Dr. Taylor, if you would just agree to go to dinner with me, I wouldn't have to injure myself to spend some time with you." He winked.

"Ah, charming and handy. What more could I want." I giggled, filling out the rest of his chart. Derek was a massive flirt but he never meant it. He was about 30 years older than me, and had a wife at home.

"So what? Same routine?" he asked, grabbing his bag.

I nodded. "Keep it dry and clean, and let me know if it's getting tender or red in the next few days."

"You got it." He patted my shoulder. "See you soon, Dr. Taylor."

"Don't make it too soon, Derek." I chuckled, watching as he made his way to the check-out desk of the ER.

I ducked into the staff lounge for a quick break before seeing my next patients. Glancing up at the clock, I winced. Was it really only noon? I had only slept about two hours last night and despite Alessandro getting up to make me coffee, I was seriously dragging today. Despite the six shift hours still ahead of me, I didn't regret a single second of last night.

Everything had happened so quickly. One minute we were arguing and the next, his lips were on mine and our clothes were on the floor. Well, his were anyway. I hadn't even gotten back into mine after my shower had been interrupted by the giant mutant creature Alessandro called a camel spider. I didn't really care what it was called as long as it was gone.

Alessandro had come to the rescue like my knight in shining armor and the rest was history. My body was still aching as thoughts of last night fluttered in my mind. I wondered how in the world I was supposed to concentrate today when all I could think about was the way Alessandro's body looked with the moonlight barely dripping in through the curtains and how his strong hands had felt on my body. If I didn't have the persistent ache in my thighs, I would have thought I dreamt the entire thing.

What was he doing to me? I was so hung up on him that I thought I was hearing his voice.

Wait. Was I hearing things or was that actually his voice? Was he here? Was something wrong with Ty?

I stood up so fast that I nearly knocked the chair over, getting strange looks from a few of the nurses on break as well. I composed myself, before hurrying out into the ER lobby.

Sure enough, Ty and Alessandro were standing there talking to Dr. Bauer.

"It's been a long time, Alessandro. How are you doing?"

Alessandro's jaw was hardened and I could tell that he wasn't here to speak with Dr. Bauer. But why were they on a first name basis? Did they know each other?

"Fine, thanks," Alessandro said flatly. "I'm actually here to see one of your..."

"Daisy!" Ty shrieked, racing towards me. He slammed into my legs and wrapped his arms around them in a tight hug, nearly knocking me right off my feet.

─────── ⟿ ───────

"Woah! Slow down, buddy." I chuckled, bending down to his level. "What are you guys doing here? Is everything okay?"

"We wanted to bring you lunch!" Ty beamed, looking back towards Alessandro.

Alessandro gave me a guilty smile, holding up a paper bag.

"You two know each other?" Dr. Bauer asked, with a frown on his face.

"They're friends, definitely not boyfriend and girlfriend," Ty interjected immediately, luckily depleting some of the awkwardness that hung in the air. I had to fight the urge not to burst out laughing. Alessandro looked like he wanted to crawl under a rock but started chuckling himself.

"Oh." Dr. Bauer gave a nervous laugh. "Well, don't let me stand in your way. Daisy, come by my office when you're done, will you?"

"Absolutely, Dr. Bauer." I nodded with a smile.

He nodded back, scurrying off like he couldn't get away from Alessandro fast enough. There was a strange air between the two of them and I couldn't help but wonder why.

"Come on, Daisy! Let's eat!" Ty squealed, grabbing my hand and pulling me towards the front doors before I had the chance to ask Alessandro anything about Dr. Bauer.

"Definitely not boyfriend and girlfriend, huh?" I smirked, teasing Alessandro as we walked out into the courtyard.

"I swear, the kid has a mind of his own." He shook his head, chuckling. "He put me on the spot this morning and I didn't know what to say."

"I'm just giving you a hard time. Trust me, I am not one of those girls that is going to pester you to define our relationship right away. Far from it actually." I smiled.

Alessandro turned towards me, pressing a quick kiss to my lips. "I think that just makes me like you more, Daisy."

I looked back at him, trying to figure out where this charming, thoughtful guy had come from. Coffee this morning, now lunch. And he had only ever called me Daisy in bed. I was so used to his tough-to-crack demeanor that he was catching me a little off guard.

"What?" He smirked as we sat down at the picnic table. Ty started running after some of the ducks from the nearby pond. "Ty, slow down, bud!" Alessandro yelled after him before turning his attention back to me expectantly.

"Nothing." I blushed. "You just never call me Daisy."

"Yeah, well, if my son gets to call you by your nickname, I figured I should be able to as well." He winked.

"I guess that's a fair point." I sat down next to him. "So what's for lunch?"

"Sushi!" Ty chimed in, finally joining up, completely out of breath. "I wanted to make it, but dad said no, we had to buy it." He rolled his eyes dramatically.

I smiled, ruffling his hair. "Well, I appreciate the thought."

Alessandro started getting all the food out of the bag and we all laughed as we ate together. Pretty soon, Ty had had enough and took off running again. He was certainly getting his stamina up.

"Hey, I was thinking..." Alessandro started. "If we're going to try this, like for real, I should take you out on a date."

A smile tugged at my lips at the prospect of a date with Alessandro. My mind was already swarming with possibilities. "Okay. What did you have in mind?"

Alessandro grinned, probably not having expected me to agree so easily. "Actually, it's a surprise. How does tomorrow night sound?"

"I'll have to check my schedule," I teased. "Maybe I can pencil you in."

Alessandro rolled his eyes, catching on to my sarcasm. "Okay, let me rephrase. I'm taking you on a date tomorrow night. Be ready at 7PM."

"You know, for my definitely-not-boyfriend, you sure are bossy."

Alessandro smirked. "Trust me, you haven't seen bossy yet."

"You mean you get worse?" My eyes widened, playfully.

"I can show you, if you'd like." His hand landed on my knee, fingertips grazing my thigh. Even beneath my scrubs, his touch was electrifying. "Ty seems occupied here, we can go find a supply closet or something and I can show you."

"As tempting as that offer sounds," I smiled, standing up and leaving before he made me change my mind, "I have patients to see." Alessandro looked hurt that I was leaving. "But I could be persuaded to see when I get home tonight."

"The longer you make me wait, the worse it's going to get." Alessandro's grin was menacing and sent butterflies fluttering through my stomach.

"Looking forward to it." I winked at him and waved to Ty.

"Bye, Ty! Thanks for lunch! See you later."

"Bye, Daisy!" He waved wildly, tossing some pieces of bread to the ducks.

"Goodbye, Dr. Taylor." Alessandro smirked, with a smoldering look on his face that made me consider heading home with him right now.

"Goodbye, Mr. Bosio." I waved, teasingly. Two could play this game.

I stole one more glance over at Ty and Alessandro before heading inside. Alessandro had joined Ty down at the pond, and it almost hurt my heart how cute they were together. Soon, Ty was running and Alessandro was chasing after him laughing the entire time. Alessandro scooped him up in his arms, tossing him over his shoulder and hanging Ty upside down. Ty dissolved into giggles and pounded his tiny fists on his dad's back. I loved seeing the two of them together.

Reluctantly, I headed inside and put my coat back on. I remembered that Dr. Bauer wanted to see me, so I headed up the stairs towards his office. Damn, I had completely forgotten to ask Alessandro what the deal between the two of them was.

I knocked twice on Dr. Bauer's office door and he called for me to come in.

"Good, Daisy. Shut the door behind you, and come have a seat."

For the first time, I was getting the feeling that something was off. It was rare that Dr. Bauer asked to see people in his office in the middle of the day, and I could count on one hand the number of times I had met with him at all. Usually, he was the type to catch up while we were rushing down the hallway from room to room.

"Is everything okay, Dr. Bauer?" I asked, sitting down nervously.

"Of course, dear. I wanted to talk with you about your plans after you graduate. I received your request to be placed here, along with a rather pointed letter from Mr. Bosio." He narrowed his eyes at me. "Apparently, he thinks you'd be a great addition to this hospital.

As do I. But I wanted to also let you know about a position that opened up at St. Jude's research hospital. I know you enjoy working with children and this truly is a once in a lifetime opportunity. You'd have my full support if you wanted the position, and I think we both know how prestigious this would be for you. I just need to know your decision by the end of the month so that I can put in the papers."

"Wow." My eyes were wide. "That's... thank you Dr. Bauer! That's amazing. I will definitely consider it."

"Good." He nodded. "I would hate to see you turn down the job of a lifetime because something is holding you here."

He was talking about Alessandro. The look on his face gave me an uneasy feeling; I knew I needed to find out what was going on between the two of them.

I left Dr. Bauer's office completely stunned. He was right, this was my dream job, and the opportunity of a lifetime, I would be stupid not to consider it. I had worked my entire life for this, and I could finally prove myself to my family. It would mean moving away from Alessandro and Ty, but could I really let that hold me back? We had joked about it today, but it wasn't like we were in a relationship. We had slept together once, and a million things could go wrong between us in the next few months. There was no way I could turn something like this down because of that, right?

I had a lot to consider, but I already felt myself getting excited about the possibility of going. How could I ever give that kind of opportunity up?

CHAPTER 13

ALESSANDRO

Adrenaline was pumping through my veins before I even pulled into the parking lot of the warehouse. After Ty and I had taken Daisy lunch, I had gotten a call from Joe. They had a little surprise waiting for me at the warehouse, and I was fucking ecstatic. My boys had done good. They hadn't just brought me any Chavos gang member, they brought me the one that had actually pulled the trigger at the park, and they had strong reason to believe that he was one of the men that had attacked Talia. This was like a Goddamn dream.

Since Daisy was working until six, I dropped Ty off with Joe's wife, Emily, and raced to the warehouse. This wouldn't be quick, I wanted him to suffer at my hand with every last breath he took. I wanted him literally pleading with me to kill him by the end. There wasn't a lot that was frowned upon in our world, but going after an innocent woman or child, that was crossing the only strict line in the book, and he had picked the wrong man to mess with.

Joe was waiting for me outside, pacing back and forth. He didn't look up until I slammed my car door, and when he saw me, a huge grin blanketed his face. "We got him, Alessandro. We fuckin' got him."

I couldn't stay up on my smile as well, clasping hands with Joe and hugging him. "I can't believe this is finally going to be over."

Joe huffed. "Well, he's swearing the order came from above, but he's not talking. It might be a while before we actually get the shot collar."

"I figured as much, but this is a step in the right direction," I agreed.

"Oh fuck yeah!" Joe chuckled, following me into the warehouse. "Where is he at?"

"We've got him in a block. Q and I have been having a little fun while we waited for you." He snickered, unlocking the door to the tombs for me.

I followed him down the narrow pathway to one of the back rooms. I could hear a high-pitched, squeaky voice pleading Q about something, but couldn't make out what he said.

"You've got this all wrong!" The man dangling from the ceiling shrieked when Joe and I burst through the door.

He was stripped down, already a little bloodied up. They had his wrists secured and locked with the chain hooked to the ceiling, and he stood on his tiptoes on a stool waiting for me. As soon as it was out from under him, he would be dangling by his arms, his wrists broken from the jerk of the cops.

I smirked, walking towards him menacingly. "It's nice to finally meet you, I've been waiting for this moment for a long time."

"Look, Bosio, you've got this all wrong. I didn't..." Before he could even finish, I sent the stool flying out from under him with a swift kick.

"Ahhhhhhh!" He gasped in sheer pain, jerking his body around as his wrist bones shattered.

The cuffs were laced with razor blades that had now sliced into his skin, sending a cascade of blood down his body. They were positioned so that each movement caused searing pain. "Keep flailing around like that, it's just going to hurt worse."

"Please," he begged, his voice hoarse. "You have to believe me, I was just following orders."

I pursed my lips, stalking back-and-forth in front of him. "I can appreciate that. And if you tell me who gave the orders, I might consider letting you go." I wouldn't, but I needed to see how hard I was going to have to push him for the information. I rubbed the brass knuckles on my hand, flicking off a piece of dried blood.

"I don't know!" he shrieked, jerking against his restraints. "I swear."

I started chuckling. "Wrong answer." I reared my fist, landing it sharply on his jaw. Teeth and blood flew across the room. It was like the second I hit him, a huge relief washed over me. I had waited so long for this moment, and it was every bit as satisfying as I had expected. I hit him again, over and over, never giving him a single second to catch his breath. When I finally did stop, he hung against his restraints completely deflated.

The knuckles clambered to the ground, and I fisted his hair, jerking his head up so he had to look at me. " I want to know why."

"It was nothing personal." The guy sighed.

"Nothing personal?" I scoffed. "You shot my son and left my wife for dead."

"I'm sorry." He sputtered blood as he spoke. The guy was in bad shape, and I knew if I didn't stop soon, he wouldn't live for me to do this another day.

"Get him out of here," I growled, rubbing the sweat off of my forehead. I must've had some of his blood on my face, because when I wiped it, my forearm was bloody. I was definitely going to have to take care of that before I saw Daisy or Ty.

"What do you want to do Alessandro?" Q asked as we walked up the stairs to my office.

I sighed, running my fingers through my hair. If it was possible, I was even in a worse mood than when we started. It felt good to hit that guy, but it didn't bring me any closer to finding out who had ordered the hit. "He didn't give you guys anything?"

"We know the name of his boss, but from what I can gather, he's just a low-level banger himself. We have no idea who's calling it from above."

"I want eyes on anybody that you think is even associated with this gang. Press them for information until we get what we want. Somebody has to know something, and this has to end."

Q and Joe both nodded in agreement.

"How are things with the naughty nurse?" Q asked, trying to lighten the mood. Little did he know he just enraged me more.

"Don't ever let me hear you say that about her again. Her name is Daisy. Have some fuckin respect."

"Sorry man!" He held his hands up in the air. "I just thought..."

"No, you didn't think," I spat. "Don't let it happen again."

Q recoiled away, afraid to even speak, but Joe eyed me suspiciously. "I knew this was gonna happen." He shook his head.

"What are you talking about?" I snarled.

"You really like this girl, don't you?"

Q's eyes got wide as he came to the same realization that Joe had.

"So what if I do? Is that such a bad thing?"

"No." Joe shook his head. "In fact, I think it's a great thing. I, for one, think she's great."

"Why didn't you tell us sooner?" Q asked.

"Because. If you couldn't tell, we've been a little busy." I gestured to the warehouse, and all the information we had been gathering about Los Chavos.

"Does she know how you feel?" Joe pressed for more details.

"Yeah, I think the point was pounded home last night." I chuckled at my own innuendo. "Look, it's not that big of a deal. We're just trying things out and seeing where it goes."

"I'd say that's a pretty big deal, wouldn't you Q?" Joe asked, while Q nodded his head wildly.

"Have you taken her on a date yet?"

I shook my head. "We are going to dinner tomorrow. And before you two idiots even get started, I don't need any help."

"Yeah, you do." Joe smirked. "It's been years since you've been on a date. Are you sure you even know how to do it?"

"It's dinner, you morons. How hard can it be?" I rolled my eyes, becoming a little skeptical myself.

Joe and Q shared a concerned looked.

"Look, Alessandro, you want to impress this girl, right?" Q got a silly grin on his face.

I narrowed my eyes at him, ignoring the question. I think that went without saying.

"Let us help you. Do you know what kind of food she likes?" Q asked.

I shrugged. "Ty said something about sushi."

Joe burst out laughing. "Yeah, you definitely need us. Your son has more game than you do."

"You should take her to the top of the stratosphere, women love that shit." Q suggested, putting his hands on his hips.

"What if she's afraid of heights?" Joe frowned in deep thought. "How about Mandalay Bay? I hear they have a restaurant where you can pick your lobster out of the tank."

I held my hand up to silence them. They didn't have terrible suggestions, but I already had something in mind that was going to blow Daisy away. "I realize it's been a while, but I think I still know how to treat a woman. I do need someone to watch Ty though."

"Say no more." Q chuckled. "I'd love to hang out with little man."

"I appreciate it." I stood up, grabbing my bag to take some work home with me. "I'm gonna get out of here, see you guys tomorrow."

"Wow. Running home to the family, this is new." Joe chuckled and I shot him an icy glare.

"You guys are ridiculous."

I left the warehouse, ready to get home. I had taken a quick shower to get the blood off before picking Ty up from Emily's. Ty had already been involved in my work too much for a boy his age, and I was finally starting to feel like my old self. That meant I could get a handle on things and keep my family and work separate.

"What sounds good for dinner tonight?" I asked Ty as we headed inside. Daisy had been cooking nearly every night, but I didn't like relying on her for that. Technically, she was a guest in my home, and I needed to step up a little bit.

"Isn't Daisy going to cook?" Ty arched his eyebrow at me, already judging my skills.

"She doesn't have to every night. It might be nice for you and I to do it sometimes."

Ty shrugged. "How about we order pizza?"

"Now that sounds right up my ally." I chuckled, ruffling his hair.

Daisy's car was in the driveway when we got home, and Ty skipped inside.

"We're home!" he called, throwing the front door open.

"There's my favorite Bosio man." Daisy grinned, coming around the corner and giving him a hug.

"Hey!" I frowned at her suggestion that Ty was the favorite.

Daisy wrapped her arms around me, pressing a kiss to my cheek. "And there's my second favorite Bosio man."

"You think you're funny, don't you?" I chuckled, gently tapping my fingers on her ass. I loved the feel of her body nestled against mine, and I could feel myself getting revved up already.

"Dad said we can order pizza," Ty said, reminding us both that he was still here.

"As long as we don't get anything with pineapples." Daisy smiled.

"You got it." I grinned, pulling my phone out to order.

Daisy and Ty started chatting about their day and I headed upstairs to change. When I came back down, they were both sitting at the piano. Daisy's fingers moved across it like magic, beautiful music floating through the entire house.

Ty looked on cautiously, keeping his promise to just watch as she continued to play. She smiled at Ty, eliciting a small smile from him as well. My heart was nearly bursting out of my chest as I watched them, watched the way she was with him. Everything felt like it was moving in fast forward, but each time I would start to get too worried about it, she would do something to show me just how right this really was.

She fit into our lives so perfectly that I couldn't remember how we ever functioned without her. Even before she and I had slept together, she had been making life better for Ty and I. Damn, I had it bad for this girl.

I watched them, completely enthralled with the way they interacted, while we waited for our pizza. We had dinner together, sitting at the table like a normal family. Ty was having a normal childhood for the first time since even before his mother had passed away and it was making me emotional. It was all thanks to Daisy, and it was terrifying how much she was ingraining herself in us. If things didn't work out between the two of us, I had no idea what we would do.

After dinner, I took Ty upstairs to bed and came back down to see Daisy doing the dishes. She had her back to me and I could tell even by her posture that something was off.

"How was your day?" I asked, wrapping my arms around her waist and kissing her neck.

She jolted at my touch, quickly wiping at her cheek, and I realized she had been crying.

I frowned, immediately pulling back a little bit. "Daisy, what's wrong? Is everything okay?"

"I'm fine," she insisted, giving me a half-hearted smile. "Really."

"Why are you crying?" Tears weren't exactly my forte. Normally I would run at the first sight of them, but something about the look on her face concerned me.

"I just..." She paused, the wheels in her mind turning. "Ty told me that Talia was teaching him how to play the piano before she died and sometimes my heart just breaks for him when I think about all that he's gone through."

I bit my lip, studying her face. It was a plausible story, but something told me there was more to it than that.

"Are you sure that's all?" I pressed, pulling her in closer to me.

She looked back at me again as if she wanted to say more but she bit her tongue. "Yeah, I'm fine, really. I just hate that you guys had to go through this."

"Thank you." I smiled, pressing a kiss to her forehead. "You know, it's been a lot easier on Ty having you around. On both of us."

Daisy closed her eyes, blocking more tears from falling, and somehow I knew that was the wrong thing to say. There was something else going on with her.

"I think I am going to head to bed, too," she finally said. "I've had a long day."

"Hey." I pulled her towards me, getting even more concerned. "Stay with me tonight. I just want to hold you in my arms."

For a second, I thought she might fight me on it, but she gave in. "Okay."

We turned things off downstairs and headed up to my bedroom. She fell asleep in my arms quickly, but I lay awake for hours, wondering what was going on in that pretty head of hers.

CHAPTER 14

D^{AISY}

I stared at the transfer papers in my hands, pain rippling through my chest. All I had to do was sign them and I'd be heading off to St. Jude's for my absolute dream job in a few months. If it was that easy, then why the hell had I been sitting here frozen for the last hour?

I knew exactly why. There was a picture on the front of my locker staring back at me that Ty had drawn. It was a picture of me and him and of Alessandro all together. For the first time in my life, I was second guessing my choice to put my career first, and it was because I met a guy. Alessandro wasn't just any guy though. He was infuriating and stubborn and so arrogant sometimes I couldn't hardly stand it. But the more I got to know him, I saw how passionate and caring he was. How much he loved his son and how guilty he felt about what had happened to Ty's mom. He was grasping at anything he could in order to not completely fall apart, and his brokenness only made me fall for him harder. And made him human, and was a side of him I was pretty sure he didn't let many people see.

It wasn't just Alessandro and Ty that were holding me back, though. It was the entire concept. I was about to get everything I ever wanted, but what if it wasn't actually what I wanted? I had been so caught up in proving myself to my family that I lost sight of what was really important. What did it matter what they thought if I wasn't happy? It was terrifying that I was questioning whether or not this made me happy. I had put all my eggs in this basket, and never once second guessing it until this moment. Alessandro and Ty aside, what if I wanted kids of my own someday? What if I met a really wonderful guy who loved to travel and experience the world and I couldn't ever go because I was busy at work? That had been my father my entire life, and I came to resent him for it.

I hadn't told Alessandro about the transfer, or even asked him about what happened with Dr. Bauer, because by the time I got home I was so emotionally drained. This had been on my mind nonstop since I found out yesterday, and as hard as I tried, I could hardly think about anything else. I hoped by this evening that would change. Alessandro was planning a night out, and I desperately wanted to enjoy it with him. The very last thing I wanted to do was bog it down because of my own indecision.

"You are alive." My friend Peyton peeked her head in from the door of the break room, smirking. She was another med student at the hospital, and our schedules had been so busy in the last few weeks that we hadn't seen each other in a while.

"Hey!" I let out a huge sigh of relief. Maybe I needed to vent to someone, and Peyton would be the perfect person.

She walked in and sat down at a table across from me. "Don't hey me. You've been keeping some seriously huge secrets from me."

"What do you mean?" She was right of course, both Alessandro and the transfer, but I wasn't sure how much I wanted to get into all of that right now.

"Everyone is talking about the guy who brought you lunch yesterday." She grinned.

"Oh, that."

"Yes, that." She clicked her tongue flippantly. "Spill girl."

I let out a heavy breath. "I've been seeing him."

"I figured that much." She rolled her eyes. "Alessandro Bosio? How come you didn't tell me about that?"

"It's still pretty new. How do you know who he is anyway?" Alessandro was gorgeous and had a lot of money, but he wasn't exactly a household name.

Peyton clamped her mouth like she was considering not telling me, but she was my best friend. We literally shared everything the last few years, and I doubted she was going to stop now. "I shouldn't know this, but I heard Dr. Bauer talking. Apparently, your boyfriend has a big beef with the hospital. A lawsuit of some kind, I don't know the details." She waved her hand in front of her face as if blowing it off. "Whatever happened must've been pretty major. He basically owns Dr. Bauer and this hospital now. And you're dating him." She squealed with glee.

I let her words sink in. A lawsuit with the hospital? I guess that would make sense. He hadn't wanted to bring Ty here, and had pulled strings for me virtually overnight. What could've happened though? Did it have something to do with Talia? I thought he said she was killed by the same person that went after Ty? Either way, I would make a stop by medical records on my way out today.

"Tell me all about him."

I smiled, feeling giddy just thinking about him. Yeah, I had it bad for this guy. "He's really wonderful. Passionate about what he does, but always finds time for his son. He's always making me laugh and we just have a really good time together."

"You're totally blushing. This guy really means something to you, doesn't he?" She grinned.

"He does." I smiled. "I haven't felt like this in a really long time. It's still so soon but I already feel so comfortable with him. Like I've known him forever."

"Are you going to bring him to the gala?" Actually, I completely forgot about that. In three weeks, the biggest fundraiser at our hospital was happening, and we were all expected to be there.

"I'm not sure," I said. "I hadn't really thought about it."

"Well, that's great, Daisy." She beamed. "I'm really happy for you."

"It is really great," I agreed, pushing my transfer papers towards her. "The only problem is this. Dr. Bauer gave this to me yesterday."

Peyton read them over, her eyes widening. "St. Jude's? Daisy, that's incredible. When do you leave?"

I swallowed the lump growing in my throat. "I don't know if I am."

"What?" Peyton nearly fell out of her chair. "You can't be serious. You're considering staying here for a guy?"

"I'm not considering turning it down for Alessandro, Peyton." I sighed. I knew it would be hard for her to understand—hell, it was hard for me to understand, but I couldn't ignore what I was feeling. Something about the transfer just didn't sit right with me. "I just... I don't know if it's what I want anymore."

"Daisy, ever since I've known you, this has been all you ever talked about. What do you mean it's not what you want anymore?"

I shrugged. "Honestly, I'm not sure it ever was. Of course, I love helping kids, but there are a million other ways to do that. I wanted to be a doctor because I thought I could prove myself to my father, and I'm starting to realize how ridiculous that is."

"Look, don't do anything about this yet." She set her hand on the papers. "This is all happening really fast, you need to give yourself time to process it. It wouldn't be until the end of the semester, right?"

I nodded.

"Then don't rush this. I think you need to talk to Alessandro if he means as much to you as you're saying."

"Peyton, I'm not basing this decision off of him... " I tried to defend.

"I know," she assured me. "But he is influencing the doubts that you're having, whether or not you want to admit it."

She was right. If I hadn't met Alessandro, and let myself consider the possibility of something else, I would've been content to do this for the rest of my life. I would've been on the first plane out to Tennessee to take this job.

"All I'm saying is consider all of your options. It's not like you to make a rash decision like this."

"I know." I nodded. "You're right, I need to talk to Alessandro about it."

"I'm sorry to run out, but I've got a patient in three that's been paging my ear off. Dinner this week?"

"Sounds great." I smiled as Peyton ducked out the door.

I shoved the transfer papers into my locker, determined to put it out of my mind for now. Ty was spending a half day at school today, and I told Alessandro I would pick him up. Monday he would be back in school full-time, and I could tell he was a little anxious about it. He had missed three full weeks after the shooting, and had gotten used to playing video games on the couch and spending time with his dad.

I grabbed my stuff, and before I left, dropped by the medical records office. Alessandro obviously wasn't offering much information about his relationship with the hospital, and I didn't want to pry. If nothing turned up from this, I would let it go.

I quickly filled out a request sheet and handed it to the tech on duty.

"Let me just check..." She started typing furiously on the keyboard, staring at the screen. "Hmm. Are you sure this is the name? There's nothing coming up."

I nodded. "That's strange. I'm sure it's Talia Bosio. It would've been about six months ago."

"Nothing." She shook her head.

"How about Alessandro Bosio?" I frowned. I really thought this would turn up something, but maybe it really was nothing. Maybe Payton had misunderstood. It wouldn't be the first time her eavesdropping had sent us down a rabbit hole.

The tech reentered the information, but shook her head. "Sorry Daisy, nothing is coming up under either of those names."

"Okay." I bit my lip, defeated. "Thanks for checking."

I left the hospital quickly so I wouldn't be late to pick up Ty. Alessandro said we were leaving at 7 for our date and my stomach was fluttering with nerves. It wasn't exactly a first date since we have been living together the last several weeks, but I was still nervous. I had no idea what he had in store and was really looking forward to it.

I pulled up to Ty's school and walked to the door, just as Alessandro had explained. There was a big group of moms waiting to pick up their kids and I stayed as far away as possible. I only had a few minutes to spare before the bell rang and was anxious to hear how Ty's day went. When it finally rang, he came out of the door and his face lit up as he saw me.

"Daisy!" He raced towards me. All the mothers turned to look at me as they realized I was here for Alessandro Bosio's son, and I could see the wheels already turning in their minds wondering who I was.

"Hey! How was your day? As bad as you thought?" I grinned, taking his backpack from him.

Ty rolled his eyes. "Worse. The only good thing was that my teacher and my friends were happy to see me."

"I bet they were, you're like a real-life superhero."

"I know." His grin quickly turned into a frown. "But dad said I can't tell them what happened so everybody just thinks I had the chickenpox. It's not fair."

I smiled sympathetically, ruffling his hair. "I'm sure it's hard not to tell them, but your dad is right. He just wants to keep you safe."

Ty rolled his eyes dramatically. "Can we get ice cream on the way home?"

"How about lunch first?"

"Hi Ty." A woman gave a sly smile as she walked over towards us with her son in tow. "We're so glad you're back. Elliott really missed you. What happened?"

Ty glanced up at me before responding as if considering whether or not he was going to share the real story. Thankfully, he stuck to the chicken pox route. "I had the chickenpox," he grumbled.

"I'm sorry to hear that. I'm sure your dad is so busy taking care of you, maybe I'll drop off a pot of my famous Chicken noodle soup." Could she be any more obvious? She was seriously using Ty to get to Alessandro? I had to fight the urge to laugh at how pathetic the entire thing was.

"That's okay. Daisy has been cooking for my daddy." He grinned up at me. Apparently, Ty could see right through the woman too.

"Oh, Daisy." The woman turned her attention up to me for the first time, sizing me up. "You must be the new nanny."

I opened my mouth to speak, but was cut off by the sound of Alessandro's voice behind me. "Actually, Jill, Daisy is my girlfriend." He pressed a kiss to my lips, effectively silencing her. Ty beamed up at us, thoroughly enjoying the moment as well.

"Oh." She stared at Alessandro in disbelief.

"Thanks for your offer for the soup, but like Ty said, she takes great care of us." Alessandro smirked, well aware of just how much he was flustering both me and Jill. Not only was it the first time he called me his girlfriend, but he had never touched or kissed me in public like this.

"Glad to hear that." Jill gave them a tight-lipped smile. "Come on Elliot. We'll set up a playdate soon."

She turned on her heels, dragging her poor son along with her.

"These women are like sharks." Alessandro chuckled, wrapping his arm around my waist. "How do you two feel about lunch?"

"Yeah!" Ty cheered, running towards the parking lot.

"I'm surprised you're here, I didn't think I was going to see you until dinner." I smiled, interlacing my fingers in his as we followed Ty.

"I know, I couldn't help myself. I just can't seem to get enough of you Dr. Taylor." He smirked, winking playfully at me.

"Well, Mr. Bosio, the feeling is definitely mutual."

CHAPTER 15

ALESSANDRO

"Is that what you're wearing?" Ty scrunched his nose in disgust at me as if I had walked out in a clown costume. He and Joe were sitting on my bed, watching me get ready for my date with Daisy. I didn't appreciate the audience, especially when they were so critical of my attire, but it was hard to say no to Ty.

I shook my head, throwing my arms in the air. "What's wrong with this one?" He'd already nixed two other outfits I had put on, and at this rate I was going to run out of options in my closet.

"You look like the guy at Home Depot." Ty dissolved into giggles. Leave it to my son to diss Armani.

Joe smirked. "I agree with Ty, jeans are too casual. Aren't you trying to impress her?"

"She sees me in a suit nearly every day. And what we are doing isn't exactly black-tie material..." I rolled my eyes. I was taking Daisy to the Italian restaurant at my vineyard where she and I were going to make wine. I wanted this to be more than just the traditional first date, and this seemed like it was right up her alley. I could tell something was on her mind the last few days, and tonight would be carefree and fun and hopefully make her forget about whatever was bothering her.

"I think it's perfect." I checked in the mirror one last time. Daisy wasn't about the fancy stuff—that was one of the reasons I picked this as our date to begin with. Besides, if I got my way, we wouldn't be in clothes for very long.

Ty shrugged, shaking his head at me. "We tried to help."

"Get out of here." I chuckled, tossing a pillow at the two of them.

Joe grinned, batting it away. "Alright, alright. Come on, little man."

With a few minutes to myself, I sprayed on some cologne and grabbed a leather jacket out of my closet. I highly doubted Joe and Ty would approve of that choice, but I rather liked it.

As I came down the stairs, the sound of music filled the house again. It was the third time this week that I had had to catch myself. For whatever reason, nothing got to me quite like hearing music in our house again.

I walked into the living room, and just like the times before, Daisy and Ty sat at the piano. He was still just watching, not allowing himself to play yet, but he was completely enthralled with her. This time, she really was playing the Batman theme song, just as he said. I had to laugh out loud at how funny it sounded being played so classically, but it fit him perfectly and brought a huge smile to his face.

"You want to give it a try?" she offered to Ty when she finished playing.

Ty shook his head. "I like when you do it."

"I hate to break up the concert, but Daisy and I have to get going." I smiled, walking towards the two of them. I wiped a little bit of ketchup off of Ty's cheek. "You'll be good for Q tonight, won't you?"

Ty nodded. "Can I stay up until you get home?"

"Not this time, bud. You'll be back at school full-time next week and you need to be rested." Ty stuck his lip out in a pout, and Daisy gave him a sympathetic smile. "But if you take a bath and brush your teeth when Q asks you to, then you can stay up an extra hour."

"Thanks dad!" He beamed, throwing his arms around my neck. "You still have time to change, you know," he whispered in my ear.

"Get out of here." I chuckled, patting him on the butt. He was spending too much time with his uncles.

He snickered, giving Daisy a hug. "Bye Daisy."

"Bye buddy, see you tomorrow." She kissed the top of his head. Once again, it struck me how close they were getting.

Once he was gone, I offered Daisy my hand to help her up from the piano bench.

"Is this okay?" She gestured down to her outfit. "I didn't know what we were doing, so I wasn't sure what to wear."

"It's perfect." I kissed her gently to silence her. "You look beautiful."

"Thank you." She smiled. "Where are we going?"

"You'll find out soon enough." I winked, grabbing her hand and leading her towards the garage.

"Would this be a bad time to tell you I'm allergic to almonds?" I opened the car door for her and she climbed inside.

"Not at all. I already knew that, so we're having an almond-free evening." I chuckled.

"How did you..." She trailed off. I could tell by the look on her face she connected the dots. "Oh right. The background check."

"Tonight, why don't we focus on learning things that can't be found on a report?" I reached over, setting my hand on her thigh.

"That sounds perfect to me." She smiled, setting her hand on top of mine. The silence between us was comfortable as we drove to the restaurant.

She looked confused as I passed the exit for the strip. "We're not going somewhere on the strip?"

"Nope." I shook my head. "I hate the strip, actually. I hope you don't mind, I picked something a little different for us tonight."

"Now I'm even more intrigued." She smiled.

We drove for a little while longer before I pulled into the Italian restaurant at a nearby Vineyard. This place was like a one stop shop. Winery, restaurant, teaching kitchen. Daisy and I would be the only ones in the lesson tonight, and I couldn't wait to show her what we were doing.

"Wow. This place is beautiful," Daisy said as she surveyed the area, stepping out of the car.

"It's one of the oldest wineries in all of Nevada," I boasted, putting the keys in my pocket and taking her hand.

"It's hard to believe that something like this even exists in Nevada. It's so dry." She continued to marvel at the grapevines as we walked towards the entrance.

"Actually, this is the perfect climate for grapes. We're just far enough out of the desert area and close to the mountains. The grapes can't handle harsh winters, but somewhere tropical with too much moisture can kill them off too. This is the perfect balance for them."

Daisy smiled, clearly impressed. "You sure know a lot about grapes."

"I should." I chuckled. "This is my vineyard."

"Your vineyard?" Her eyes widened.

I nodded, leading her up the steps. "Come on, there's something I want to show you."

The tasting and restaurant area was bustling when we got inside. Daisy was still in shock, and I hadn't left her with much explanation. I watched her in wonder as she took in all the sites around her.

"Alessandro, this is... it's really yours?"

I nodded, grinning. "It's kind of a side project. But this isn't the best part. How do you feel about getting your feet dirty?" I winked, and tugged on her hand taking her towards one of the backrooms.

"My feet?" She scrunched her nose. I had her thoroughly confused now, and I was enjoying it. I couldn't get enough of the smile on her face. It was everything to me, and the more I saw it, the more I wanted to keep her smiling for the rest of her life.

She started to connect the dots as soon as we got into the back room. There were high platforms with wine barrels underneath them, and large containers of grapes were scattered about.

"What is all of this?"

"This is an age-old Italian tradition." I grinned. "You and I are going to make our own wine, and grape stomping is the first step."

She let out a sharp laugh. "Grape stomping."

I nodded, stepping out of my shoes and throwing them into a locker. "What do you think?"

"I love it." She smiled, joining me. "This is so cool."

"Mr. Bosio." Max, one of our stomping room attendants grinned. "Everything is all set up for you guys. Jen is waiting for you in the barrel room once you finish up here."

"Thank you Max. This is Daisy, it's her first time here."

His smile grew. "Well, welcome! Ever been grape stomping before?"

"Never." Daisy smiled, interlacing her fingers in mine.

"Ah. Well, you're in good hands with Mr. Bosio. Let me know if you guys need anything."

Daisy took her shoes off and put them in the locker next to mine. Max already had everything set, so I helped Daisy up to the platform.

"So I literally just stomp on them?" God that grin of hers was mesmerizing.

"Yep." I nodded, rolling my pants up a little bit. "There are barrels underneath that capture all the juice to use for wine and then we use the pulp to compost and fertilize."

"Isn't that a little unsanitary?" She arched an eyebrow at me.

"Dr. Taylor, the germaphobe," I teased her. "Lucky for you, the actual stomping is more about the experience. Although when it ferments, all the bacteria is killed off anyway. The juice we use for our wine comes from our mechanical crushing system. It has to sit for a few weeks so people couldn't make their own wine after just stomping juice."

"I see." She smiled. "Well, what are we waiting for?"

"After you." I gestured.

Daisy shot me a smirk, hesitating before she stepped into the tub. I offered my hand to steady her and she climbed inside.

"Oh!" she cried out. "It's cold."

I kept her hand in mine, climbing over the ledge as well. "The colder they stay, the juicier they are."

"I'm seriously impressed. I had no idea you knew all of this."

"Well, tonight is all about learning new things about each other." I leaned forward, hovering just a few inches from her lips. "Now get to stomping."

Daisy threw her head back in laughter, moving her feet up and down. We spent an hour in there just joking around and laughing, and it was the lightest I felt in years. I almost felt like a kid again, thoroughly enjoying every moment we were spending together. By the time we had had our fill, we were both drenched head to toe in purple.

"That was incredible. I had no idea making wine was so fun." She had a small fleck of grape on her cheek and I leaned forward, kissing it off of her.

"You haven't seen the best part yet." I winked. "I figured you might want to get cleaned up after this though, so there's a bathroom right in there and something you can change into."

"You really have thought of everything haven't you?"

"People get killed in my line of work if you don't pay attention to the details." Fuck. Why did I say that? It was out of my mouth before I could stop myself. Great topic of conversation for a date, Alessandro. "I'll meet you out here and then we can go pick out flavors," I said quickly, hoping to distract her.

"I just need a few minutes." She smiled, seeming to shrug my comment off completely.

"I'll be waiting."

Daisy disappeared into the bathroom and I did the same, quickly cleaning myself up and heading back into the stomping room. I only waited a few minutes more for Daisy; she didn't fuss over her appearance like most girls I had dated, which was so refreshing.

"All set?"

"All set." She smiled. "I know this kind of thing shouldn't surprise me anymore, but this dress fits me perfectly."

"I have a feeling you could make a potato sack look beautiful."

Daisy blushed. "Flattery will get you everywhere, Mr. Bosio."

"Then I'll keep it coming." I grinned, wrapping my arm around her waist and kissing her gently.

We went into the barrel room, meeting with the sommelier. She explained all of the flavors and the process to Daisy, letting us try and sample anything we wanted. Daisy was enthralled with every single bit of it, and I was equally as in thralled with her. I loved watching the joy on her face, finally letting go and relaxing. Whatever had been bothering her earlier this week, was now just a distant memory. Eventually we decided on a smooth honey and pear blend and sent our mixture off to be created. We walked through the vines for a little while, sipping on some of the stock wine as we searched for constellations in the crystal clear sky. It was hard to imagine in a place like Las Vegas where the stars were constantly muted by the bright lights, but out here it was breathtaking. By the time we had gotten to our table in the restaurant, there was a bottle of our creation waiting for us.

"This is incredible. Everything about tonight has been perfect." She reached across the table, grasping my hand.

I brought it to my lips and kissed it gently. "I'm glad you think so, but it's not over yet."

"Ty told me you like seafood, the chef makes an incredible cioppino. How does that sound?"

"Whatever you recommend." She took a sip of her wine. "Should I be concerned that you're taking dating tips from your son?"

"I call it using my resources. The kid likes you almost as much as I do."

"Well, what a coincidence. I like you almost as much as I like your son too." She eyed me playfully.

"Ouch!" I grabbed my chest, feigning hurt. "Cut me a little slack, I don't have the advantage of being a seriously adorable first grader."

"True. He is pretty damn adorable. You do have some other advantages going for you though," she conceded.

"Yeah?" I arched my eyebrow at her.

She nodded wildly. "Irresistible charm, annoyingly handsome, blew my mind in bed, you came to my rescue when I was being attacked by the spider... Although I don't have to compete with the moms at school for Ty's attention like I do for you."

I let out a sharp laugh. "Trust me, Daisy. It's absolutely no competition. In fact, when you're in the room, it's like every single other woman disappears"

"Again with the flattery. If I didn't know better, I'd say you're trying to get me to sleep with you on the first date."

"That's certainly assuming of you. I'm way too much of a gentleman to do that," I teased. "I'll at least buy you dinner first."

"Good, because I'm starving."

Jesus Christ, this woman had my number. She was so different than anyone else I had ever met, from a completely different world than Talia, and I had never felt so refreshed in all of my life. She was playful and endearing and sexy and tempting all at once. I was only falling deeper and deeper into her web, and I was damn close to not being able to get out. I appreciated the way she challenged me, not treating me as if she was terrified of me like most people in my life did, and it was as if my money meant absolutely nothing to her. Every time she opened her mouth, she surprised me, and I had never been called a great listener, but it was like the sound of her voice cast a spell on me and I could listen to her speak all day.

Tonight had only further confirmed what I already knew. I was starting to fall hard for Daisy Taylor and the thought of that was enough to bring me to my knees.

CHAPTER 16

D AISY
    "How exactly did you get into the wine business?" I asked, as we shared an appetizer of bruschetta and caprese skewers. This place was amazing and everything about tonight so far had been perfect. Alessandro wasn't his usual serious self and was finally starting to break down some of the barriers between us. He had promised that tonight was about getting to know each other and I was planning to take full advantage of that. There was still so much about him that I didn't know, although at this point, there wasn't a lot that could change my feelings. I was falling hard and fast for Alessandro.

"This place has been in my family for years. My grandmother started it and passed it down to my mother, who eventually passed it down to my brother and I. Emmett isn't as interested in it as I am, he's more of a wall street guy so he signed everything over to me a few years ago," he explained, sipping on his wine.

"I didn't even know you had a brother," I said, shocked that I hadn't known that. It wasn't like Alessandro had a lot of family pictures hanging up in the house, and the ones he had were of him and Ty and occasionally Talia.

He nodded. "He's a year older than me. We're very close, but I don't see him very often. I said he was a wall street guy, but that's being modest. He's one of the most successful stock brokers in the world. He travels quite a bit and splits his time between London and New York."

"He was never interested in what you do?" I pressed me for more details, fully expecting him to put his guard back up and think twice about sharing all of this with me. it surprised me when he continued to speak.

He shook my head. "Emmett is older than me, so he should have inherited both the winery and my father's business, but he wanted nothing to do with it. He's more of a free spirit and didn't want to be tied down. My dad worked a lot when we were young and hardly ever had time for us. He was a great father when he was around, but that was rare. I think Emmett watched how the business kind of consumed him and he didn't want that. I didn't either, but I felt a responsibility to take over when Emmett declined. I try to be really conscious of how much time I spend working though and always try to be available for Ty."

"You're a really great father." I smiled, again feeling the weight of all he and Ty had to go through. I couldn't imagine marrying someone, only to lose them a short time later. I didn't envy Alessandro having to navigate his own grief all while also being there for Ty. "You can see how much Ty loves you, and even though he doesn't have a traditional family, he knows how much he's loved."

"Thank you for saying that." Alessandro softened even more, staring off into the distance. "Tell me about your family. I know you have two brothers but that's about it."

"Well, yes." I laughed nervously. "I have two older brothers who both work for my father at his practice in St. Louis."

"Is that why you decided to go into medicine? Because your whole family is?"

I sighed heavily. That was a loaded question. That was the answer I gave everyone who asked, that I started because my family was in it, but that wasn't really the case. "Sort of. It's more in spite of them

I guess. They didn't think I could do this. I know this sounds stupid but even when we were young, I would always have to be the nurse when we played hospital. I never got to be the doctor because my dad and brothers said I couldn't. They tried to steer me in so many different ways. Nursing school, physician's assistant. My dad even offered to buy me a house if I dropped out of med school and came to work for him as a nurse." I rolled my eyes, laughing at the memory. "So when I finally did head off to school, I was determined to prove them wrong."

"Well, it looks like you've done exactly that." Alessandro smiled. "It's hard when the people who love you most aren't supportive of your dreams." He was holding something back but I couldn't quite tell what it was.

"It is." I nodded. "I'm the only girl and the youngest of the family and I think they just didn't like the idea of me leaving. Las Vegas was about as much as I could get them to compromise. I wanted to go to LA."

"What's in LA?"

"Everything." I grinned. "Their hospitals see some of the worst possible cases in the emergency room and I wanted that experience. Although I have to say I don't think I would have gotten the experience of removing a bullet in a moving car if I had gone there."

Alessandro smirked. "Glad I could help with that. I am sorry, you know. I realize I shouldn't have kidnapped you like that, but you have to admit, it seems to have worked out for the both of us."

"You know, if you weren't so damn cute, I would be walking out on you right now. You realize how crazy that sounds right?" Alessandro really did live in his own world sometimes.

"Alright, alright." He held his hands up in defense. "I'm sorry. I shouldn't have kidnapped you regardless."

"Or blackmailed me into staying." I narrowed my eyes playfully at him.

"Or blackmailed you into staying," he said begrudgingly.

"Or tried to push me away when you realized you had feelings for me." I might as well go for it all while I had him where I wanted him. It wasn't often Alessandro apologized, even if it was under duress.

"Cut me some slack." He chuckled, rubbing his thumb along the top of my hand. "I've been out of the dating game awhile."

"I find that hard to believe. Women flock to you. I'm sure you could have your pick of any of the mothers at Ty's school."

"Don't even joke about that." He shook his head. "I'm serious. This is the first real date I've been on in... well, ever."

I threw my head back laughing. "Okay, now I know you're joking."

"I'm not," he insisted. "I was seventeen when my parents told me I had to marry Talia. We went out on dates, but at that point, we already knew we were getting married so it kind of lost its effect."

"Your parents forced you to marry Talia?" My eyes widened. Was he serious? I had no idea that kind of thing happened in real life. I certainly had no idea that Alessandro had been through it.

He nodded. "Talia's father was a powerful businessman before he passed away and our parents thought that a union between families would make them both stronger."

"And you went along with it?" That was even more surprising. Nobody made Alessandro do anything he didn't want to.

"Yeah." He shrugged. "If I didn't agree to marry her, it would have only been someone else. In the world of arranged marriages, it could have been a lot worse than Talia. We grew up together, and she was one of my best friends. I really cared about her."

"Did you love her?"

"As the mother of my son, I did." He nodded. "But I was never in love with Talia. Everything between us served a bigger purpose. A business purpose."

I had so many questions I wasn't even sure where to start. "Does Ty know that?"

"Definitely not. I always treated Talia well and never slept around on her while we were married, even if we weren't in love. I wanted Ty to know how to treat a woman, and knowing the truth about Talia and I wouldn't change things for him. He adored her." Alessandro bit on the inside of his cheek and I could see the emotion in his eyes.

"Alessandro, I don't even know what to say. I'm so sorry."

"Hey." He grabbed my hand, pulling my chair closer to him. "Don't be sorry. I'm a firm believer in everything happens for a reason, and now you're in our life and I am actually starting to feel what real love feels like."

We both froze, as if absorbing the weight of what he just said. Love. He was starting to fall in love with me, too.

"Anyway," he said, changing the subject. "How are things going at work?"

I immediately tensed up. I hadn't told him about the transfer yet, and I certainly didn't want to ruin the mood by bringing it up right now. I still had no idea what I wanted to do, and I had a lot of thinking to do before I said anything.

"It's...good," I said quickly. "You know, I still don't really know what you do for work."

I had a vague idea, but now that I knew he had an arranged marriage, I was even more intrigued.

Alessandro shifted in his seat, gathering his thoughts. "Daisy, I think you know that what I do is very dangerous. It's part of what got Talia killed and Ty hurt. I am crazy about you, and I love what is developing between us, but before it goes any further, I need to be honest with you about what you're getting into."

"Okay..." I sucked in a sharp breath in anticipation. There wasn't much that would change my feelings but Alessandro was a man of many surprises.

"The short answer, and the one you will say if anyone ever asks you, is that I run an international import and export line. But the longer story is that I run a section of the Italian Mafia and we use the line to control counterfeit money distribution..."

My eyes widened. At a certain point, I wasn't even hearing his words, just focusing on the way his lips moved. The mafia. Alessandro was a part of the mafia. In my mind I had expected it to be some kind of gang, but this was... this was even bigger than that. He was a criminal in an organized crime ring. Everything was starting to fall into place for me. The shooting, the warehouse, the complete disregard for rules. "Okay," was all I could bring myself to say in that moment.

Alessandro let out a sharp laugh, stunned at my response. "Okay? I just told you I am a mafia Don and all you can say is okay?"

"Well, I just... I mean I knew what you did was dangerous. Albeit, I thought it was a little smaller scale than the Italian mafia." I laughed nervously.

"Daisy, I'm not telling you all of this to intimidate you. I am telling you this because I want you to be able to make the best decision for you. Like I said, I am starting to fall in love with you, my son adores you, and I'm excited about what comes next for us, but this is pretty life changing. If you want to leave, I understand. You can go tonight and we never have to talk about this again."

I hesitated for a second. "You thought I was going to leave because you're in the mafia?"

Alessandro looked at me strangely. Yes, that was exactly what he thought.

"Alessandro, I stayed, knowing full well the dangers of being with you. Just because you named it now, doesn't change anything. I'm starting to fall in love with you too, and you're not going to get rid of me that easy."

Alessandro looked at me as if my words had completely shocked him. "You're incredible, you know that?"

"Just don't start talking like those old-school mobsters from Jersey and we'll be good." I smirked playfully. It certainly was a lot to take in, but I had expected something along these lines.

"Of all the things associated with the mafia it's the accents that scare you?" Alessandro chuckled, leaning back in his chair.

I shrugged. "What can I say, danger has become pretty attractive to me in the last few weeks."

"What do you say we get out of here and can explore that fascination with danger a little bit more?" He winked seductively, and I knew exactly where his mind was at.

"Lead the way."

CHAPTER 17

A LESSANDRO

By the time Monday morning rolled around, I was in a state of bliss I had never experienced before. This weekend felt like I was living someone else's life, one I had never imagined I would have for myself.

My date Friday with Daisy had only been the beginning. I woke up with her in my arms early Saturday morning, and we sat on the balcony sipping coffee before Ty woke up. Somehow, I let the two of them talk me into going to the zoo, and I spent the day watching in sheer amazement at the joy both Ty and Daisy were having. We made homemade pizzas for dinner, and curled up on the couch to watch the new Despicable Me movie. Ty had barely fallen asleep when I whisked Daisy upstairs, desperate for a moment alone with her. As much as I loved watching her with my son, I enjoyed our alone time.

Sunday was equally as perfect. I woke up in bed alone, but followed the smell of pancakes and the sound of laughter to the kitchen where Daisy and Ty were hard at work. We had a lazy day, going to the park and getting Ty ready to start school full-time again. I had expected him to be hesitant since the last time we had been there was the shooting, but he felt safe with both Daisy and me around and I was exploding with pride watching as he explored. It was the most normal weekend I had ever had in my life, and I was left wondering why I had waited so long for something like that. Ty didn't need fancy trips and excursions to be happy and I had no idea how much I could love something so mundane and usual.

I had put off dealing with the Chavo we had detained the whole weekend, and the coming of Monday meant it was back to reality. Ty was less than thrilled about going back to school and right now, I was wresting him into something semi-presentable. He didn't understand why he couldn't wear his pajamas all day like he had been, and trying to convince him otherwise just wasn't happening.

"Come on, bud." I sighed in exasperation. "If we don't get going, you're going to be late."

"I don't want to go," he growled, eyes fixated on his iPad.

I snatched it quickly from him. "Ty, I'm serious. You're going to school. You've already missed enough."

My words seem to go in one ear and out the other. Ty tried to grab his iPad back from me, but I jerked it away. "Ty, I'm going to count to five and if you don't have your shirt changed, you'll be grounded from video games the whole week."

It wasn't often that I had to dish out consequences to Ty, but when I did, you would've thought it was the end of the world. He burst into hysterics and threw himself back onto the bed.

I groaned, throwing my arms in the air. Now we were three steps backwards. What was his deal today?

"Everything okay in here?" Daisy frowned, peeking her head into Ty's room.

"Ty's having some trouble listening this morning."

"No!" Ty jumped on the defensive. "I just don't want to wear that shirt."

"Ty, this is the third shirt I brought out for you. I'm not getting another one. This is ridiculous. You love this shirt."

Ty ignored me, rolling over to face the wall.

Daisy looked at me, suppressing a smile. "Do you want me to try?"

"Be my guest." I handed her the shirt and waved my arm out.

Daisy took it and sat down on the bed next to Ty. "Isn't this your favorite shirt?"

Ty nodded silently.

"Then why don't you want to wear it? Don't you want all your friends to see how cool you are on your first day back?"

Ty hesitated, and lifted his head up. "I just don't want to."

Daisy shrugged. "Well, if you're not going to wear it, can I?"

Ty gave her a strange look, and I bit back my own laughter. "It's for boys, and it won't fit you." He took it out of her hands.

It was quiet for a few minutes and I was about to jump in again when Ty finally sat up. "I like my shirt, I just don't want to go to school."

"Are you feeling nervous to go back because you've been gone so long?"

Ty nodded. "What if my friends don't like me? And what if my teacher is mean? What if I miss daddy?"

I let out a heavy sigh, realizing this was never about the damn shirt. He was having a hard time adjusting and I should have seen that immediately. The kid was so mature most of the time, I had a hard time remembering he was only six and he had been through hell in his lifetime.

"Bud," I bent down and put my hands to his cheeks, "your friends are going to be so excited to see you. Remember how happy they were on Friday when you were only there for a few minutes? Think how excited they will be that you get to spend the whole day together! And you love Miss Hodges! I already talked to her and she is going to make sure everything goes smoothly for you. And if you miss me, all you have to do is call. I can be there in a second."

Ty didn't look completely convinced, but he was coming around to the idea.

"Sometimes I get nervous too." Daisy smiled, reaching into her pocket. "But you know what helps me?"

She pulled out a clear marble stone and set it in his hand. "When I was a little girl, my brother gave me this and when I get nervous, all I do is rub it and it makes me feel better. Try it."

Ty started rubbing the stone and like magic, looked up at Daisy with amazement in his eyes. "I think it works."

"Of course it works." She giggled, ruffling his hair. "I was thinking you could take it with you today."

"Really?" He looked up at her like she was giving him a stack of gold.

"Sure! As long as you promise to take really good care of it." She smiled.

"Okay!" Ty exclaimed, jumping up. Before I even knew what was happening, he had slipped the shirt over his head and was packing his backpack for school.

"You're a miracle worker." I chuckled, wrapping my arms around her and gently kissing her forehead.

"I didn't do anything. All he needed was reassurance from you." She smiled.

"Well, whatever it was, thank you."

"Come on dad!" Ty called, traipsing down the stairs.

I laughed, shaking my head. "Want to ride with us?"

"I wish I could." She frowned. "Dr. Bauer called me in for a shift today."

"Damn, I thought we were finally going to get some alone time. I had big plans for you."

She smiled. "Rain check? I shouldn't be too late tonight."

"Dad!!!" Ty hollered.

"I'm coming!"

"I have no idea where he gets that impatience." Daisy smirked, putting her hands on her hips.

"Funny." I kissed her one last time. "I'll see you tonight."

It physically hurt me to leave Daisy standing in my hallway but I had to get Ty to school. Maybe with a little time off today I could actually get something done. I hadn't been planning on going to work, but since Daisy would be gone all day, maybe I should.

Ty hopped in the truck and we headed towards his school. Luckily, he seemed back to his exuberant self.

"You gonna crush it today?" I asked, smirking at him.

"Of course. They're not going to know what hit them." Ty grinned, and I tried to suppress my laughter. He was so damn adorable that sometimes I had a hard time believing he was mine. I hated seeing him as upset as he was this morning, and was thankful that Daisy could pull him back to himself. She really was incredible with him.

"Alright, bud," I said, pulling up to the curb of the drop-off line. "I'll pick you up after school. Call if you need me."

"Thanks dad, but I think I'll be okay." He grinned sheepishly, grabbing his backpack. When he picked it up, a picture fell out.

"Hey, Ty, wait!" I called, but it was too late. I picked the paper up and looked at it. All of a sudden my heart stopped. This couldn't be happening.

I threw my truck into gear and headed towards the office. I barely put it in park before jumping out and tearing in to find Joe and Q, fuming the entire time. What the fuck was this guy thinking? He had no idea who he was messing with and when I found out who he was, I was going to rip him limb for limb with my bare hands. I'd break every bone in his body, and let them heal just so I could do it again. He was getting too cocky for his own good and had to be stopped.

"Alright, my turn." Joe chuckled, taking a spot at the end of the table. He and Q were playing some form of table football.

"We've got a problem," I hissed, slamming the picture onto the table.

"Well, good morning to you too." Q chuckled.

I swept my arms across the table, knocking everything off and leaving no question how serious I was. "The mother fucker was in my house. He left this in Ty's backpack."

Joe frowned, picking the picture up and scanning it.

"I'm coming for you." Joe read the words on the paper, the color draining from his face. "You found this in his backpack."

I nodded. "It fell out in the truck this morning. This has to end. I don't want Ty to live in fear."

"We'll get him, Alessandro," Joe said definitively. "How do you think he got in the house?"

"Fuck if I know. We were gone a lot of the weekend but security has been locked down since the shooting. No one gets in or out unless I know about it." I shoved my fingers through my hair in frustration. The longer I sat here without any kind of answer or plan, the more reckless I was feeling.

Joe and Q shared a panicked look, before Joe finally spoke. "Look, Alessandro, don't take this the wrong way, but the only person in and out of your house that is unusual has been Daisy. Are you sure there isn't something to do with her?"

"Of course not!" I growled, nearly coming across the table at him.

"Easy," Joe cautioned. "I'm just saying we need to cover all of our bases. How do you know?"

I picked the picture up and threw it at him. "I know, because he threatened her too."

I watched as Joe studied the picture again, zoning in on the picture drawn beneath the words. It was of her and me and Ty from the zoo this weekend and she and Ty had red x's drawn through them.

"Okay." Joe let out a heavy breath. "We'll get him. Q, get this to analytics and see if there is anything they can get off of it. We'll go visit the guy in holding and see if he's got any information for us."

"I want someone at Ty's school in the meantime posted outside his classroom. And put someone at the hospital too. I don't care what you have to do, but don't let Daisy know things are off until I can tell her tonight. Have him pose as a janitor or something."

"Got it boss." Q nodded.

"We've got to get this bastard." I gritted my teeth, gripping onto the table so hard that my fingers were turning white. This was what I had been afraid of. Daisy was in danger now, and I had no fucking clue who was behind it.

CHAPTER 18

DAISY

I sat at my desk, typing away on my keyboard and charting the patients I had already seen this morning. It was a crazy day in the ER. Three other doctors had called out and Mondays were crazy enough as it was. Our emergency department doubled as an urgent care during the week, but over the weekend, there were just emergency doctors there. That meant higher prices and higher wait times, so Monday mornings were always jam packed with people who were waiting to get in. Mondays were the days people came in through the emergency room with a cold or food poisoning convinced they were dying.

I finally had a small break and was trying to catch up on the charting I had neglected all morning. I had no idea when I would get out of here today, especially since I wasn't even supposed to work to begin with.

My cell phone started buzzing in my pocket and I pulled it out, groaning when I saw the caller ID. Just what I needed today.

"Hi dad." I grimaced, trying to sound as upbeat as I could.

"Hi Mads! Hope I didn't catch you in the middle of anything."

I rolled my eyes, shoving the mountain of paperwork to the side. "Not at all. How are you?"

"Doing well. Busy this week with the practice's 30-year anniversary this weekend. You're still coming, right?"

I slapped my hand across my forehead, silently cursing myself. I had completely forgotten. "Of course I am. I'm looking forward to it!"

I quickly jumped on my computer to book a flight. As excruciating as the idea of flying home for the weekend sounded, there was no way I could miss this, I'd never hear the end of it. For a brief moment, I considered asking Alessandro to come with me, but thought better of it. That would be like walking into a forest fire, and we were already going to have enough to talk about.

"Can't wait to see you, sweetie!" he said. "Hey, Dr. Bauer told me that St. Jude's offered you a position next year, that's wonderful Daisy. Mom and I are so proud of you, and you'll be closer to home!"

I rolled my eyes, fighting the urge to scoff out loud. I had waited my whole life to hear those words from him, and somehow they were much more lackluster than I expected. Maybe because proving myself to him didn't matter to me anymore. I had busted my ass for this my entire life, and it wasn't until I was offered a nationally prestigious job that it mattered to him. So many things about what he just said irritated me but something really struck me as odd. "You know Dr. Bauer?"

"We're acquaintances. He was in my class at med school, I'm sure I've told you that." I was sure he hadn't. I never would've taken a job from someone tied to my father just on principle. "Anyway, I've got to run. Mom and I have dinner Friday night, you'll be able to take a taxi from the airport, right?"

"Yes, I'll figure it out. Bye dad."

"Bye Daisy."

I hung up the phone, letting it fall onto my desk in frustration. I don't know why I let him get to me like that, but it happened every time. Honestly, I would rather walk on hot coals than go back home this weekend and suffer through his practice's anniversary party. But I would do it, just like the dutiful daughter that I was.

"Daisy, I'm so glad I caught you." Dr. Bauer peeked in my office. He was probably here to grill me on whether or not I had made my decision. And now that I knew whatever I said to him might make it back to my dad, that was the last thing I wanted to talk about. Could this day get any worse? Before I even finished that thought, three young and impressionable faces appeared behind him.

"I'm actually heading back to see a few patients." I plastered a fake smile on and grabbed my stethoscope.

"Even better." He waved his three companions in. "These guys are first years who need some observation time in the ER, and I just don't have the time. They're going to follow you around today."

———— ❧ ————

I pressed my lips into a thin line, containing my real thoughts. "Great."

He was passing his responsibility off to me. These three looked like deer in the headlights, having no idea what they were getting into.

Dr. Bauer said goodbye and I headed towards the emergency room with my new entourage. We were immediately hit with three patients. One suture job, a little girl who fell off the monkey bars onto her wrist, and someone with alcohol poisoning from the night before. Two of the students watched eagerly, taking notes as I worked, but the other one hung back. It didn't take me long to realize he wasn't like the others. He didn't even know the basics of medicine and hardly knew which end of the scalpel to use. Something seemed odd about him, and my suspicions were confirmed when I noticed a tattoo on his forearm. It was the same one I had seen on Alessandro's chest. Unbelievable.

The last thing I wanted was one of Alessandro's men playing bodyguard and following me around the hospital. It was already nerve-racking enough, and I knew it was just a matter of time before someone else realized he wasn't actually a medical student. I could handle myself, and this was a hospital emergency room in Las Vegas for crying out loud. It was crawling with police, what exactly did he think happened to me at work?

He had mentioned sending someone to the hospital with me for safety purposes at one point, but we had never talked about it again. I would've thought he would at least give me a warning instead of just dropping someone into my life posed as a medical student. If I knew Alessandro, he was probably counting on me not having any idea who this guy was.

When the other two stepped out of the room for a minute, I took my opportunity. "How long is Alessandro making you follow me around for?" I asked, snapping my gloves off and tossing them into the trash.

"I don't know what you're talking about, ma'am." He stood stone faced, not making eye contact with me.

"You can tell Alessandro that I don't need to be babysat. This is absurd."

A small smile tugged at the corner of his lips. "I think you're the only one who can get away with talking to Boss like that, ma'am. And this isn't about someone babysitting you, it's a precaution. There was a security breach."

A security breach? I sucked in a sharp breath. What exactly did that mean? Was I in some kind of danger? Was Ty? Or Alessandro? "What happened?"

He shrugged. "I just do what I'm told. Everybody is fine, we're just amping up security. I'm sure the Boss will have more information for you when you get home."

I fought the urge to roll my eyes, and bit my tongue keeping my thoughts to myself. This guy was just following orders, and I needed to talk to Alessandro myself.

"Can you at least tell me your name?" I huffed, crossing my arms over my chest defiantly.

"Ernie." He smiled.

"Nice to meet you, Ernie," I repeated. "And I'm Daisy. You can stop with the ma'am thing."

He chuckled to himself as the other students came back in.

I was irritated that Alessandro took this upon himself without even talking to me. And if something had happened, why didn't he call me? When I had a spare minute, I tried to call him, but he didn't answer. Apparently this was just going to have to wait until I got home.

For the rest of the day, I did my best to ignore Ernie, which wasn't hard to do because he barely spoke. It was harder to ignore the anxiety building inside of me. What if Alessandro wasn't answering or calling me because something had happened to him? Ernie had said everyone was fine, but he had been with me the last 6 hours, what if something happened during that time? I kept checking my phone obsessively, but nothing came from Alessandro.

When I pulled into the driveway and saw Alessandro's car at the house, I felt like I could finally breathe. As soon as I walked in the house, I could hear Ty and Alessandro laughing and a huge relief washed over me.

"Hi guys!" I smiled apprehensively as I came into the kitchen. Things certainly seemed business as usual around here. Alessandro even had dinner started.

"Daisy!" Ty threw his arms around my legs. "Dad said we can go see the sharks at the aquarium this weekend!"

"Wow!" I chuckled, arching my eyebrows at Alessandro. "That sounds fun!"

"Hey now, I said as long as you don't fight me about going to school anymore this week, we can go." Alessandro chuckled, walking towards me and pressing a hungry kiss to my lips. "How was your day?"

"Interesting." I clicked my tongue. "Did you send one of your men to the hospital to babysit me today?"

Alessandro pressed his lips into a thin line and narrowed his eyes at me, gesturing towards Ty. "We'll talk about it later."

I sighed in frustration that he was brushing me off so easily. Wanting to press him on it, I opened my mouth to speak but thought better of it. He was right, there was no reason to scare Ty.

Something felt off the entire time we ate dinner, but I couldn't put my finger on exactly what. Alessandro was especially short fused and I could tell he was stressed. Ty didn't seem to notice though, chattering away about his day and the deal Alessandro had made him with little to no response from me or his father. It was a completely different climate and it was shooting my anxiety through the roof.

When Alessandro finally sent Ty upstairs to brush his teeth, I was a mess of nerves. He came back into the kitchen and leaned onto the counter with his back to me. Every muscle was tense and I could see his shoulders rise and fall with each breath. I hadn't seen him like this since the day Ty was hurt and I hated it.

"Alessandro, talk to me," I begged, biting my lower lip. I was already almost in tears and didn't even know what was going on.

He let out a heavy sigh and turned towards me. He leaned back against the counter, pushing his sleeves up and exposing his decorated forearms.

"I'm sorry I didn't tell you Ernie was going to be at the hospital. I wanted to be the one to tell you this, and I didn't have time." I could see his breath starting to even out but still every muscle was clenched.

"Tell me what?" I stood up, approaching him cautiously.

"This morning, when I dropped Ty off, I found a note in his backpack. It was a threat to both you and Ty, and someone was close enough to us to put it into his backpack."

I sucked in a sharp breath, blindsided and unsure of how to respond.

Luckily, I didn't have to. Alessandro handed me the note and I scanned it, taking in all the details.

"Daisy, I'm not going to let anything happen to you or to Ty, do you hear me? Nothing. I'm going to get this guy and make sure no one comes after us again. But in the meantime, I need you to humor me. I don't want you to leave the house alone. Either Ernie or I will be with you at all times. It's just temporary, and I'm sorry it has to be this way, but I've got to cover my bases. I'm not taking chances when it comes to you or my son."

"Alessandro, I get your concerns, but don't you think this is a little overkill? This is just a drawing, we don't know..."

"Someone was in my house, Daisy. Someone got past my security and into my house and was close enough to my son and close enough to you to leave this. I don't care if it's a goddamn paint by number, it's serious. I've lost too much..." Alessandro was shaking, he was so angry, emotion clouding his eyes.

I reached out for his hand, regretting any fuss I had put up. I hadn't even thought about how triggering this would be for him. Of course, he'd go overboard to make sure nothing happened like it did with Talia.

"Okay." I squeezed his hand. "I understand. I'll do whatever makes you feel better."

"Thank you." Alessandro seemed relieved that I was on board. "I swear I won't let anything happen to either of you."

"I know you won't." I gave him a sympathetic smile. "But if you're so busy keeping Ty and I safe, who's going to keep you safe?"

Alessandro grinned, leaning forward and pressing a gentle kiss to my forehead. "You don't need to worry about me. I can take care of myself."

"You don't have to though." I put my palm to his cheek, rubbing gently with my thumb.

Alessandro smiled, trapping me against the counter with his hips. "I'll tell you what, when we're inside these walls, you can take care of me all you want."

He was trying to make light of the situation, but I couldn't help but worry. Alessandro carried so much guilt that I couldn't imagine it not eating at him. He had taken my comment sexually, but I found myself wanting to take care of him on every level. I wanted to be there for him, and listen to him, and be a support for him. And I wanted him to want me to. Alessandro's lips dragged along my neck and I knew I wasn't going to get anywhere tonight.

"I have to go out of town this weekend," I said, resting my arms around his neck.

"Where?" He furrowed his brow.

"St. Louis. To see my family." The timing couldn't be worse and I could already see the concern on his face.

"I'll come with you," he said definitively, snaking his arm around my waist.

I sighed, not wanting to rock the boat. "Alessandro, I need to do this myself. I'll only be gone a few days."

"I don't like being away from you, especially with everything going on."

"I'll be gone 48 hours. My dad's practice has a 30th anniversary party and I just need to make an appearance. I feel like I need to at least talk to my parents before I show up with a boyfriend and his son."

"I like when you call me your boyfriend." He snickered, his tongue grazing my ear.

"I'll call you every day." I smiled, melting into his touch.

"Make it every hour and you can go. "

"I can go?" I let out a sharp laugh. "I wasn't asking for permission."

Alessandro playfully slapped my ass. "You're so damn stubborn."

I had to roll my eyes. "And you're insane."

"Only for you, babe."

CHAPTER 19

ALESSANDRO

"Wow!" Daisy's eyes were wide in amazement as she listened to Ty recount our adventure at the aquarium today. He had insisted on coming right home and Skyping with her to tell her all about it. She had literally flown out this afternoon and we were both already missing her desperately. "That sounds really cool. I'm sorry I missed it."

"That's okay." Ty shrugged. "Dad said we can go again, and this time I can actually get in the tank!"

She arched her eyebrows at me trying to figure out if he was telling the truth or not. I chuckled, ruffling his hair. "They have a program where you can snorkel in one of their tanks, we talked about doing it for his birthday possibly."

"But my birthday isn't until January," Ty whined, throwing his head back dramatically. I could tell he was tired. We went to the aquarium right after I picked him up from school and now it was nearly 10 PM here.

"Well maybe I want to go for my birthday." Daisy shrugged, smirking.

"Yeah!! See dad? We have to go sooner!" He beamed up at me.

"Oh, now you two are conspiring against me?" The sound of Daisy's giggle made me weak through the computer. It was nothing like real life, but I would take what I could get.

"We can't disappoint Daisy, dad." Ty grinned mischievously.

"No, we certainly cannot." I winked at her, inducing a slight blush to her cheeks. "Ty, why don't you tell Daisy good night? It's time for bed."

"What?" Ty's face scrunched up in horror. "It's not even a school night!"

I gave him a stern look, and he eventually conceded. "Fine. Good night Daisy," he mumbled, sulking up the stairs.

"Goodnight Ty!" Daisy called.

"I'll be up in a minute to say goodnight, bud. Make sure to brush your teeth," I reminded him. I couldn't help but laugh at how dramatic he was being. He was moving at a snail's pace, his shoulders slumped forward like I told him Santa Claus wasn't real.

"It sounds like you two had a great day." She smiled, covering her mouth as she yawned.

"We did. It's been a long time since we've done something just the two of us like that," I agreed. "How was your flight?"

"Not too bad. There was a little bit of weather coming in, but I've been on worse."

"Good, and Ernie still with you?" I asked, already knowing the answer to that question. Ernie had been in touch with me all night like I had asked. I didn't like being away from her, but Ernie was one of my best guys and I knew he would keep her safe.

Daisy rolled her eyes slightly. "Yes. He's outside sleeping in a van. I tried to get him to come inside, but he refused. I still think this is a little overkill. My parents live in the safest suburb in all of St. Louis. Security and everything."

"Daisy," I sighed heavily. I knew she wasn't thrilled about this, but that didn't mean we had to rehash it at every turn. "My men are internationally trained in security and somehow these guys got through them. I highly doubt a bunch of neighborhood watch guards would be able to hold them off."

"That's a lovely thought right before I go to bed." She narrowed her eyes at me.

"Well, good. I'm glad it makes you nervous." I gave her the same look as the one I had given to Ty. "If you're nervous, you might not give me such a hard time about keeping you safe."

She sighed sheepishly. "I know, I'm sorry. I get it. It's just going to take me a little while to get used to this kind of thing."

"I know it's weird to be followed around all day, but I'd do anything to keep you safe."

<hr />

"I know, I just wish you were the one here with me." Her bottom lip stuck out in the most adorable pout I'd ever seen.

"I distinctly remember offering to come."

"I know." She smiled. "But trust me, I wouldn't even be here if I didn't have to be."

"How is it going with your family?"

She let out a heavy sigh. "It's fine. They're all too occupied with the party to remember what a failure I am." She tried to mask her disappointment with a giggle.

"Daisy, I don't ever want to hear you talk about yourself like that again." I frowned, wishing more than anything I could be there to wrap my arms around her right now. "Just because they had different ideas for you doesn't make you a failure, and you shouldn't let them sell you short like that. Just because your dad is living in the 60s and thinks women should only be nurses doesn't mean he's right. You're brilliant, and you don't need anybody's validation but your own. If you're doing what you love, then who the fuck cares about anything else?"

Daisy's lips turned up into a smile, but I could see her mind still swirling. "Thank you for saying that. I can't wait to get home."

"I can't wait for you to get home either." I couldn't mask my smile at the way she had referred to being here with me and Ty as her home. It wasn't the first time she had done it, but I loved the sound of it even more when she was sitting in her childhood home surrounded by her family. I loved that she was more comfortable here with us.

"I better get going. My family is waiting on me to eat." Sadness filled her smile. "Tell Ty goodnight and I'll see you both on Sunday."

"Text me before you go to sleep." I smiled.

"I will." She grinned. "Bye Alessandro."

"Hey Daisy?" I interrupted.

"Yeah?"

"I love you."

My words caught her off guard and she paused for a second, but then a warm smile blanketed her face. "I love you too, Alessandro. I'll talk to you later."

Daisy disappeared from the screen and I stared at it for a second as if it would make her come back. What was wrong with me? I was seriously strung out for this girl and that was a dangerous place to be. It was a relief to know she at least felt the same way. I was putting all of my eggs in this basket, leading both my son and I full force at this, banking on things with Daisy working. Each day I fell deeper and deeper under her spell, letting her work her way into my life, crafting it and spinning it in unimaginable ways.

I shut the computer, heading up the stairs to check on Ty. He was lying on his bed in his rocket ship pajamas, staring at the iPad screen in front of him.

"Ready for bed, bud?" I smiled, sitting down on the bed next to him.

He nodded, a big yawn tugging at his lips.

I helped him under the covers, kissing the top of his head as he settled himself in.

"Daddy, is Daisy going to be my new mommy?"

His question caught me off guard, so much so that I found myself stumbling over the words, unable to give him an answer. "I...I don't know, Ty."

"Well can she be? I really like her and she makes you happy." He smirked.

"What makes you say that?" I let out a sharp laugh, amazed by how perceptive he was. Nothing got past him, and the connection between Daisy and I was no exception.

"You smile more, and your eyes don't look sad." He giggled, putting his palm to my cheek.

"You're too smart for your own good, you know that?" I chuckled, tickling him and sending him into a fit of squirming.

Ty giggled wildly until I stopped and then settled down again.

"She's not going to go away like my other mommy is she?" Seriousness washes over his face.

I sucked in a sharp breath, running my fingers through his hair. "Buddy, your mom didn't just go away, she never would have left you if she had the choice. You know that right?"

Ty nodded hesitantly. "She got really hurt right? By a bad man?"

"Yes." I bit my lip. "A very bad man. Like the one who hurt you. And I promise, I am going to do everything I can to keep both you and Daisy safe."

"And you?"

"Yes, bud." I smiled. "No one is going to get hurt."

Fortunately, he didn't pick up on the uncertainty in my voice. I couldn't guarantee that until I had this guy. I was doing everything I could, but the truth was, I couldn't rest until this guy was dead. I couldn't promise anyone's safety until that happened.

We were closer, but that wasn't good enough. Q and some of his men had worked the captive over until he gave us a location. It wasn't current, but my guys were combing it now for some kind of clue.

My answer seemed sufficient enough for him and a soft smile grazed his lips. "I love you, daddy."

"I love you too, Ty. Sweet dreams." I kissed his forehead one more time before turning out the light and heading back downstairs.

It was dark and quiet as I descended the stairs. I let out a heavy sigh, rattled by my conversation with Ty. I had been so desperate to move us past this that I hadn't even considered how deeply he had been affected by it. He needed to talk it through and I had tried to sweep everything under the rug thinking he needed to forget. That was just another thing I hadn't been equipped for when Talia passed away.

A sharp creak coming from the kitchen caught my attention. I turned quickly, just in time to see a flash of black rush past me. Someone was in my house. I reached quickly for my gun, realizing it wasn't on my hip. I had put it away before Ty and I Skyped Daisy.

An excruciating pain seared through my abdomen as I stumbled back. Blood seeped through my fingers as I pressed the wound, watching as the intruder scurried out the front door. I leaned against the door for support, stumbling into the kitchen to get to my phone. A trail of blood followed me, and I slumped into the chair, grunting in pain and grabbing a towel to absorb some of the blood. The bastard had sliced clean through, just deep enough that it was probably going to need stitches.

I could feel myself getting dizzy from the blood loss and clumsily punched Joe's number into my phone.

"Hey man. I was just about to call you," Joe answered.

"Someone was here." I grunted, still applying pressure to the wound. "They broke into the house while I was upstairs with Ty. He stabbed me."

"What?" Joe shrieked. "Is he still there?"

"He snuck out the front." I winced.

"I'll be right there, man. How bad is it?" I could hear Joe already firing up his car.

"I'm okay. It's a flesh wound but it's deep. We've got to find this guy."

"On it. I'll be there soon," Joe said, hanging up quickly.

I tried to take a few deep breaths to take my mind off the pain, but it wasn't working. It felt like the world was closing around me. Why couldn't I stop this guy? Why was he always one step ahead of us?

CHAPTER 20

DAISY

By the time all of the schmoozing and speeches were over at my dad's party, I was absolutely drained. The afternoon had been full of playing the part of perfect daughter for him, and listening as he bragged to his friends about my position at St. Jude's. It was odd considering he and my entire family had been so adamantly against me becoming a doctor for the last several years.

I had been home for less than twenty-four hours and I was already over it. I had hope that coming back here would rejuvenate some of the passion I had for medicine a few years ago, but it had actually done the exact opposite. I was reminded of how practicing medicine had monopolized my dad. He had touted it as dedication in his speech today, but the reality was much bleaker. Truthfully, my dad was always at the office, and I had very few childhood memories that involved him at home with us. He never made it to a single dance recital, or sporting event, or play that me or my brothers were involved in. In fact, when I was a child, I almost drowned in our pool because he had been too occupied on a call to be watching me. I had never told a soul that that was what actually happened that day, but it was always in the back of my mind.

I thought about all of the trips my dad had to take when I was growing up, and the way my brother Jake had missed the birth of his first child because he was on call at another hospital. And the way Sean's high school sweetheart had walked away, breaking his heart, because she didn't want to come second to his work and Sean couldn't make any compromises. I had seen that job rob my family of so much, and the more I started to realize that, the less I wanted to become a doctor.

What I loved more than anything was helping children, and I didn't need a medical degree or fancy title in order to do that. There were thousands of jobs I could do, many still at the hospital that wouldn't consume me the way I was used to the medical profession doing. Of course I knew that not all doctors were like that, but I also knew myself. I had become so infatuated with proving myself to my dad that I had completely overlooked whether or not I even wanted to do this job. It was never because I really wanted to become a doctor, it was because I wanted him to be proud of me. The only problem was, I was beginning to see that may never happen. I could bend over backwards trying to be good at this, but would it ever be enough for him? It wasn't like taking the St. Jude's job and becoming a doctor would make my dad love me more, or see me as a professional in his same field. I'd be fighting that battle the rest of my life, or die trying.

On top of that, spending time with Alessandro and Ty had only made me realize how much I wanted a family. A family that I would raise and be active in, not one that sat on the shelf as some sort of decoration to me. I had battled with this the last several days, because I wanted to be sure I wasn't just making this decision because of Alessandro. I needed to be sure this was what I actually wanted, and not because I was making a frivolous decision based off of a boy and the wedding bells and butterflies in my mind. At the end of the day, even if things didn't work out with Alessandro, the life my father and brothers lived was not the life I wanted.

My parents were thrilled about the prospect of me moving to Memphis since it was only 3 and a half hours away. It would be difficult to tell them I was having second thoughts about everything, but I also knew I couldn't drag this out much longer. In my heart, I knew St. Jude's wasn't right for me, and I had no intentions of coming back home anytime soon. And I was seriously starting to doubt if being a doctor was the right thing for me either. It had nothing to do with Alessandro, and if things didn't work out with him, I still knew I was doing the right thing. I also knew there wasn't a shot in hell my family would see it that way.

I was a little apprehensive about giving up on my dream of becoming Dr. Daisy Taylor. It had been all I could think about my entire life, I never even considered doing something else. But now, with the prospect in front of me, I was oddly excited about pursuing something else. If this trip was worth anything, it had solidified that decision for me.

I had spent the better part of the afternoon googling other career paths that might interest me and settled on one thing in particular. Many children's hospitals were now hiring Child Life Specialists, and I had even worked with a few of them in the ER at St. Luke's. They worked with families of children in the hospital to help them all feel at ease with what was happening. They could help prepare the child, and even be in the room with them during the procedure so that they had a familiar face. Once, I had a child come in who needed stitches but was desperately afraid of needles. No matter how much the mother tried to calm her down, she was screaming at the top of her lungs and wouldn't let anyone near her with a ten-feet pole. When the child life specialist arrived, she showed the child on a stuffed bear what was going to happen and helped keep her calm so the doctor could sew her up quickly. It was amazing, and like nothing I had ever seen before. Unlike being an emergency pediatrician, it was something I could really see myself doing, and something that I truly felt could make me happy. At the very least, I wanted to look more into it, and would discuss it with Dr. Bauer when I got back to Las Vegas.

The decision was weighing heavy on me, and it was all I could think about right now. I hadn't been able to talk to Alessandro much today and I knew he was probably worried. At least Ernie would let him know I was okay, but I knew he would see right through me if we spoke to each other. I wasn't ready to let him in on this decision yet, even though I was confident I wasn't doing it for him. It made me feel oddly vulnerable in a way I had never felt with him before, not even when he kidnapped me and held me captive in his house. I had given myself to him in every way but this was something from the deepest parts of my soul and it was hard to share that with anyone. It's never fun to admit that you're doubting yourself or your decision.

Right now, I had to focus on telling my parents, and that was even more daunting.

"It's so good to have you home Mads." My brother Sean pulled me in for a hug as I sat down at the dinner table in the chair next to him. "I can't wait until you're just down in Memphis."

Memphis? How did he know about that already? "You told them?" I stared back wide-eyed at my father. I had only told my parents the news, but apparently they had taken it upon themselves to share it with Sean and Jake. This was only going to complicate things.

"I'm sorry, sweetheart. I know it was your news to tell but we're just so excited for you." He smiled at me as if he couldn't help it, setting a heaping salad bowl on the kitchen table.

"We all are, Daisy." Jake slid into the seat next to me. "That's so awesome. We knew you could do it. And you'll only be three and a half hours from home. We'll get to see you all the time."

"Hallelujah!" my mother chimed in, walking in from the kitchen with a bottle of wine. "We have so much to celebrate." She beamed, pouring a little bit into all of our glasses.

I grimaced, unable to pretend like there wasn't a giant elephant in the room. "Thank you guys, but it's not official yet."

"Dr. Bauer made it sound like the only thing left to do is sign the paperwork." My dad frowned as he cut into the barbecue chicken my mother had made.

I had half a mind not to get into this now, to let them all continue on in this blissful state, thinking my move to Memphis was a sure thing. In the back of my mind, I knew that wasn't right. I couldn't shy away from this any longer. I was used to their disappointment, what difference would this make?

"It is." I nodded cautiously. "But I'm taking my time in making the decision. I don't want to rush anything."

"Make the decision?" Sean looked at me with wild eyes, dropping his fork onto the plate loudly. "What decision is there to make? You have a chance to leave a shitty state hospital and go to one of the most reputable research hospitals in the country. Sounds like a no brainer to me."

"Yeah, I mean it is a great opportunity, I just..."

"It's a once in a lifetime opportunity." My father frowned condescendingly, as if he already knew where I was headed with this. "You can't possibly be considering turning it down."

I bit my lip hesitantly, but then it started coming out like word vomit. There was no turning back. "Well, the thing is I'm not even sure I want to be a doctor anymore. I think there are a lot of things I could do that I would enjoy and I'm not sure I want..."

My mother dropped the fork she was holding, sending it clattering to the ground. Both Sean and Jake looked at me wide eyed and then turned to my father anticipating his reaction.

He leaned back in his chair and let out a sharp laugh. "You've got to be kidding me. After all the time and money and fight you put up for this, you're having second thoughts about being a doctor?"

"Sweetheart, you've got to be reasonable here. You've spent the last several years dedicating your life to this." My mother tried to smooth over the situation.

"Not to mention throwing away all that money for what? To prove some kind of point to us? You can't honestly be serious about this, Daisy. Turning that job down would be vastly irresponsible. You simply can't," my father growled, already not taking this well. It was strange though, the more he talked, the more confident in my feelings I became.

"Well, first of all, it was my own money that I have thrown away if I decide I don't want to do this. And you've never wanted me to be a doctor, I would think you'd be happy about this." I gritted my teeth, nearly shaking with anxiety. I had never stood up to my father in such a way and it was both thrilling and terrifying.

His eyes turned to daggers. "That's because this has always been about sticking it to me. You acted like a petulant child, uprooting your life and spending thousands of dollars to prove some idiotic point to me, and now you can't even follow through enough to do that. You've never stuck with anything, Daisy, even when you were a child. And that's precisely why I didn't want you to pursue medical school. I knew it would be a fleeting thing for you, and here we are, exactly where I thought we'd be."

His words stung worse than I would have liked to admit. I felt a burning hole in my heart, staring back at him and realizing this was all I was ever going to get from him. Nothing would ever be enough and I had to accept that. He had never given me any indication that he would change, and I had to quit hoping because it only made me more disappointed.

"Daisy, your father just means..." My mother reached for my hand, trying to soothe me.

"It's fine." I stood up quickly. Suddenly, I couldn't get away fast enough. This only helped to make my decision easier. I wanted no part of the job, or the profession, or even my father right now. Maybe someday that would change, but right now, all I could think about was getting back to Alessandro and Ty. I turned towards my father, sighing heavily. "I'm sorry to disappoint you. I think it's time for me to go."

"Daisy, please don't..." My mom tried to stop me.

"Let her go," my father said harshly. "Running away from this just proves how childish she is. We can't even have a conversation about it."

Every part of me wanted to turn around and unleash my rage on my dad. To tell him how I had spent my entire life trying to please him, that the main reason I didn't want to be a doctor was because I didn't want to turn out like him, to tell him all the bottled-up emotions from the last few years I was feeling burning on the end of my tongue. In the end, I decided it wasn't worth it. He wasn't worth it.

I packed my stuff up quickly and said a quick goodbye to my mother and brothers. I was equally frustrated with them that no one had stood up for me.

Ernie was completely confused when I came out to the truck and asked him to take me to the airport. Luckily, there was a flight heading out soon and Ernie and I were able to get on it. I let myself cry for a few minutes on the airplane, but by the time we touched down in Las Vegas, I was over it and content with my decision. My father had essentially made it for me, and now there wasn't a doubt in my mind. As harsh as he was, there was some truth to what he was saying. I had gone about this in completely the wrong way, setting my happiness aside to impress someone else. That would never happen again.

The house was dark when Ernie and I pulled up, and I knew Ty and Alessandro were probably both sleeping. I didn't care though. I would wake them both up and tell them how much I missed and loved them. The people in my life would never have to wonder how I felt about them.

I used my key and opened the door quietly.

"Do you want me to take your bag upstairs?" Ernie offered.

"You don't need to do that, you've already done enough. Thank you for everything." I gave him a hug. "Go ahead and head home, I'll see you tomorrow."

"See you tomorrow." Ernie gave me a tight squeeze. "And Daisy, for the record, I think your father is a sack of shit for saying the things he did."

I bit my lip to stifle my laughter. How had Ernie heard? I should be surprised. "Thank you."

Ernie smiled one more time before closing the door behind him. I let out a heavy sigh, happy to be home and excited to see Alessandro. It was amazing how much lighter I felt after having made the decision. I had no idea how much it was weighing me down in the last few months, and it was such a relief.

There was a creak on the stairs and I turned towards it.

"Alessandro?" I asked, moving towards the noise cautiously.

Silence. Another creak.

"Hello?"

CHAPTER 21

D^{AISY}

"Hello?"

No one answered and I watched paralyzed as a dark figure moved towards me. Why the hell had I let Ernie leave without making sure Alessandro was here? Especially after everything he had told me the other day. The person had been in the house and now he was back to finish the job.

"Who are you?" I sputtered, backing away slowly.

"Daisy? Is that you?" Just as the figure stepped into the light, I recognized the voice as Joe's.

"Jesus Christ, Joe!" I let out a heavy breath. "You scared me to death."

"Sorry!" He chuckled, opening the fridge and grabbing a beer. "I didn't expect you home. Aren't you supposed to be in St. Louis until tomorrow night?"

I shifted my weight uneasily, not in the mood to get into everything with Joe right now. "My plans changed." I left it simply.

"You should have called. Alessandro likes to know when plans change."

I rolled my eyes. "I can make my own decisions, Joe. I don't have to clear everything with him."

"Easy killer, who pissed in your Cheerios?" He arched his eyebrows and held his arms up in defense.

"Is Alessandro upstairs?" I ignored his banter, my patience with today running thin. I had had just about all I could take.

"Uh, actually..." Joe diverted his eyes, shoving his hands into his pockets. "Alessandro is at the hospital."

"The hospital? Why? What happened?"

"He's okay," Joe tried to soothe. "There was an incident last night. An intruder got into the house and stabbed him, but he's completely fine, it's just a precaution."

"Oh my god." I covered my mouth, tears rushing to my eyes. How had someone gotten inside again? Alessandro and Ty both could have been seriously hurt. The thought of anything happening to either of them was enough to send me right over the edge tonight. "Why didn't anyone call me?"

"Hey." Joe recognized my tears and put his arm around me. "He's fine, Daisy. I promise. We weren't even going to go in but he was worried it might get infected. They've already treated him and only kept him overnight as a precaution."

"I want to go see him," I said, my lips quivering, wanting to see for myself that what Joe was saying was true.

"Okay." Joe nodded, grabbing a bag off of the kitchen table in front of us. "I just came to get a few things for him. Ty is at my house with my wife."

I nodded, having trouble forming words. It had already been an exceptionally emotional day for me and it was only getting worse. I needed Joe to get me to Alessandro as fast as possible.

Joe seemed to understand my need, and ushered me to the car. We drove in silence, my mind swirling in a million different directions. It was a relief that Alessandro was going to be okay, but he should have told me what happened. I shouldn't have to find out like this. Everything was fine this time, but it was a harsh reminder of the present danger in our lives. Nowhere was safe. Alessandro was attacked in his own home, and someone was close enough to do it.

Joe parked in front of the hospital and we both hurried inside. He showed me down the hall to Alessandro's room and I burst inside with Joe close at my heels.

Alessandro was sitting up in the bed, tapping away at his laptop, and looked up at me wildly when I rushed towards him.

"Daisy?" Without even saying anything, I threw my arms around his neck and draped myself over his body, holding on for dear life. The world felt like it was crashing around me and all the emotions of the day were converging on me at once. It was all I could do to keep my composure right now. His arms wrapped tightly around me and he kissed the top of my head, already sensing something was off with me.

"I found something I thought you might like back at the house." Joe chuckled, slinging the bag he had brought onto the recliner.

"Why don't you give us a few minutes?" Alessandro said softly. He kept one arm around me and set his computer to the side with the other.

Joe nodded and shut the door to Alessandro's room behind him. With him gone, and my own confirmation that Alessandro really was okay, fury began to replace my concerns.

"Why were you home? You're supposed to be in St. Louis with your family." He brushed my hair off of my cheek with his thumb.

"Why didn't you call me immediately?" I clenched my jaw, ignoring his question entirely. He wasn't the one in charge right now.

A small smile tugged at Alessandro's lips, as if teasing me for my reaction. "I didn't tell you because it wasn't a big deal. I thought we could talk about it when you got home."

"Not a big deal?" I reeled back. "Alessandro, someone attacked you in your home and you're in the hospital. Of course that's a big deal! Do you have any idea how worried I was when Joe told me? How would you have felt if something like this had happened to me and I hadn't told you because I didn't feel like it was a big deal?"

"I'd be pretty pissed," he said contemplatively. What I was suggesting was completely new to him. It wasn't how he normally functioned.

"Exactly." Hot, angry tears pooled in my eyes. "So from now on, you don't get to keep things like this from me. That's not fair, it's not how a relationship works."

"Okay." Alessandro nodded solemnly. "It won't happen again."

"And don't just say okay to placate me. Say it because you mean it. We're a team, I shouldn't be the last one to find something out like this. I was so worried when Joe told me. It felt like I had been stabbed myself."

"I do mean it, baby." He put his palm to my cheek, pulling me close and giving me a gentle kiss. "I'm sorry, okay? I'm not used to having someone to tell these types of things to, but I swear, I will call you immediately next time."

Next time. I hated that phrase.

"But I promise you, I'm fine. In fact, this might even be a blessing in disguise. We were able to get a clear picture of the guy off the surveillance camera and Q and his men are already tracking him down. We're that much closer to getting these guys."

"But at what expense?" I bit my lip as the tears finally released and started to roll down my cheek.

"Daisy, relax. I am fine. I promise. It barely even hurt. Do you want to tell me the real reason why you're so worked up? You can't possibly be this upset about me getting a little knife scratch. Did something happen when you were back home?" He put his hand to my cheek, stroking gently.

"I don't want to talk about that. I want to talk about you." I shook my head, not allowing him to shift my attention in that way. The things that happened back in St. Louis were the least of my concerns. "Was Ty home?"

Alessandro rolled his eyes playfully. "You know, I haven't seen you in two days, and I can think of a lot more enjoyable things we could be doing than reliving all of these details right now."

I glared at him harshly, letting him know I meant business.

"Okay, okay." He chuckled, wrapping his arm around me and pulling me back so that I was lying on the hospital bed next to him. "Ty was home. It happened almost right after I hung up our Skype call. I went up to tuck him in, and came back downstairs and there was somebody in the kitchen."

"And he stabbed you?" The words left a bad taste in my mouth, almost like poison.

Alessandro nodded. "As he was running past me, so it really is just a flesh wound. The only reason I am here is because the blade must've been rusty, and it started to fester and they were worried about an infection. Your buddy Dr. March cleaned it out and stitched it up to try to keep it as clean as possible. I called Joe after it happened, and he came over immediately. Ty has been staying at his house with his wife and is completely safe. He doesn't even know I was hurt."

"Can I see it?" I propped myself up a little bit. Alessandro pulled his shirt up, exposing a long wound on his abdomen. I gently ran my fingers along it, counting each individual stitch. Twenty-five in total, which was a lot for a knife scratch as he had called it. He was lucky, Doctor March was a great physician and took good care of him by the looks of things.

"Does that hurt?" I asked.

"Not at all." He grinned smugly. "In fact, you rubbing my chest like that is the best I've felt since it happened."

"Very funny. You know three centimeters to the right and he would have nicked your abdominal aorta, and we'd be in a much different situation," I cautioned. It was amazing he hadn't actually. That artery went directly to the heart and Alessandro would have bled out quickly. The thought made my stomach turn.

"God, you are so sexy when you use medical words like that." Alessandro certainly hadn't lost any of his spitfire and that was a comfort. His banter was starting to calm me down a little bit, too, and I could almost feel my heart rate slowing.

"Yeah, well, don't get your hopes up. I work in this hospital, there's no way I'm having sex with you here." I rolled my eyes at him.

"Then can you at least get them to release me so we can go home and do it?" He winked.

I glanced up at Alessandro's IV drip and noticed they were giving him some pretty strong antibiotics. Maybe it was a little worse than he was letting on. "I'll tell you what, I'll go find Dr. March and see what's really going on, and if he thinks I can take you home with special care, we'll get out of here."

"Oooo, I like the sound of special care." He slapped at my butt as I stood up from his bed.

"Would you stop?" I laughed, my cheeks blushing red.

"I just missed you." He flashed a smile at me that made him look just like Ty. Totally sweet and innocent. Too bad I knew the real Alessandro. He probably had never been described as sweet and innocent in all of his life.

"I missed you too." I kissed him, brushing my tongue along his bottom lip. "Now, please behave while I'm gone."

"Yes ma'am." He smirked, fake saluting me. He was such a child sometimes, and it was both infuriating and adorable.

I snuck out the door, letting Joe know that he could go back in, and continued down the hall to find Dr. March.

Instead of finding Dr. March, I found Dr. Bauer standing at the end of the hall at the nurses' station, and he turned around right as I approached.

"Daisy." He seemed shocked to see me. "What are you doing here? I thought you were in St. Louis for your dad's event?"

"I was." I nodded. "But I came back tonight. My, um, Alessandro was injured and I was just looking for Dr. March to see if I could take him home."

"Of course. I heard that Mr. Bosio was here. Give him my best for a speedy recovery, will you?" He grabbed a stack of files quickly, trying to walk away.

"Actually, Dr. Bauer, I was hoping I could talk to you about something." I guess now was as good a time as any.

"Yes?"

Suddenly I felt flustered, having trouble finding the words. "Well, I just wanted to thank you for helping me with the opportunity at St. Jude's, but I just feel like it may not be the best place for me."

Dr. Bauer looked back at me like I was insane. "Daisy, are you sure about this? The opportunity at St. Jude's is very rare, and something like this won't come up again."

"I know." I bit my lip. "I just want to be sure this is right for me before I make a big decision like that."

He let out a heavy sigh. "I think you're making a huge mistake. You've worked tirelessly for this, and you're going to let that guy in there change your mind?"

"This has nothing to do with Alessandro." I was immediately defensive against his accusations. I had made sure that this decision was for me, and not for Alessandro, and I certainly didn't need to explain myself to Dr. Bauer.

His call light went on. "I have patients I need to attend to, why don't we meet after the gala and talk more about this?"

"There's nothing..."

"Goodnight Daisy." He cut me off abruptly and turned down the hallway.

I thought about going after him and insisting that there was nothing he could say to change my mind, but realized it wasn't worth it. Especially not tonight.

I was able to find Dr. March quickly and he said that I could take Alessandro home. He expected him to heal up well, and would follow up next week.

Right now, getting Alessandro home and lying in bed next to him sounded like a perfect ending to an otherwise terrible day.

CHAPTER 22

A LESSANDRO

———— ⬥ ————

"I'm not so sure about this." Daisy frowned, pushing her plate of tacos towards the center of the table. She had hardly touched it.

I had met her for a quick lunch before I had to head into work, and she had been distracted the entire time. In fact, she had been a little aloof since she came back from St. Louis but I hadn't pressed her on it. I knew how raw and personal family issues could be, and she would come to me on her own time.

It didn't mean I was happy with that, or that it wasn't irritating the fuck out of me that I couldn't figure out what was on her mind. I was trying this new thing though where I was respectful of people's boundaries, so instead of prying it out of her, I decided to focus on the issue she was talking to me about. The gala at the hospital this weekend.

"What exactly aren't you sure about, babe?" I reached across the table and took her hand gently in mine. "Going to the gala or me going as your date?"

Daisy rolled her eyes. "Trust me, you aren't the issue. If you hadn't agreed to go with me, I wouldn't even be considering going at all."

That was a relief. I was suspicious she was having second thoughts about mixing our relationship and her work like that, and was glad to hear that wasn't the case. "Then what is the problem?"

She left out a heavy sigh, staring off into the distance. "I hate this type of thing. It's just a big dog and pony show, I'd much rather be at home watching movies on the couch with you and Ty."

"As much as I like the sound of that, I'm looking forward to the opportunity to show you off as my girlfriend. And think of how much fun you and I will have sitting in the shadows making fun of all the pretentious people there." I had been to things like this a million times before and if nothing else, they were always entertaining. You could count on some rich guy getting drunk off his ass and making an idiot of himself. A mistress, desperately trying to act like she belonged in a place like this. Usually a fist fight or two. The list went on. You'd think that a room full of Las Vegas elite would have more class, but fundraisers like the hospital gala never ceased to surprise me.

"Do we have to?" Her lips formed a tiny pout.

"Yes." I let out a sharp laugh. "It's not like this is some sort of torture. Most girls would love a night to get dressed up and be wined and dined. And besides, you're required to be there for work, remember?"

Daisy bit her lip. "Yeah, but what if..." Her voice trailed off, conflict blanketing her face.

"What if what?" I pressed, her expression sparking my curiosity.

"Nothing." She shook her head. "Fine. I won't complain about it anymore. But we're leaving early. That's non-negotiable."

"As long as we're agreeing to terms." I smirked, pulling a card out of my pocket. "This is my friend Rebecca's shop. She's expecting you this afternoon to pick out a dress. Another non-negotiable."

Her eyes widened. "You're not buying me a dress."

"Trust me, I'll figure out some way for you to repay me." I smirked, letting her mind wander. Truthfully, I wanted to buy her a dress for this event out of the goodness of my heart, but if she was going to make it difficult on me, I had plenty of ways in mind for how she could work it off. Every single one of them involved her being naked in my bed.

"You're impossible, you know that?" She gave me a half smile.

"What can I say, I'm used to getting what I want." I chuckled, finishing what was left of my beer. I normally didn't drink in the middle of the day like this, but I needed something to take the edge off of what I had to do this afternoon.

Joe and Q had tracked down a bastard high up in the Chavo organization. We were so damn close to breaking this wide open that I was almost salivating in anticipation. I couldn't wait to put this shit behind me so Daisy and I could move on and have a normal life with Ty. He deserved that, she deserved that. And never in my life had I craved such a thing. Right now, it was all I could think about though.

"Have you ever thought that maybe what you wanted all along isn't what you really wanted at all?" Daisy sighed, leaning back in her chair.

I frowned, trying to read her expression. I didn't like not knowing what was going on with her but it was starting to irritate the hell out of me. "Daisy, what are you talking about?"

"I..." I could see the wheels turning in her mind, words hanging on the tip of her tongue. "It's not a big deal. I guess I'm still just irritated about something my dad said."

"Do you want to tell me about it?" God, I so badly wanted to know. I was already furious with the bastard for making her feel this way and I didn't even know what happened.

"Just the same old stuff." She shook her head in an attempt to brush it off. "It's not even worth mentioning. I don't know why I'm so hung up on it this time. I'm fine, I promise. Let's just forget about it."

"Are you sure?" It didn't sit right with me. I was big on confronting things immediately no matter how abrasive it may be.

Daisy needed time to process and mull it over which was difficult to me. Talia had been the same way, maybe it was a female thing.

She nodded. "I'm sure. I'm not gonna think about it anymore. Besides, aren't you supposed to be at work at one?" She glanced at her watch.

"Damn," I growled, looking down at my watch. "I am. But I can always rearrange things for you."

"I appreciate it, but I promise I'm fine." She smiled, squeezing my hand gently. "I'll see you for dinner?"

"I'll be counting down the seconds." I nearly vomited as the words came out of my mouth. What the hell was happening to me?

A smile tugged at Daisy's lips. "You know for such a big, tough mafia leader, you're kind of a big sap," she taunted.

"Don't you dare ever repeat that to my men." I couldn't help but smile either. There was that sass I loved so much. "Or I'll have to show you just how scary of a mafia man I can be."

"I'm not scared of you." She pursed her lips confidently, almost begging for me to kiss them.

I happily obliged, pressing my lips to her hungrily, and pulling away at the exact moment I felt her relax into the kiss. "You should be." I smirked, standing up and grabbing my jacket off the chair.

"I love you." She fluttered those lashes up at me like a damn butterfly. This was bad, we hadn't even been together all that long and she already knew exactly how to get to me.

"I love you too." I brushed my lips against her forehead quickly so as not to fall even deeper under her spell. I needed to get some work done today, and if she kept looking at me like that, I would never leave. "Even if you are a tease."

She giggled, waving innocently at me. I didn't even look back because it was already taking so much restraint to walk away from her. The sooner I could get this over with though, the sooner I could thoroughly enjoy her.

Dr. Daisy had been holding out on me since my injury, claiming sex was too much activity and I might bust my stitches. She cleared me this morning when I all but threatened her life, and I was planning on taking full advantage of it tonight. I had it in my mind that a good fuck was what we both needed.

The warehouse where Joe and Q were holding the guy was a short drive away and I spent the ten minutes trying to clear my mind. I wanted this to be over as soon as possible, and I needed to be sure I was giving it my full attention. All distractions needed to be on the back burner until I got what I needed from him. And that was a name. The name of the guy who was behind all of this.

We were so close I could almost taste it, just that one piece of information and I could break this thing wide open.

I found my way to the back room and Joe and Q were already eagerly waiting for me.

"It's about time you got here." Joe chuckled. "Daisy let you off the leash for the afternoon?" He and Q shared a smirk.

"I have a lot of pent-up aggression saved up this afternoon, boys. I'm sure our prisoner would be glad if I took some of it out on you two morons." I rolled my eyes at them. It was a good thing they were my best friends because they were seriously irritating me today. Their banter was interfering with my focus.

"Alright, alright." Joe smirked, walking over to the chair in the center of the room. The prisoner was tied to it tightly, with a bag pulled over his head. Joe removed it roughly, and the guy looked around like a deer in headlights. "Alessandro, meet Ryker. He's a Lieutenant in La Eme and was the one who ordered the hit on both Talia and Ty, and fingerprints were found all over your house."

"That's not true. I had nothing to do with your old lady, I swear to God." He shook his head wildly, trying to backtrack. It was amazing how much men like this preached loyalty, but sang like songbirds once they were in a situation like this.

Q reared his fist back, landing it squarely on Ryker's jaw and sending blood sputtering across the room. His brass knuckles clamored to the floor.

I bent down to his eye level, meeting his glare. "Ryker, I think you'd say just about anything right now to save your own skin. I think you killed my wife, targeted my son, and I think you came back the other night to try to finish the job. You have 30 seconds to convince me otherwise."

"I don't know!" he shrieked, jerking against his restraints. "I swear, I never met the guy. I don't even know anybody who has. All I know is he is some rich white guy, doesn't even live in Vegas. They call him Doc."

"Doc?" Joe repeated.

Ryker nodded wildly. "He never shows his face but everything runs through him. Every time he sends an order, it arrives in a brown paper bag of takeout food from a Chinese restaurant on 1st. That's all I know, I swear."

I stared at him intently, trying to determine whether or not he was telling the truth. He had no reason to lie to us, we were his only hope of staying alive. Either we killed him, or we let him go with a target on his back. Whether or not he told us anything wouldn't matter, it would look like he did to his group.

"What do you think?" Joe sneered, the same thoughts running through his mind.

"I think we aren't in a position to overlook any leads." I gritted my teeth. If Ryker was telling the truth, we were closer. I hated the thought of this dragging on even longer, but I wanted to be sure. I had to be sure, there was no room for mistakes.

Joe nodded to Q and he left the room, ready to chase down the lead. They were ready for all of this to be over, too. Our entire business had pretty much been on hold the last few months.

"Look, you've got to protect me. I can get you to Doc, but I need some assurances first," Ryker stuttered, pleading with us. He was well aware of his fate the second he walked out of my door.

Joe let out a sharp laugh. "Protect you? You're lucky you're still breathing right now."

I rubbed my jaw, contemplating my options. Unfortunately, he was right. He had the closest ties to whoever this guy was and was our best chance of ending it swiftly.

"You can have 3 days," I offered.

"It's going to take longer than that. I told you, this guy doesn't do face to face."

Joe looked at me curiously, but watched, clearly intrigued with what I was going to say. Bargaining wasn't a method that I tended to use very often.

"Three days. If you don't deliver him by then, La Eme can have you." I turned and looked towards Joe.

"I want eyes on him at all times," I ordered. "And taps on the phone."

Joe nodded, hauling Ryker off.

I let out a sigh of frustration. I had waited so damn long for this and now that it was here, I was anxious. I had a lot to lose if a war broke out, but I'd do everything I could to avoid it.

CHAPTER 23

A LESSANDRO

"Daaaaad," Ty called from the top of the stairs. "She's ready!"

He was insisting on treating this like some sort of prom night introduction—not letting me see Daisy all afternoon, and making me stand in the foyer as she walked down the stairs. I had no idea where the kid got his ideas on romance, because they certainly didn't come from me.

"Okay, bud." I chuckled, standing up and brushing one lone wrinkle out of my suit pants. "I'm coming."

A small part of me was actually enjoying this. I hadn't experienced dating jitters like this...well, ever, and this was exciting. I was more than ready to take Daisy out in public and show her off as my girlfriend. We had been out before, of course, but attending a fundraiser like this together was the next level. Many of my business associates were donors to the hospital and would be there, and it would for sure be photographed. I felt more confident than ever with Daisy on my arm and I was determined to show her a good time tonight. She had been settling down a little bit as the week went on, showing her endearing sass more and more, but I could tell she was still a little restrained and I was going to get to the bottom of it tonight. I hated seeing her conflicted, and not being able to do anything about it.

Daisy had picked out a dress at Rebecca's shop but both of them were refusing to show it to me until tonight. All I knew was that it was black and I was instructed to dress accordingly. Rebecca was an old associate of mine, and she and Daisy had hit it off immediately. She had even offered to come over tonight to do Daisy's hair and make up for the night. The anticipation had absolutely skyrocketed my sex drive and by the time Ty announced she was ready, I was chomping at the bit to see her.

"You gotta close your eyes, dad," Ty insisted, standing at the top of the stairs with his hands on his hips.

"Bud, seriously, we're already running late. Can't we..." I threw my arms in the air in impatience. Hadn't I waited long enough?

"Do what he asks, Alessandro." I heard Daisy chuckling from behind him somewhere, still out of my sight.

"Fine, fine." I caved, glancing at Joe who was standing a few feet away from me, smirking. He didn't need to tell me for me to know exactly what he was thinking. He enjoyed giving me a hard time, but the truth was, he was just as indulgent to his wife, Emily. It was no secret who wore the pants in their relationship. At least I hadn't given up full control to Daisy yet.

I covered my eyes with my hand. "Everybody happy?"

"Okay, go ahead," Ty whispered loudly, encouraging Daisy down the stairs. The wood creaked with each step she took, building up my anticipation.

"Can I open them?" I couldn't help but smile at this silly game. It was so mundane but it clearly made both of them happy.

"Okay, now, daddy!" Ty exclaimed. Was he actually jumping up and down in excitement?

When I opened my eyes, Daisy was halfway down the stairs, the long black dress flowing in the air behind her. It took the breath right out of my lungs. She was an absolute smoke show in the form-fitting dress, her blonde hair secured in pins at the base of her neck and her lips painted a deep red. The dress cut down dangerously low in the front, and a long diamond necklace drew my eyes right to her chest.

"You look..." My mind turned to complete mush and I couldn't seem to form a sentence, imagining all the ways I wanted to take this thing off of her tonight. It was beautiful, and I had insisted on us going to this thing in the first place, but one look at her dressed up like that and all I could think about was bending her over my bed instead.

It wasn't until Joe elbowed me in the ribs that I could finish my thought. "Absolutely incredible."

She smiled, scrunching up her nose. "You don't think it's too much?"

"Not at all. I think it's perfect. Every guy in that room is going to wish he was with you." For the first time, I was having second thoughts about this whole thing. I was going to have to fend guys off of her all evening with her looking the way she did. And while I enjoyed being on the receiving end of other people's envy, I wanted to enjoy the evening with her.

"You clean up nicely yourself." She blushed, reaching for my hand.

"You both look great." Rebecca smiled, rushing down the stairs herself and handing Daisy a matching bag. "Your lip color should stay, but I put the tube in your purse just to be safe."

"Thank you so much for everything Rebecca, this is like a fairytale," Daisy gushed, hugging her tightly.

"Well, it helps when the canvas is already beautiful." Rebecca smiled. "Good to see you Alessandro." She stood up on her tiptoes to kiss me on the cheek.

"You as well. Thanks for the suit, too." She was a fashion designer and almost everything I owned came from one of her lines or another. She had hand delivered this one today through, apparently not trusting me to pick something suitable enough to be seen with

Daisy, and I couldn't blame her. Daisy was the most beautiful thing I had ever seen in the entire world, and even I felt out of my league with her tonight.

"You two better get going." Joe chuckled. "The carriage turns back into a pumpkin at midnight."

"Hey!" Daisy gave him a teasing glare. "Does that make me Cinderella?"

"What's wrong with that?" Ty asked curiously.

"You don't ever want a girl like Cinderella, Ty." She smiled, bending down and giving him a tight squeeze. "She waited around her whole life for a man to come rescue her, couldn't do anything for herself."

"Okay." I laughed, reaching for her hand. "Let's get out of here before you turn my son into a feminist."

"What's a feminist?" Ty scrunched his nose up.

"I'll let your uncle explain that to you tonight." I chuckled, shaking my head.

Daisy and I said our goodbyes and I called the car around. We talked the entire way to the fundraiser about the evening and she was actually starting to look forward to it.

The gala was at the Bellagio and by the time we got there, it was already crawling with elitists. I could feel Daisy hesitate as if she didn't belong there, but I held her hand firmly, and let her inside.

"I'm nervous," she whispered as we picked up our name plates and headed into the dining room.

"You have no reason to be." I turned to her, cupping her chin in my hand. "You are the most beautiful person in the entire room. Hell, you're the most beautiful person I have ever seen in my entire life. You're compassionate and brilliant, and you're going to make an incredible doctor in a few months. You belong here more than about seventy-five percent of these morons. So stop doubting yourself, everything is going to be fine."

I pressed my lips to her, watching as a strange look clouded her eyes, almost as if she was about to cry. I could tell she was going to tell me something when we were rushed by another woman.

"Daisy! I am so glad to see you! When your name wasn't listed at our table, I was worried you decided not to come." The woman threw her arms around Daisy, and I stepped back.

"Hi Peyton." Daisy smiled, regaining her composure a little bit. "It's good to see you."

"So what's the deal? Does Bauer have you sitting with the St. Jude's visitors tonight?" Peyton grinned widely at Daisy.

Daisy's face got white. "The St. Jude's doctors are here?"

"Well, yeah... Is that a problem?" Peyton frowned, confused by Daisy's reaction as well.

"Daisy is sitting with me tonight, I'm sorry to steal her away from you guys." I gave her a charming smile, stepping in. "I don't believe we've met, I'm Alessandro Bosio."

"Of course!" Peyton turned her all too positive attention towards me. "It's so nice to finally meet you, I've heard a lot about you. Daisy and I have been friends for years. I guess if I have to give her up tonight, you're a good enough reason."

"I appreciate that." I chuckled, wrapping my arm around Daisy's waist.

"Well, come find me later." Peyton gave her one last squeeze. "And it was lovely to meet you Alessandro."

She flitted away before either of us could respond.

"Are all of your friends so bubbly?" I smiled, turning to Daisy.

She bit her lip, letting out a small laugh. "No. That's just Peyton's personality, and she's even more excited tonight because she loves this kind of thing."

"A rare breed."

"That she is." Daisy smiled, loosening up a little bit again.

Before we could even catch our breath, Dr. Bauer appeared. "Daisy, Alessandro, so nice to see the both of you."

"Nice to see you too, Dr. Bauer. It's a beautiful event." She smiled, turning on the charm.

"It is, isn't it? This is always one of my favorite nights of the year." He grinned, staring right at her and hardly acknowledging my presence. I could feel my blood pressure start to rise already. The guy was a smug bastard and I hated the thought of Daisy having to work with him.

He was one of the most arrogant people I had ever come across, and watching the way he operated made me sick. Daisy hadn't noticed the way his eyes grazed her breasts, but I did. She wasn't the only one he was ogling either. He was here with his wife, but that didn't stop him from watching all of the young female doctors. He was a slime ball and my hatred for him ran deep.

When Talia had been taken to the hospital, a mistake was made. She would have survived the attack, had a doctor not given her the wrong dose of medication and killed her instantly. Dr. Bauer was the head of trauma at the time and knew exactly who had done it. I begged him to tell me who the doctor was but he flat out refused. He hid behind legalities and paperwork and tried to throw all kinds of money at me to make the problem go away. He denied all knowledge that a mistake had been made and there was no proof so even when the cops got involved, the hospital couldn't be held accountable. It plagued me to this day, the way he had held the one tiny detail I coveted most this entire time and held it over my head like a goddamn carrot in front of a race horse.

"I have to go speak with one of our esteemed guests, but Daisy, find me later will you? You and I have to finish our discussion from earlier this week." He eyed her carefully and turned to walk away. Like hell I would let her find him alone. It was a ticking time bomb having men like that in a place like this with all the free booze. I'd be keeping close tabs on her all night.

Daisy watched as he walked away, with the strange look in her eyes again. Was she upset about her family, or had something happened with Dr. Bauer?

"Everything okay?" I asked.

"Yes." She smiled, a little too enthusiastically. "I could certainly use a drink, how about you?"

I let out a hesitant sigh, but followed her. "That sounds great."

I ordered a champagne for Daisy and a whiskey for myself and we wandered around until we found our seats. We were seated with a few of the men I had done business with in the past, which was perfect. I wanted Daisy to feel as comfortable as possible and I had a feeling she would click with one of the wives in particular. We sat down and I introduced her to the people at our table. This was a fundraiser for the hospital, but it was also a ploy for them to get more funding. That meant most of the people in this room had nothing to do with the hospital, and Dr. Bauer and other board members would spend the evening trying to convince Las Vegas' wealthy to invest in them. It was probably why he insisted on having Daisy and the rest of the graduating med students there.

I watched her all night, mesmerized as she interacted with everyone, as comfortable as if she had known them her entire life. She could fit perfectly into any situation and she had no idea how incredible she was. Everyone at the table was eating up every word she said as she told stories about the ER and all of the wild things she had seen. I found myself beaming with pride for her, so lucky that I was the one she was with.

"And how did the two of you meet?" Craig, one of my associates, asked.

I was taken aback at first, not going to admit that I had kidnapped her from a park. We hadn't talked about what we were going to tell people about how we met.

"I treated his son earlier this year. We just kind of clicked." Daisy smiled, resting her hand on my knee. I swelled with pride at her gesture.

"I knew there was no chance I could let her get away," I echoed, putting my arm around her shoulder and pulling her into me.

"I'm surprised he didn't kidnap me." She winked, teasingly.

"I am, too!" Craig chuckled. "Alessandro certainly has a way of getting what he wants."

"I'm going to get another drink while you all harass me." I chuckled, standing up and grabbing our empty glasses. "Another champagne babe?"

"Sure, thanks." She smiled, her cheeks already turning a soft shade of red from the buzz. I couldn't contain my smile as I walked away from the table, she was so damn adorable.

"Whiskey on the rocks and a champagne, please." I set our glasses on the bar as I ordered.

A man came up next to me and at first, I didn't realize who it was. When I turned to see Dr. Bauer, I looked away in disgust before I could do something I would regret.

"Alessandro." He slapped me on the back as if we were old friends. "Enjoying the night?"

"Yep," I answered shortly. Conversing with him wasn't high on my priority list. I could play nice because he was Daisy's boss but that was about it.

"I'm glad I caught you alone. I've been wanting to speak with you for weeks. Ever since you brought lunch to Daisy."

I shot him a harsh glare. "Well, here I am."

"What exactly are you trying to pull by dating Daisy? Is this some kind of way to get back at me for not telling who made the mistake with Talia?"

"What?" I let out a sharp laugh. This guy had a lot of nerve thinking my relationship with Daisy had anything to do with him. "You're out of your mind. I love Daisy and I haven't given a fleeting thought to you in months. Except for two hours ago when I watched you checking out my girlfriend right in front of me."

"Alessandro, let's be real here. What are the chances you wind up with one of my most promising med students after everything you and I have been through?"

"I don't know what to tell you, old man. This has zero to do with you. Now if you'll excuse me..." I turned, but he caught my arm.

"It's pretty selfish don't you think? Making her give up her dreams to stay here with you?" He arched his eyebrow at me curiously.

"What the fuck are you talking about?" Giving up her dreams? Making her stay? What was this all about?

"St. Jude's. Ever since I have known her, that's been her dream. You expect me to think it's another coincidence that you show up and she turns the job down?"

Job? What job? I didn't even know what St. Jude's was. It seemed my confused expression convinced Dr. Bauer, and his face broke into a smile.

"Oh, I see." He started chuckling. "She didn't tell you."

"My patience is running thin, and I don't like being jerked around." I gritted my teeth. "You better tell me what the fuck you're talking about."

Dr. Bauer smiled widely as if he was relishing in the fact that he was the first one to tell me this. "Daisy was offered a job after graduation at one of the most prestigious research hospitals in the nation. St. Jude's in Memphis."

CHAPTER 24

D AISY
  I hated to admit it, but Alessandro was right. The gala had been more bearable than I expected, I might even say enjoyable. I had managed to avoid Dr. Bauer and his judgmental opinions for most of the evening, and it was great to get to know some of Alessandro's business partners. It was like seeing a whole new side of him, one that he had kept the mask over since we'd met, and I felt oddly proud that he was finally choosing to include me in it.

I had been to these things a million times over the last few years, and had always sat back with Peyton, poking fun at all of the rich clowns who paid a pretty penny to attend. I had always regarded the hospital donors as deft investors who didn't have the faintest idea what we actually did on a daily basis and only contributed to make themselves look good. Tonight, I was realizing how wrong I was, that Alessandro's friends were actually very active in the hospital and trying to make positive changes. Many of them were even the engineers who designed the very technology I used on a daily basis.

After a few minutes, I glanced around the room trying to spot Alessandro. He had gone to get drinks, but the bar area was empty. Maybe he had stepped outside for a few minutes. I excused myself to go look for him, and hopefully convince him to join me on the dance floor. We were here after all, might as well fully immerse ourselves.

I stepped out onto the balcony into a cloud of smoke. Several men were outside enjoying cigars, but Alessandro wasn't among them. Thinking I might catch him by the bathrooms, I started that way, but was quickly stopped.

"Daisy." Dr. Bauer stood in front of me, another man I didn't recognize stood to the side of him. "I'm glad I caught you. This is Frank Martin, the head of surgery at St. Jude's. He's the man who offered you the job."

I sucked in a sharp breath, realizing what he was doing. He was backing me into a corner by introducing me to Dr. Martin, trying to railroad me into agreeing to the job. My chest started to constrict, a mix of anger and angst making it hard for me to concentrate on anything.

"Hello, Dr. Martin. It's so nice to meet you. Dr. Bauer throws a lovely party doesn't he?" I smiled politely, trying to mask my racing heart.

"That he does." Dr. Martin shook my hand. "He was just telling me that you haven't made your final decision about joining our team. Are there any questions I can answer to ease your mind?"

"I'm afraid Dr. Bauer might have misunderstood me, Dr. Martin. I am so thankful for your offer but I am unfortunately going to have to decline. I am thinking about using my degree in a different capacity and would hate to waste your time."

Dr. Martin gave me an understanding grin. "One thing I appreciate in a person, Daisy, is sincerity. Good luck with whatever it is that you decide to do, and please keep me in mind if you change your plans."

"Of course." I smiled, shaking his hand again.

"Now if you'll excuse me, I have to find my colleague." Dr. Martin turned and headed back towards the ballroom.

"I was hoping our little chat the other night had made you reconsider." Dr. Bauer narrowed his eyes at me. "You're throwing your entire career away, Daisy."

"I'm throwing away a career I don't want, Dr. Bauer. I have other plans now and St. Jude's just isn't part of them. I'm sorry if that puts you..."

"That man will ruin you, Daisy. He'll use you just long enough to crush every bit of spirit inside of you and then throw you out with the trash. I've seen it happen before."

"Dr. Bauer, you have no idea what you're talking about. This has nothing to do with Alessandro and even if it did..." I couldn't get away from this conversation fast enough.

"It got his wife killed, you know. Alessandro and his bogus business dealing. Did he tell you that?" His face was reddening as he spoke, clenching his fists tightly.

"You knew Talia?" I frowned, suddenly curiously about what he was saying.

"Of course. Everyone around here did. She was murdered by someone Alessandro worked with and then he tried to blame it on my staff. I'm telling you, Daisy, take the job and get out of here before you meet the same fate."

I swallowed the lump in my throat, knowing there couldn't be any truth to what he was saying. If I was to trust Dr. Bauer or Alessandro, there was never any contest. It would always be Alessandro. But I needed to talk to him about what happened to Talia and put this to rest once and for all.

"We're not done here, Daisy," Dr. Bauer growled, catching my wrist and jerking me back.

"Ah!"

Before I knew what was happening, Dr. Bauer had released my wrist and a tall dark figure moved in between us. Thank god it was Alessandro.

"You most certainly are." His words spewed like venom. "If you ever lay a hand on her again I'll have you buried so deep in a sexual harassment suit that you'll never touch a scalpel again."

Dr. Bauer chuckled. "That's always your go to, isn't it? Take care of this one Alessandro, I'd hate to see Daisy end up like the first Mrs. Bosio, wouldn't you?"

Alessandro swung his arm backwards, slamming it against Dr. Bauer's cheek with such force that the pop echoed off of the walls.

I covered my mouth with my hands, watching as blood spewed out of Dr. Bauer's mouth.

"Let's go." Alessandro interlaced his trembling fingers tightly in mine and pulled me to the door.

I was too shocked to speak, wanting to get out of this situation as quickly as possible. Every eye was on us as Alessandro led me out, bursting through the front doors and out to the curb.

"Alessandro, slow down," I pleaded, nearly tripping over my own feet.

Once we were outside, he mumbled something into his phone and seconds later, Q pulled a car around.

"How was it?" Q grinned widely as he opened the door for us. His expression changed wildly the second he saw Alessandro's scowl.

"Just take us home, Q," Alessandro hissed, scooting over to the far side of the car, leaving a canyon between us.

Q nodded and began the drive towards home immediately. There was definitely more to this than Alessandro was letting on. Everything was fine one minute, and now it was like he was a completely different person.

"Alessandro, what happened back there?" I asked quietly, once I was slightly more composed.

"What happened?" He scoffed, shoving his fingers through his hair. "I didn't like the way he grabbed you so I knocked him out."

"You punched my boss, Alessandro. I have to work with those people every day. I appreciate you wanting to stand up for me, but my world doesn't work the way yours does. You can't just punch somebody every time you get upset."

Alessandro let out a harsh laugh. "Don't be so naïve Daisy. That world is a lot more like mine than you would like to think. And I'll never apologize for protecting what's mine."

"What's yours?" I arched my eyebrow. "I'm not some kind of possession Alessandro, I'm your girlfriend."

"You're damn right you are, and he's lucky I didn't get another punch in. The guy may be your boss but he's a total prick and If he ever tries to touch you again, he won't be getting up."

"You know, I am able to stand up for myself Alessandro, which I was doing before you showed up. You don't need to go around punching everyone just to prove a point." I narrowed my eyes at him, a little frustrated.

"Well, excuse me for trying to defend you." It wasn't that I was ungrateful that he was defending me, it was that I could see something else was going on. His issue with Dr. Bauer was obviously much bigger than he would like me to believe.

"Is everything okay?" I tentatively reached out and put my hand on his knee.

"Everything is fucking perfect Daisy." He cut me off abruptly, jerking away from my touch. With his jaw clenched, he stared out the window silently, lost in his own mind. It wasn't until a few minutes later that he finally broke down.

"When were you going to tell me you're moving to Tennessee?" His voice was completely flat, void of all emotion.

His words hit me like a sharp punch to the gut. How had he even found out about that? I was obviously going to tell him about the job, but I wanted to wait until I had a decision made so he couldn't talk me out of it one way or the other. I hadn't officially told them anything until tonight, but now I didn't even have the chance to tell Alessandro myself. And worst of all, he thought I was actually going.

"Alessandro, I don't know what you think..." Words seemed to be failing me right now, and I could hardly form a coherent thought. Maybe this was what had prompted his reaction to Doctor Bauer.

"What I think, Daisy, is that you've been sitting on this news for the last few weeks, leading my son and I along, all the while knowing you were going to take this job and leave." His tone hinged on the edge of hurt, but was mostly anger.

I could feel my own anger start to brew. "Who told you about St. Jude's?" I bit my lip gingerly.

"That's what you're concerned about right now?" he roared, causing Q to glance back worriedly.

"Of course I'm concerned about it, Alessandro." I threw my arms in the air in exasperation. "I had every intention of telling you once I had time to process it myself. I only just found out about the job, and didn't want to say anything to you until I was sure."

"Well," he gave me an evil, sarcastic grin, "Dr. Bauer made it sound like you're pretty fucking sure now. Were you just planning to disappear out of our lives one night or what? If that's your plan, why don't you just go now? Ty can't handle much more loss."

Dr. Bauer, of course. I was almost at a loss for words. How could he honestly think so little of me? I was well aware that Alessandro could be harsh, it came with the job, but his spite had never been turned on me. I never reacted well to being backed into a corner and could already feel myself teetering on the edge of an explosion. Alessandro had made his mind up without even allowing me a second to explain myself. He had taken the word of my boss whom he absolutely hated over me, and that stung more than I would like to admit.

"Can you pull the car over, Q?" I pursed my lips, needing to put a little bit of space between myself and Alessandro right now. There was no way for me to reason with him when he was this upset and we would just end up in a great big fight, both of our tempers flying.

"What the fuck are you doing? You're actually going to leave right now?" Alessandro's face twisted in rage.

"Nope." I shook my head, trying to remain calm as I unbuckled my seatbelt. "I'm giving us both some space. You've obviously made up your mind, without even asking me my side of things, and I don't want to say something I'm going to regret." I opened the door, stepping out into the brisk air.

"So what? You're going to sit on the curb?" He rolled his eyes petulantly at me. The way he was brushing me off only irritated me further.

"No, I'm going to walk home alone."

"Not in that outfit you're not," he spat at me before I slammed the door.

I took my shoes off so I could walk faster, hoping to put enough distance between us that he wouldn't catch up to me. Not even Alessandro would dare to chase me down on the crowd strip. I fumbled with the strap, jumping when I heard the sound of his door slamming.

"Damn it, Daisy." He shoved his fingers through his hair, tearing around the side of the car. "Just get back in the car."

"The last thing I want to do is go somewhere with you right now." Angry tears threatened to fall from my eyes. I was so damn mad at him I could hardly see straight.

"I'm the one that should be upset, Daisy. You've been lying to me for weeks." He put his hands on his hips, reaching out and catching my arm when I finally stumbled out of my stubborn shoes.

"I haven't been lying to you, and if you had given me half a chance to explain to you what actually happened, instead of taking that bastard's words over mine, this wouldn't even be an issue," I hissed, relinquishing my hope of getting any space between the two of us tonight. He was ready to have this out, and apparently it was happening whether or not I wanted to.

"Then explain it to me, because from where I'm standing it looks pretty shitty." For the first time, I heard a hint of hurt in his voice. It broke with the slightest bit of emotion, and I could tell he was softening.

I crossed my arms over my chest, debating my next move. I could continue to be mad and argue with him childishly, or I could explain my side of things to him and have an adult conversation.

"Please, let's just take a walk. Let's go somewhere quiet and talk," he begged, releasing his grip on my elbow and gently caressing my hand.

Hesitantly, I intertwined my fingers in his and we made our way towards the Gardens behind the Bellagio. It wasn't exactly private, but it was as close to quiet as you could find on this strip. And at least Q wouldn't be hearing every word of our argument.

There was so much we needed to talk about.

CHAPTER 25

ALESSANDRO

Daisy was livid as we walked to the gardens. Her hand was intertwined in mine, but it was reluctant, every muscle clenched like my touch was foreign to her. My life relied on my ability to read people, and I could already feel her withdrawing from me. As we made our way through the gardens to find a bench, I couldn't help but wonder how the tables had turned so quickly.

I was the one that should be pissed off. I was the one that had been lied to, and strung along like some lovesick school boy. Me and my son. I was the one that would be left to pick up the pieces when she left us behind. And now she wanted to play victim because I had been trying to defend her and she had been caught.

So why wasn't I more angry with her? Why wasn't I reading her the riot act and making sure she knew she was the one in the wrong? It was because for the first time in my life, I felt completely out of control. Like my fate was in her hands, and would be determined by whatever came out of her mouth next. I had never experienced vulnerability like this, and it was a terrifying, debilitating feeling. I knew I was acting irrationally, but I felt like a train without brakes, speeding full steam ahead a brick wall. How had I let this woman get so woven into my heart?

The silence between us was almost comical, a perfect depiction of just how stubborn we both were. Neither one of us wanted to make the first move, but the longer we sat here like this, the more my anxiety grew.

"Why didn't you tell me about Tennessee, Daisy?" I finally said, wincing at how pained and weak my voice sounded. I was too wound up to be ashamed though. I was hurt, and I wanted her to know it.

Daisy took a deep breath, chewing tenderly on her lip. "Alessandro, I didn't tell you because it didn't concern you."

"Like hell it doesn't concern me!" I bellowed, my face twisting in disdain as I pulled away from her. Was she serious?

Daisy narrowed her eyes at me. "Are you going to let me talk, or are you going to interrupt me every two seconds?"

I set my jaw, not wanting to admit defeat, but also desperately wanting to hear what she had to say. If I had to bite my tongue for a few minutes, so be it.

"I just mean that I had to be sure I was making this decision for me, not because I fell love with you." Tears welled up in her eyes. "Alessandro, my entire life, all I have ever wanted was to be a doctor. I wanted to work with kids and St. Jude's was like the top of that world. It's everything I had ever dreamed about and to be offered a job there right after school was incredible."

"I guess congratulations are in order," I grumbled sarcastically.

Daisy sent me a harsh glare and I rolled my eyes, holding my hands up in defense. I needed to keep my mouth shut if I was going to get any answers. "Sorry. Go ahead."

"I always thought I'd be thrilled when an opportunity like this came around, but the second Dr. Bauer told me, all I felt was dread." She sighed, pursing her lips slightly.

My brow furrowed. Dread? What was she talking about? Hadn't she just told me what a dream-come-true it was?

"For the first time ever, I was questioning everything about my career and everything I had dedicated to it. I couldn't shake my doubts and I was scared that it was because of you. I don't want to be that girl who drops everything for a guy and totally changes who she is. That's why I didn't tell you right away. I needed to make sure that what I was feeling was real, and not just because I fell in love with you and didn't want to leave. I needed to know I didn't want to be a doctor with or without you."

My chest started to tighten as I realized that I had made a terrible mistake in reacting the way I had. Of course, I wish that she had told me sooner, but I couldn't fault her for this. It was exactly the way I had felt to begin with, wanting to be sure of my own feelings for Daisy before I let Ty get too attached to her.

"Daisy, I feel like an absolute moron." I raked my fingers through my hair, swallowing my pride and ready to grovel at her feet. "If this is something you really want we can figure it..."

"I didn't take the job, Alessandro. And it's not because of you, despite what Dr. Bauer, or anyone else, thinks." Her face hardened at the mention of Dr. Bauer. It made me feel even worse, because I knew he must have been giving her a hard time about this, and I had taken his word as truth. The word of a man who I detested more than just about anything in life. How had I been so stupid? I must have played right into whatever scheme he had going.

"I didn't take the job because I don't think I want to be a doctor anymore," Daisy continued, pausing to gauge my reaction.

"You...you don't?" I stuttered, staring at her wide eyed. She had just dropped two bombs on me. First that she hadn't actually taken the job, and second that she didn't even want to be a doctor anymore. What had changed? Did that mean she was staying? Where was all of this coming from? I was bouncing somewhere between relief and confusion.

I was ready to start rapid firing my questions when she shook her head. "No, I don't. In fact I don't know if I ever really did. Becoming a doctor has always been about proving something to my family, to my father. And it took me all this time to realize how ridiculous that was. I don't owe him anything, and I certainly don't have to prove anything to him. And I was ready to work myself into the ground, and give up any resemblance of a normal life to please him. It almost makes me sick to think of that now."

I absorbed what she said, holding my thoughts in. "So what changed?"

She shrugged, wiping a few errant tears off of her cheek. "I met you."

I frowned at her admission. Although it was flattering, I never wanted to be the reason for holding her back. What if she changed her mind again? What if she passed up on the job and ended up resenting me?

Daisy could see where my mind was wondering and immediately jumped in. "Let me explain. I am not turning the job down because of our relationship. I love you, and I want things between us to work, but I also don't want to be the person who makes life-changing decisions like this just because she fell in love with some boy. What I mean is, until I met you and Ty, I didn't really even consider life outside of the hospital, let alone having a family. I was so focused on my career and getting ahead and becoming the kind of doctor I thought my dad would be proud of, but these last several weeks, I've gotten a taste of the family life I missed out on my whole life. My dad was always gone, constantly working and then completely distracted whenever he was at home. And even if I don't end up with you and Ty, I don't ever want to be that way."

"Daisy, you have way too big of a heart to ever be that way. You're amazing with Ty, and you will be no matter what you do for a living. Who cares if you don't want to be a doctor? The only thing that matters is that you're happy and you're doing something you enjoy." I snaked my arm around her shoulders, pulling her in close to me. I could feel her soften into my hold and she laid her head gently on my shoulder. It was a small reprieve from the conflict between us, but I would take whatever I could get. I planted a soft kiss on the top of her forehead in reassurance.

"I'm glad you think so. Unfortunately, that's not good enough for everyone." Her pained sigh nearly broke me.

"Is that why you came home early from seeing your family?"

She nodded. "I told my parents, and my dad pretty much laughed in my face. Said he always knew I couldn't do it. And maybe he's right, maybe now that it's a reality, I'm scared so I'm running away."

Fury filled my veins. I hated seeing her doubt herself, and I hated it even more than it was at the hands of her father. Someone who was supposed to love her unconditionally and build her dreams up. Not tear her down and make her feel like a failure.

"Daisy, look at me." I put my finger under her chin, tilting it so I could look into her beautiful eyes. The distraught look inside of them was like a dagger to my heart. "You are one of the most driven and determined people I've ever met, I don't believe for a second that you're scared of this. Do you?"

"I guess not." She bit her lip. "What I'm scared of is that I don't have any kind of plan. I'm about to throw away my entire education and hundreds of thousands of dollars and I don't have the slightest idea what I'm going to do."

"First of all," I smiled, pulling her even tighter into me, "I don't believe for a second that you're doing this without some sort of plan. That's just not who you are. I think you've put a lot of thought into life after making this decision or we wouldn't even be having this conversation, am I right?"

Daisy blushed, a small smile on her lips. "Sort of. I have a few things I want to look into."

"Good. You're young, who cares if you don't have your entire life figured out yet? So spend some time exploring those and find something that excites you. Find something that makes you proud. Not your dad, not me, not anyone else."

"You know, it's kind of ironic that you're the one giving me this lecture." She laughed softly. "You went into your family business to please your family also."

I chuckled. She did have a point. "Yeah, but the difference is, I'm doing what I'm doing because I enjoy it. Making my dad happy was a nice side effect, but I knew this was what I wanted. There was never a shadow of a doubt in my mind, and I know that if I had said I didn't want to take over for him, my dad would have supported me in whatever I chose to do. The thought that you don't have the same support from your dad makes me want to bash his skull in."

Daisy winced. "Thank you. I know you're just trying to make me feel better, but I really appreciate you saying all of that. It just makes me love you even more. And I'm sorry I didn't tell you right away, I hate that you found out from someone else. I just couldn't let your feelings about it sway my own one way or another. It's terrifying to think that everything I've built my life around since I was a child, suddenly isn't what I want anymore."

Pieces were starting to fit together for me. Her return from visiting her family so quickly, how off she had been lately, the way she had spoken about uncertainty the other night. I had thought she was talking about me, but she was actually talking about this. "Daisy, I don't even know what to say. I fucked everything up. Dr. Bauer told me that you were taking the job, and I just saw red. The thought of losing you nearly paralyzed me, and obviously I wasn't thinking straight. I should've found you to talk about it immediately."

"Of course it was Dr. Bauer." Daisy rolled her eyes, shaking her head softly. "He won't let it go no matter what I say to him. That's what we were talking about when you came up."

"Look, I want you to know that no matter what you would have decided, I would have supported you. I don't ever want to hold you back from your dreams, and even if you decide to quit and join the circus, you'll have my love and support and we'll make it work."

Daisy burst out laughing. "The circus?"

"It got my point across." I smiled wryly. "I love you, and I'm so sorry for overreacting. I should have given you the opportunity to explain before I jumped to any conclusions. And I sure as hell never should have taken Dr. Bauer's word for it."

Daisy shifted her weight, withdrawing slightly again. "Alessandro, what's the deal between you and Dr. Bauer? There's obviously more between the two of you than you've told me."

I sucked in a sharp breath, trying desperately to plan out my next move. I had told Daisy the gist of what happened to Talia, but not as it related to Dr. Bauer. At first, it was out of respect for her job, but I was pretty sure that excuse went out the window when I punched him in front of half the hospital staff. It wasn't just that though, I hadn't really talked to anyone about Talia's death, like keeping it inside was some form of self-inflicted punishment I was putting myself through. This was the final wall I had up. Daisy had broken down every single barrier I had, and now I was seconds away from letting her tear down this last one. The one thing that was holding me back. After she knew this, every secret of my heart would be laid out for her, for better or worse.

"After Talia was attacked, her mom called an ambulance. I didn't get there in time to control the situation and she was taken to St. Luke's. While she was in surgery, there was a mistake made, I never got to really know the specifics. But Dr. Bauer was in charge of the emergency department at that time. He knew who killed her, and he wouldn't tell me. We went back and forth in court for months but I got nowhere. All I wanted was a name." I gritted my teeth, envisioning what I would have done to the guy if I had been given the opportunity. It sent adrenaline pulsing through my veins, only to be reined in by the soft touch of Daisy's fingertips on my forearm. There was a soft sympathy in her eyes that wrapped around me like a warm embrace and I found myself compelled to continue.

"Alessandro, I'm so sorry. That must have been so terrible for you."

Terrible was an understatement. It changed the entire course of my life. I became a single father, hell bent on revenge and neglecting nearly every responsibility I had in the meantime. If it hadn't been for Joe and Emily, Ty and I probably wouldn't have survived. The guilt consumed me and I was half the man I once was, letting it eat away at my soul. It wasn't until I met Daisy that I even felt like a resemblance of my old self. It was a slow process but it was happening.

"I guess Dr. Bauer has become my scapegoat. I don't know who was really responsible, but he's the closest target I can get. And the way he was treating you tonight..." I clenched my jaw, reliving the moment. "Something in me snapped."

Daisy put her palm to my cheek, rubbing gently. "You don't have to carry this around forever, Alessandro. I know you feel responsible and like you have something to avenge, but that's a horribly sad way to live. You need to give yourself a break."

"But it was my fault."

"No, it wasn't. You just said yourself that what killed Talia was a mistake made by someone in the hospital. And from the way you described it, she knew what she was getting into when she married you. You can't carry a burden like this forever. You owe it to Ty to let it go, and honor his mother in a productive way. Not like this. I know you think knowing who was responsible will help, but all it will lead to is more violence. Is that really what you want for Ty?" Daisy continued to rub my cheek as tears sprung to my eyes.

I was torn between knowing she was right, and staying loyal to the crusade I had been on for the last several months. She had no way of understanding, but I had no intention of arguing with her anymore. There was nothing in the world I hated as much.

I reached for her hand and brought it softly to my lips. "Let's go home."

CHAPTER 26

A LESSANDRO

⎯⎯⎯⎯⎯⎯◦◦◦⎯⎯⎯⎯⎯⎯

When we got home from the gala, adrenaline was pumping so strongly between Daisy and I that there was no way we would make it up the stairs before pulling each other's clothes off. There was something electric about makeup sex, and the way my body was magnetized towards her was like nothing I had ever experienced. It must have been a combination of the jealousy and possessiveness I felt watching the way Bauer grabbed her and the paralyzing thought that she might be leaving, but I felt out of control. I had to have her right this very second and I wasn't sure if I would ever get enough.

The gorgeous black lace that had covered her body all night was now in pieces in the kitchen, and I had thrown my jacket to the side, buttons popping off of my dress shirt as she ripped it off. Daisy felt the same thirst that I did as she dragged her nails down my bare chest.

"We should go upstairs." She bit gently on her lip.

I grunted, lifting her up onto the counter. "I can't wait. No one is home, I want you right here."

Daisy wrapped her legs around my waist, rubbing her hips up and down against mine. I was already so hard for her that the aching in my groin was almost too much. "Then get to it," she whispered,

197

dragging her tongue against my ear. The sensation sent chills down my spine.

The thing about Daisy was that her body was just as brilliant as her mind. She dropped her head backwards, exposing her chest to me. Her breasts spilled out of the bra she was wearing and she fumbled with the clasp, letting them fall freely against her. Sliding one hand behind her head and fisting her hair, I kissed her neck hungrily and made my way down. Her moans just solidified her desperation for my touch, daring me to go further. I grazed my tongue against one nipple and then the next, flicking my tongue against her mercilessly as her body writhed in pure pleasure.

"Oh my god, Alessandro." She was already nearly out of breath.

Lowering her gently onto the counter, I climbed on top, throwing what was left of my clothes to the side. The chill of the granite made Daisy shiver as she bent her knees and let them fall open to the side.

"You are so beautiful." I kissed her knee first and then down her thigh. Her fingers trailed through my hair as I lapped my tongue against her, just close enough to where she wanted me but not close enough. I enjoyed teasing her, watching the way her body squirmed in anticipation, ready and longing for the next touch. I knew I was testing her patience, but it only added to the fun. If she was on the edge, it would make the release that much more intense.

"Please, Alessandro," she begged, her desperate eyes locking with mine.

I couldn't help but smirk, pressing my fingers against her slick flesh. "Is this what you want?"

"God, yes. Please." I fucking loved hearing her beg. It felt so primal and raw.

I chuckled, returning my attention to her breasts. "Be patient, baby."

Daisy knew exactly what I was doing, reaching for my length and stroking it with her fingertips. Her touch caught me off guard, momentarily throwing me off of my game. "You want to play games, huh?" She winked, grabbing my hips and easing them over her.

"Ugh, yes." I moaned, lowering myself into her mouth.

Daisy closed her fingers around me and flicked her tongue against the tip.

"Mmmm." I groaned again, my erection throbbing.

"Is this what you want?" she teased, throwing my own words back at me. She let me in a little deeper.

"Mmmm." I couldn't even form a sentence.

"How about this, baby?" She licked up and down my length, her tongue twisting and sucking against me.

"Fuck yes, Daisy. You feel so incredible." My head fell back and I allowed the feeling to consume me. It was literal heaven.

Immediately, she pulled away and propped herself up on her elbows a little bit. "What was that you said about patience a few minutes ago?"

I shook my head, pressing my lips to hers. "Okay, you got me. No more games."

"Perfect." She smiled, leaning into my kiss and pulling me down.

Her knees fell open again and I stroked my fingers against her vigorously. She was dripping wet for me, and I could tell she was right on the edge. My wallet was sitting on the counter and I grabbed a condom out of it, ripping into it hastily. Daisy took it from me, sliding it on me.

I slipped inside of her, her body clenching around me. My hips rocked against hers roughly. My hunger and need for her was driving me over the edge and I was through being gentle. Daisy arched her back, clinging onto me as she moaned and called out my name. Harder and harder I plunged inside of her and it was driving her absolutely wild. Daisy shrieked, digging her nails into my back hard enough to scratch.

"Harder," she whispered, egging me on.

I pounded into her over and over again, and Daisy took every inch of me. At the last second, I spun her around so she was on her knees and I slid my cock in from behind. She gasped at first, and then tilted her hips against mine. After a few hard thrusts, I couldn't take it anymore, exploding inside of her. My orgasm sent Daisy over the edge and she fell against the counter, both of us writhing against each other. I held her against my chest as we both tried to catch our breath. Soon, our chests rose and fell in sync.

"You know, this whole makeup sex on the kitchen island was really hot, but do you think we could move the cuddling part upstairs?" She grinned.

"I completely agree, this granite is going to murder my back." I chuckled, sliding off to the side and reaching my hand out to help her down.

"Now you sound like an old man," she teased. "I just meant I'd like to continue this with a little bit more privacy."

"Old man?" I arched my eyebrow, reaching over and slapping her ass. "You're going to be sorry you said that."

Daisy grinned and started up the stairs, playfully gesturing for me to follow her. It didn't seem like we were going to bed anytime soon but that was perfectly fine with me.

CHAPTER 27

D^AISY

The sound of my alarm the next morning was like nails on a chalkboard. Alessandro and I had gotten home late, and we spent the next few hours making up. When the alarm went off, it felt like I had just barely closed my eyes.

I reached out for Alessandro, but his side of the bed was cold. He had long since been up, and I could hear the running water in the bathroom. He hadn't elaborated on what exactly he had to do, just telling me that he would be occupied for most of the day. I had a shift at the hospital, but was looking forward to a night at home. Last night had been a roller coaster of emotions, and I was just as exhausted mentally as I was physically.

Bits and pieces of the evening ran through my mind, including when Alessandro had knocked Dr. Bauer out cold on the marble floor of the banquet hall. I could still so vividly see Dr. Bauer's head snapping back with the force, and the sound that Alessandro's fist on his jaw made. Although Dr. Bauer had fully deserved it, it still made me cringe. I knew well that that side of Alessandro existed, I just didn't like having to experience it firsthand so much.

Out of everything, though, Alessandro's story about Talia was weighing on my mind the most. I couldn't imagine how terrible that must've been for him and Ty both, and the fact that he was still drowning himself in guilt broke my heart. I couldn't help but think I might be able to provide a little closure to him. If I was leaving the hospital anyways, what would it matter if I snooped around a little bit? The only problem was, I had already done that, and my search hadn't turned up anything. I could ask Dr. Bauer himself, but I highly doubted he would divulge anything to me, and the thought of facing him today after everything from last night wasn't exactly high on my priority list.

I reluctantly pulled myself out of bed and slipped a robe over my body. I had no idea where my clothes had ended up last night, but the morning light made me slightly more modest.

The bathroom door was cracked open, and as I got closer, I could see Alessandro leaning against the bathroom counter, shaving his face. In only a pair of jeans, he was humming along to whatever song was playing on his phone. I pushed the door open a little bit more, and leaned on the door frame, soaking in the details of his perfectly sculpted back.

Moments like this, where I could fully appreciate him, made me weak in the knees. My eyes traced the lines of every single tattoo on his body, and no matter how many times I had seen his bare back, I felt like I always found something new in his artwork. This morning, it was a pair of song birds right at the base of his neck. I hadn't noticed it before, because they were intertwined in a larger picture, but they were beautiful. Inside one, were the initials GM, and inside the other, NC. My brow furrowed in confusion. The GM was pretty self-explanatory, but the other one was baffling. NC? What did that stand for?

"Are you just going to stand there staring all morning?" Alessandro smirked at me through the mirror.

I smiled, sauntering into the bathroom. "I'm just admiring the masterpiece in front of me."

"Oh, well in that case..." Alessandro set his razor down on the counter and turned towards me, reaching out for my hand. "You're in luck, this isn't a look, don't touch type of exhibit. In fact," he tugged me forward, trapping me between his knees, "touching is encouraged."

"You know if I do that, neither of us will make it to work today." I smiled, reaching up and wiping a little bit of shaving cream off of his nose with my thumb, Alessandro lurched his neck to the side, pretending to bite me. He hungrily kissed my neck, dragging his teeth along the under skin and smearing shaving cream all over me.

"Alessandro, stop!" I giggled, trying to squirm out of his grasp. The more I moved, the tighter he clenched his legs around me, pulling me tightly against him.

He was usually so put together that I cherished times like this, when he let go of his tough exterior and showed me his soft and silly side. It only made me fall deeper in love with him.

"Your offer is tempting." He kissed my cheek. "But I have a few things that can't wait. I'll cash in on that promise tonight though."

"You better. It'll be the only thing getting me through the day." I sighed, breaking out of his grasp and picked up a wet washcloth to clean my neck.

"You know you don't have to go back. You could just quit," he suggested, grabbing his razor and resuming his shaving.

"I'm three weeks away from being done, Alessandro. I can't quit." I rolled my eyes, shaking my curls out gently. The mascara under my eyes and rat's nest in my hair made me fully regret just falling into bed last night.

"Yeah, done with training for a job you don't even want."

"True. But it won't look good on my resume if I quit three weeks before I'm supposed to be done. And it'll be good for whatever else I decide to do."

"Whatever makes you happy, baby." Alessandro wasn't convinced, but he played along. He put his hand to my cheek, kissing me gently. I nearly moaned out loud when he pulled away after a few seconds. "Ty is having a sleepover at Q's tonight. That means you and I have the house to ourselves." He winked. "Movie night?"

"That sounds heavenly."

"Great. I shouldn't be too late." He grinned, grabbing his t-shirt off of the counter. It wasn't often he went to work like this which had my curiosity peaked. "Ernie is going to be at the hospital with you today."

"Does he have to be? It's weird to have someone hanging around me all the time. I can't work in those conditions." I like Ernie but it was hard to be followed around all the time.

"Nice try." Alessandro chuckled, playfully slapping my butt. "He's coming. End of discussion."

"You're so bossy." I smirked.

"I'll show you bossy tonight, babe." Alessandro winked again, slipping the shirt over his head.

Even with his shirt on, the wings of the songbirds peeked out from the top of it, reminding me of the strange initials on his back. "Hey, I've never seen the tattoo of the birds on your back. It's really neat."

Alessandro smiled, continuing to get ready. "I got it for Talia. Birds symbolize immortality."

"What do the initials NC mean then?" I pressed.

"Natalia Castillo," he said. Why did that name sound familiar to me? "That was Talia's real name. She didn't take my name when we got married, she wanted to still try to keep some separation so she wasn't a target."

Well, that would explain why I had never found any records for her in the hospital. I had no idea she had a different name. Maybe this would make my search a little easier today.

"That's really beautiful, Alessandro."

"Thank you." He kissed me one more time. "I'll call you a little bit later to check in. Please don't give Ernie a hard time."

"Yes sir." I fake saluted him.

Alessandro smirked, pointing at me. "Be good. I love you."

"I love you too." I laughed, watching as he disappeared out the door.

I got myself ready quickly, anxious to get to work now that I knew Talia's real name. I had no idea what I would do with the information once I found it, but I knew I had to at least try. There was no doubt in my mind the revenge Alessandro would extract on whoever was responsible, but didn't he deserve to? A horrible mistake was made that lost Talia her life and no one was being held accountable. It went against everything I had taken an oath for, but I kind of understood it. I had no idea how he went on after something like that, and I hated that he was still suffering.

When I got to the hospital, I checked on my patients on what was a relatively quiet morning in the emergency room. By ten o'clock, it was almost like a ghost town, so I headed upstairs to the records department.

"Hey Juliana!" I smiled brightly as I approached the counter. "I'm looking for an old file a client is requesting, do you have time to look for it for me?"

"Absolutely." She smiled. "What's the name?"

"It's Natalia Castillo."

"Hmm." She frowned, sympathy filling her eyes. "I know exactly who you're talking about, such a tragedy. Dr. Bauer was actually looking at this file this week too."

Dr. Bauer had been looking into it as well? What could he possibly have up his sleeve? Did this have anything to do with what happened last night?

She grabbed it off the counter and handed it to me. "Here you go."

"Thank you!" I gave her a tight smile and turned quickly towards my office.

The file felt like it was burning a hole in my hand, but I wanted to be alone when I looked through it. I was anxious about what I was going to find, and even more anxious about what I was going to do with that information. How could I ever keep something like that from Alessandro knowing how it was eating him up?

When I finally reached my office, I shut the door behind me and nearly fell back into my chair. I braced myself before opening it.

At first, it looked like a routine case. She had come into the hospital in bad shape, but at least stable. They had rushed her into emergency surgery to stop some internal bleeding and the surgeon on call was... Dr. Bauer.

That bastard. It had been him all along.

I clenched my jaw in anger, digging into the file a little bit deeper. Talia's official cause of death had been a heart attack. It seemed strange for someone her age, so I turned to the page about medications. When I did, my heart stopped. Why was my signature on this page? Had I... Oh my god.

Things started to slowly come back to me. I had just started my training at St. Luke's and Dr. Bauer was my mentor. It was so early on that I hadn't even been cleared to participate in surgery yet, so when he was called into an emergency surgery that day, I had to wait outside. After a few minutes, he asked me to go to the med station and get a dose of pain medication. When I brought it back down, he already had an order of it. Bauer told me that he had doubled up just in case and would handle taking the extra back to the medication distribution area. He told me that he would be tied up the rest of the afternoon so he asked if I could go see the rest of his rounds. I hadn't even hesitated to hand it over to him and move on with the rest of the patients. Later that day, I asked him what had happened to the patient and he told me that she hadn't made it. Now, looking at the log, I could tell that the medication had never been returned and she had been given both doses, which was more than enough to stop her heart, mimicking a heart attack.

I felt sick to my stomach realizing that I had contributed to her death. Never in a million years had I thought it could be Talia. I had only briefly seen her when they wheeled her to the operating room, and there was no way I could have recognized her. I had just been a med student following her boss' orders, I had no way of knowing what he was actually going to do. I trusted Dr. Bauer, even more so back then, and I had played right into his plan.

That wasn't a mistake. Giving someone that amount of medication was intentional, and Dr. Bauer had known exactly what he was doing. No wonder he had tried to hide it from Alessandro all this time. I hadn't killed Talia myself, but I had practically handed Bauer the tools to.

Tears welled up in my eyes as I realized what this meant. I hadn't been the one to kill Talia but if I had paid more attention, or taken the meds back myself, or something, anything at all. Maybe I could have stopped it.

In my heart, I knew Alessandro would never forgive me for this.

CHAPTER 28

A LESSANDRO

"Damn it!" I hissed, pulling the flaming pan out of the oven. Twenty-seven minutes ago, the shit on the pan had been salmon, and now it was completely unrecognizable. Well, that was just great. I had come home early, hoping to be able to make a nice, romantic dinner for Daisy and I, and instead, I ruined the entire thing. I guess we would have to settle for take out again. I had given this cooking thing the whole college try, but it was pretty clear Daisy was the chef in the family.

I was looking forward to tonight more than I could even fathom. Last night had knocked the wind right out of me. When I thought losing Daisy was even a possibility, the pain was nearly debilitating. I had jumped the gun, but it made me realize how much she meant to me. How deeply ingrained she had become in my life. How much I wanted to spend the rest of my life with her.

That exact reason was why I had gone to the jeweler right after the warehouse and bought a ring. I had never done anything so impulsive in my entire life, but I had never been so excited either. Talia and I had never really even been engaged, we were just told we were getting married, and a few weeks later, the deed was done. This time would be so much different. I couldn't wait to see the look on her face when she saw the ring I picked out. It was practically made for her—a vintage oval diamond surrounded in a soft halo. It was unique and had character and took my breath away, just as she had. I couldn't wait until that thing was on her finger, and I could tell the entire world she was mine.

I could give her the family she had talked about last night, the one she deserved. I could give her everything she ever wanted and more, and I would relish in every second of spoiling her. I was a mess of nerves as I waited for her, but I couldn't contain my excitement at the thought of our future together. Daisy, Ty, and I.

My stomach lurched anxiously as I heard the front door open and the sound of her feet walking across the floor.

"Alessandro?" she called softly.

"In the kitchen, babe," I called, quickly shoving the burnt fish into the trash can. It didn't exactly give off the romantic vibes I was going for.

Daisy came around the corner and I could immediately tell something was wrong. She had been crying, her eyes red and swollen, and she bit on her lip gingerly. She looked completely defeated, as if she might melt into absolute hysterics at any second. I had never seen her so broken, not even when I had held her hostage at gunpoint.

"Daisy, what's going on? Are you okay?" I frowned, setting the pan on the counter and rushing towards her, engulfing her in my arms.

She didn't answer at first, just stood stiffly. Finally, she pulled away, gently shaking her head.

"Alessandro, I need to tell you something."

"Whatever it is, Daisy, we can figure it out. I promise I'll..."

She shook her head violently. "No, it's not like that, Alessandro. I... I think we should sit down."

I nodded, following her lead and sitting down at the kitchen table. Daisy set her bag on the ground and pulled a file out of it, her hand trembled on top of it. I had no idea what was going on, but I couldn't suppress the dread growing in my chest. Whatever this was, it wasn't good.

"Alessandro, I don't even know how to tell you this." Tears welled up in her eyes. "I had no idea... When I first met you..." She paused, closing her eyes as a few tears escaped them. She took another deep breath trying to compose herself, the look on her face completely shattering me. I hated seeing her in this kind of distress, especially when I didn't even know what was going on, let alone be able to fix it.

I reached for her head, but Daisy pulled away, refusing to meet my eyes. "I know who killed Talia," she said softly, barely above a whisper.

All the blood in my veins ran cold. What the fuck did she just say? "What... what do you mean?"

"Alessandro, I am so sorry." Her voice quivered as she shoved the file towards me. I opened it slowly, realizing it was Talia's file from the hospital. How had she even gotten this? They told me it was sealed.

I thumbed through it carefully, gritting my teeth as I realized Dr. Bauer was all over it. That bastard had been the one to operate on Talia and he had lied to me all this time. He had let me think it was someone else, when really I was staring the monster right in the face every time I saw him. I was shaking with anger, losing sight of everything else in the world at this moment besides finding that mother fucker and making him pay with every ounce of blood in his system. "Bauer," I growled, my voice seeping with so much anger it hardly sounded human.

"There's more," Daisy whispered, pushing me to go forward. What could possibly make this any worse?

After a few minutes, I got to the medications page. Again, Bauer was all over it. There was a different signature on this page though. Was that... No. There was no way. Why was Daisy's name on this? I looked up at her in complete shock. "What does this mean, Daisy?"

"When Talia was taken to the hospital that day, I was an intern there." She sighed, her eyes filled with fear. "Bauer was my mentor and he was pulled into surgery. I was still so new that I couldn't even be in the operating room, but I waited outside and Bauer asked me to go grab some pain meds about halfway through the surgery. When I got it back down to him though, he already had a dose, and he told me that he would take the rest back to the department after the surgery. I didn't think anything of it at the time but..." She bit her lip, a few errant tears slipping down her cheek. "I didn't even know until this morning that she hadn't made it. I should have asked, I should have made sure that Bauer took the meds back but I was so new. I had no idea that..."

"Daisy, what are you saying?" I clenched my jaw, trying to follow what was going on here. I could feel my blood pressure rising but I was trying desperately to keep it in check. She couldn't be saying she was involved, could she?

"Alessandro, Dr. Bauer used the extra meds I gave him to cause Talia's heart attack. I'm so sorry. I had no idea." She was talking a mile a minute now but all I heard was a loud ringing in my ears. I stood up quickly, nearly knocking the chair over behind me. I felt sick, like I was going to vomit right here in my kitchen. This couldn't be happening. Daisy couldn't have been involved. Not my Daisy. There was no way.

I was jolted out of my fog by Daisy grabbing my hand. "Please say something Alessandro."

"I'm going to find Bauer," I growled, barely able to get the sentence out. My mind was spinning and right now, she was only making it worse. I knew in my heart it wasn't her fault, but it didn't change the fact that she had been involved. She had practically given Bauer the tool to kill my wife. I hated myself for feeling that way, but I couldn't stop it. I had been killing myself the last several months trying to find some kind of justice for Talia and now... it was all for nothing.

"I know you're upset, but do you think that's a good idea?" she pleaded with me.

I jerked my arm away from her and recoiled. "Now you're defending him? That prick is a monster! He killed my wife, he's terrorized my family, and now he's going to pay."

"Alessandro, stop. I'm not defending him. But this isn't..." She bit her lip, shaking her head.

"This isn't what, Daisy?" I bellowed, sweeping my arm across the counter and sending the dishes shattering to the ground. "This isn't a good idea? I'm pretty sure that shit went out the window long ago. He killed Talia with drugs you gave him. I have waited for this day since I buried my wife and now that I know the truth..." I shook my head, trying to hold back my own tears. I was blinded by anger and confusion and hurt and I couldn't make sense of any of it.

"Please," Daisy pleaded, staring back at me with the same big, brown eyes I had fallen in love with. The lips I had let kiss every inch of me. The hair that had been splayed across my pillow case every morning for the last several weeks. God, how had this happened? I was such a fool. This was what I got for falling in love. For thinking that I could have a normal life.

"I think you should take that job in Tennessee." I clenched my jaw, turning and rushing out of the house without another word. If I stayed in there one more minute, I had no idea what would happen. I couldn't take that chance right now.

I had to protect my family.

CHAPTER 29

A LESSANDRO

"I'm not understanding you. You're going to have to slow down." Joe stared at me like I was growing a third head as I explained everything to him. I was so angry that the details sounded more like caveman words than actual English. Thank God Ty was already asleep because I would never want him to see me like this. I was a complete wreck after finding out the truth about Talia's death, and subsequently having just thrown the one person out of my life who ever meant a damn thing to me. Daisy deserved so much more than me. I had known from the beginning she was better than I was, praying that the day would never come that she realized that, but my actions had just been the final nail in the coffin.

This wasn't her fault, I knew that with every rational bone in my body. She had been played, just like we all had, but it still stung. As she stood in front of me, clearly torn up about what had happened, and needing me to tell her that I didn't blame her, I had never felt like less of a man. I was so blinded by my anger that I hadn't done it, and instead sent her away. Truthfully it was for the best. I was in no position in my life to give her what she needed and I loved her too much to hold her back. At least that's what I was telling myself.

"You kicked Daisy out?" His brow furrowed.

"That's all you got out of that? Bauer was the one the entire time. I think Bauer is Doc." I gritted my teeth, pushing my feelings for Daisy back and focusing all of my energy on my anger.

"You realize what you're saying here, Alessandro? You're going to accuse a decorated, respected surgeon of being part of a criminal organization," Q clarified as if I hadn't already thought all of this through. I didn't come here to hear their shitty opinions, I just felt like I should let them know.

"I'm not just accusing him, Q. I am going to make it my life's mission to take the man down."

"Alessandro, you know I will always have your back." Joe sighed heavily, sliding a glass of whiskey my way. I threw it back almost as quickly as it had been set in front of me. I needed something to take the edge off, otherwise I was going to go out of my mind. I didn't like how this was starting. "But I'm going to tell you something you're probably not going to like."

"Joe." Q tried to stop him, but Joe held his hand up.

"He needs to hear this." He turned his attention back to me. "I've known about Dr. Bauer for the last few weeks. I've known everything, that he was the one who caused Talia to have a heart attack and that he used Daisy and some other med students to do so."

"What the fuck did you just say?" I snarled, standing up so fast that I knocked the stool I had been sitting on over. Was he serious? He had known this entire time and not thought to mention it to me?

"Listen to me, okay? I did this because I care about you and I'm tired of watching you let everything else in your life suffer because you're hung up on some notion that you're going to find justice for Talia." He sighed heavily and took a big swig out of the bottle of tequila. "The night after we got Ryker and he told us about the guy named Doc, I had an idea. I had already hacked the hospital system so Daisy could steal all of that shit, so I went in and took a look at the files. I hadn't been able to do it before because I didn't know their code configuration but with Daisy's badge, I could construct one."

"Why didn't you fucking tell me?" My voice was hoarse as I yelled at him across the island. He knew how bad I wanted to know the truth and he let me go on, knowing the entire time.

"Because you're obsessed, Alessandro," Q said softly.

"What?" I hissed, snapping my neck in his direction.

"He's right," Joe interjected. "I get that you feel guilty for what happened, but Talia was a part of the mafia long before she married you, Alessandro. And she knew what she was getting into the second you guys got married."

"But I should have been..." I started, but was quickly cut off.

"No. You shouldn't have done a damn thing. You weren't home and who knows what would have happened if you were, they might have killed you too. You can't protect everyone from everything Alessandro, and you always try to. You try to control all the shit that goes on for everyone in your life but that's just not realistic. Do you feel any better knowing Bauer was the one who did it?"

I clenched my jaw, not responding at first. Joe met my eyes and I growled, shaking my head softly.

"You don't. So when is it going to be enough? You've been focused on this for the last nine months and you feel even worse now that you know the truth. And you'll feel the same way once you kill Bauer, because nothing you ever do is going to be enough to bring her back."

"I'm not trying to bring her back," I spat. "I obviously know that's not possible, I'm just..."

"Just what? Trying to prove a point? You've got to let yourself off the hook, man. You know why I didn't tell you when I found out? Because I knew you'd react like this. The last few months, with Daisy in your life, you've been a completely different person. The fun, sarcastic, adventurous guy we used to know. The one your son deserves. Not this angry, impulsive guy who can't even see how badly his son needs him, or how much that woman loves him. I thought that maybe if you realized how great life with her could be, that you'd let this thing go. She brought out the best in you, but you are so blinded by this shit that you can't see that. Did you ever stop to think the only reason she even found out was because she was trying to help you? You kicked her out for telling the truth about something she could have easily hidden. She could have gone on and never told you what she found out, and you probably would have been better off."

"Daisy deserves better than me," I said, lowering my eyes.

"You're damn right she does," Joe scoffed. "She deserves the man you are when you're not hung up on this bullshit revenge mission. Mark my words, Bauer will get what's coming to him, but you've got to move on. Otherwise you're going to drive everyone you care about away and spend the rest of your life lonely and bitter."

"She's not going to want to talk to me," I said, shaking my head. In my heart of hearts, I knew he was right. I had thrown everything I had into this the last few months, but at what expense?

"Maybe you should let her make that decision for herself." Joe shrugged.

He was right. None of this bullshit mattered if Daisy wasn't around. She had completely transformed my life, and Ty's life, and I was a complete moron for casting her aside. Fuck Bauer, all that mattered was making sure Daisy knew that it wasn't her I was upset with. Clearly I hadn't communicated that the first time, and it was time I manned up and became the man she and Ty both deserved.

I raced back to the house as fast as I could and burst through the front doors, feeling lighter than I had in a long time. I finally had the answers I wanted, and Joe was right, it was time to move on.

"Daisy!" I yelled, running into the kitchen as if she'd be in the same place I had left her. Instead, everything that I had left out from the dinner I was trying to make had been cleaned up. I headed upstairs, still calling her name. "Daisy!"

I threw the door to my bedroom open and my heart sank the second I did. All of her stuff was gone. Everything off the nightstand, the clothes that had hung over the back of the arm chair just this morning. Even her scent was gone. The bathroom was the same way. Her side of the counter completely cleared. God, I had fucked up so badly this time. I had ruined everything.

Just to be sure, I checked her old bedroom but it was dark and empty. "Okay, think Alessandro, where could she have gone?"

Her apartment lease was over so she wouldn't have gone there, and I highly doubted she would run back to her parents. No, she was still in the city somewhere, she had to be. Determined to find her and make this right, I flew back down the stairs right as the doorbell rang.

Who would be here at this hour? Ringing the doorbell no less. Maybe she had left her key and she was coming back. That had to be it!

I flung the door open expecting and hoping to find Daisy on the other side but instead, there were two police officers.

"Good evening Mr. Bosio. Can we come in? There have been some developments in your wife's case," one of them said with a sympathetic smile.

"Uh, sure," I said, moving aside so that they could come in. Having police officers in my house was a completely new concept to me. This would be interesting.

"We wanted to let you know that we have a suspect and will be making an arrest. It seems the doctor who treated her at the hospital made a mistake and she was given too much medication, causing her heart to stop. We're arresting Greg Bauer for negligent homicide."

It felt like all the air had been sucked out of my lungs. They were actually arresting him. He was going to pay for what he had done and Talia would see some kind of justice. It wasn't the justice I would have provided, but it was something. Something that would allow me to move on with the rest of my life, just as soon as I found Daisy.

"Thank you so much. That's great news." I smiled with relief. Who knew the police could actually be good for something? "If you don't mind me asking, how did you find out?"

"A woman came to us this evening with the proof we needed, we can't give you much information other than that. As soon as we locate Dr. Bauer, he'll be taken into custody." He smiled politely. "Have a good evening, sir."

"Thank you, you too."

Daisy. She must have gone to the police station after she left here. That meant she was still here, and I had to find her.

CHAPTER 30

ALESSANDRO

"Hamburgers again?" Ty rolled his eyes dramatically, glaring at me as if I had just put a plate of sewage trash in front of him. He shoved it away from him, sending his tater tots toppling over the edge and onto the table.

I let out a heavy sigh, not having the strength to fight him on this tonight. It had been like this the last week, every single thing becoming a fight. When he got up for school, what he was going to wear, why he couldn't have candy for breakfast, how quickly he needed to move so we weren't late, who was going to buckle his seat belt, where I dropped him off for the day. This was all before 8:30AM and it just continued on all day until we both collapsed into bed at night, thoroughly exhausted and frustrated with how the day had transpired.

"Bud, please just eat it. I promise tomorrow we'll get pizza or something but for tonight..." I tried to bribe him, not at all proud of my actions, but I was desperate here. We couldn't live like this any longer.

"Daisy says pizza isn't healthy and you should only eat it for special occasions."

"Well, Daisy isn't here," I snapped, rubbing my forehead. "So eat your damn burger." I immediately regretted it the second it was out of my mouth.

"I wish you had gone away and not her," he growled, knocking his glass of milk over and tearing out of the room.

"Shit," I hissed, tossing my own plate into the sink and slumping into the chair. This was a fucking disaster.

It had been a week since Daisy left. Seven days. One hundred and sixty-eight hours. I guess technically she hadn't left, I kicked her out in what could go down as the most asshole-ish move of my life. Even if I could somehow find her and convince her to talk to me, I would regret the way I had treated her for the rest of my life. I had spent every one of those ten thousand four hundred and sixteen seconds trying to track her down and find her and so far I had nothing. I had less than nothing. I had a stone wall. Daisy had turned off her cell phone, closed every account in Nevada she had, and if she was still in the city, she wasn't using her real name to stay at any hotels. She had pretty much evaporated into thin air and it was really starting to piss me off.

And apparently piss my son off as well.

I had told Ty that she was moving back to St. Louis, but he was a smart kid. He picked up early on that something had happened between the two of us and he was blaming me. Of course, he had every right to, the blame was completely on me, but it was still hard to stomach. My son hated me, the girl I was in love with was gone from my life, and the one mission that had defined me the last few months was over and done with. I had my normal work, but I couldn't help but feel out of place.

I had been avoiding going to the hospital for obvious reasons. I didn't want to chance running into Bauer, but it was my last option now. I had exhausted every other avenue and I wanted a chance to make this right with Daisy. I was also avoiding going because I knew that was true. That if I went there and she was gone, I had no other way of finding her. When she disappeared, she had made sure of that. If I waited I could still hold out hope, but not if I went and I found out that she was gone. Maybe they at least had some kind of forwarding address or something. They'd have to know where to find her.

It was Wednesday, and Daisy usually worked the night shift on Wednesdays so if I could get Q or Joe over here to watch Ty, I could go track her down. Joe was at my house within a few minutes of me texting him. I think he wanted me to find her as much as I did.

By now, I knew the way to the hospital well. It only took me a few minutes to pull into a parking spot in front of the emergency room entrance, but I hesitated to get out of the car. What was I even going to say to her? That I was sorry? That we missed her? That I was wrong? Beg her to come back and grovel at her feet? I'd do whatever it took to get her back, there was no way I would let pride get in my way.

Finally, I got out of the car and headed inside. It seemed rather quiet tonight which was a good thing. She'd be mortified enough with me showing up here, let alone making some kind of scene in front of a busy waiting room.

"Excuse me." I vaguely recognized the woman at the front desk. "I'm here to see Daisy Taylor. Is she available?"

The woman looked up from the computer screen with an irritated expression on her face. "Dr. Taylor is no longer with the hospital. You can have a seat and I will get you with the next available doctor if you'd like."

"Oh, no. I'm not here to be seen. I'm... Daisy is a friend of mine." The woman looked at me suspiciously. What kind of friend wouldn't know that she wasn't with the hospital anymore? "Did she leave any kind of forwarding address or anything?"

"No," the woman snapped. "And even if she did, we don't give that kind of information out. I'm sorry." She turned back to the screen as if I wasn't standing there anymore. Realizing she didn't want to help me in the slightest, I reached into my pocket and pulled out a hundred-dollar bill.

"Ma'am, I'm desperate, I really need to get in touch with Daisy." I slide it across the counter to her.

She scoffed, tossing it back to me. "We don't give that kind of information out, sir. Now, if I can't help you with anything else."

"Alessandro?" I whirled around at the sound of my name. Daisy's friend, Peyton. Thank God.

"Hey Peyton." I smiled, slightly relieved that I had run into her. If anyone knew where Daisy was, it would be her.

"Sorry about her." She rolled her eyes towards the receptionist as we walked away. "She's always got a stick up her ass. Can I help you with something?"

"I'm looking for Daisy," I said, cutting straight to the point.

She gave me a knowing smile. "I had a feeling that's why you were here."

"That lady said she left the hospital?" I asked, shoving my hands in my pocket.

Peyton nodded. "When she found out the truth about Dr. Bauer, she went straight to the authorities. There were no charges filed against her because she was just an intern, but the board asked her to leave the hospital."

Fuck. I ran my fingers through my hair in frustration. She had completely thrown herself under the bus to make sure I got the justice I was looking for. She wouldn't be able to graduate now, but she had done it anyways.

"I just need to talk to her, Peyton," I said softly.

"I wish I could help you Alessandro, but I think it's better for both of you if..." Her expression turned sympathetic.

"What do you mean?" I furrowed my brow, cutting her off angrily. "Fuck..." I ran my fingers through my hair in frustration. "We don't need time or space or any of that shit. She needs to know how I feel, and that I'm sorry."

"She doesn't blame you, Alessandro. She's just... kind of lost herself right now. Why don't you give her some time?" Peyton suggested, handing me a cup of coffee from the nurses' station.

"I can't do that." I shook my head. "Look, Peyton, I know you want to protect her. I get it. But you have to trust me, all I want to do is apologize. I fucked up the best thing in my entire life and I am willing to do anything I have to do to get her back. Anything. And

I know if she could just hear me out, she'd feel the same way. Please. I'm begging you. Just give me an address."

Peyton studied me carefully, trying to determine whether or not she was going to give me what I wanted. "She'd kill me if she knew I was even considering doing this right now."

"I promise, I won't hurt her, and if she says that she doesn't want to see me, I'll let it go. But I have to at least try."

"Fine." Peyton let out a heavy breath. "All I know is that she is going to be here tomorrow around lunch time to clean out her locker. I don't know where she is staying so that's your only opportunity."

A huge smile broke out onto my face. I wasn't too late. I could still make this right. I swept Peyton into a hug, nearly picking her up off the floor. "Peyton, thank you so much. You have no idea how much I appreciate..."

"Yeah, yeah." She chuckled, rolling her eyes. "Just don't make me regret it."

"You won't." I grinned. "I swear. I'll see you tomorrow."

"See you tomorrow lover boy."

I rushed out of the hospital, with a new lease on the situation. There was still time, and now I needed to pull out all the stops to make this right. I had the entire night to prepare, and that was exactly what I was going to do.

CHAPTER 31

D^{AISY}

"Are you sure you have to go?" Peyton squeezed my shoulders tightly, locking me into a hug and refusing to let go of me.

"It's not like I'm leaving forever. You can come visit me whenever you want!" I insisted, trying to ease her mind a little bit. Peyton had become somewhat of a mother hen towards me, and I knew she worried about me moving out to LA. She'd been constantly trying to change my mind since I told her, but at this point I was set. I figured a little sunshine could do me some good, or at least not make things any worse.

The last few days had been rough. When I told Alessandro about my part in Talia's death, I was a little disappointed in his reaction. I had no idea what I was expecting, I would have reacted the same way, but it still stung. I needed to make it right any way that I could, so after I left Alessandro's, I had gone to the police immediately. I gave them everything I had on Bauer, and told them my story. By the end of it, they said they had enough to put Bauer away for murder and a host of other charges. It was a small consolation, but it was the only thing I could give Alessandro and Ty right now.

Coming clean to the police also meant that the hospital board was made aware of what happened, and they politely asked me to leave the hospital. I was a few short weeks of graduating, but that seemed kind of pointless now anyways. Practicing medicine had been ruined for me on so many levels. I had entered the profession because I wanted to help people and instead, I had been a part of one murder I knew about, and God only knew what else Bauer had done. In my heart, I knew it wasn't my fault, but I still felt partly responsible and I knew I'd never be able to completely shake that feeling.

Right now, I just needed to put some distance between myself and this place, and everything that came with it. Alessandro included. I was so lost right now that I wasn't any use to anyone, and I knew I would only be a painful reminder to Alessandro for a long time. I loved him, more than I even wanted to admit, and cutting him and Ty out of my life would be torturous, but in the long run, I knew it was for the best.

"I know," Peyton whined, finally pulling away. "I'm just going to miss you."

"I'm going to miss you too." I sighed, letting my new reality sink in. It was going to be tough starting over. I had friends here in Vegas, I had life here, and now I was picking up and moving to another state, with not much of a plan. The girl I was a few months ago wouldn't even recognize who I was now. I had shown up in Vegas with my life completely planned out. My job, my career path. I thought I had it all together. And now, I was leaving with no idea what the rest of my life was going to look like. It was a little bit exciting but mostly terrifying. "I just think it's best for me to get out of here for a while."

"Because of Alessandro?" She arched her eyebrow at me.

"No, not because of Alessandro," I lied. "Just because, okay?"

"He was here looking for you last night." Peyton smirked.

My heart nearly stopped. He was looking for me? "He was here? At the hospital?"

She nodded. "He really wants to talk to you Daisy. I think you're making a mistake by not talking to him before you go."

I sucked in a sharp breath. Alessandro was trying to find me. I wasn't sure how to feel about it exactly. Of course I wanted him to, I wanted him to forgive me and tell me he didn't blame me, that nothing had changed between us, but I knew that would just make leaving all the harder. And who knows? He could be looking for me because he was still angry. "Peyton, I think it's best if I just go at this point. It's too complicated right now and I don't want to hurt him or Ty worse than I already have."

"But, Daisy, you haven't hurt them. I got the impression that he just wants to make things right with you. He loves you, Mads, and you leaving isn't going to help things, it's going to make things harder on you both," she persisted.

"I appreciate the thought, but I don't think..."

All of a sudden an alarm started blaring over the loudspeaker. "Attention all staff, we have a Code Black. Please adhere to department evacuation plans immediately."

"Stupid kids." Peyton rolled her eyes. "Do you know this is the third time this month we've had a fake bomb threat? Every time I take all my patients out, I take them all back in, just to find out it's a bunch of dumb high school kids that think they're funny."

"Attention all staff, we have a Code Black. Please adhere to department evacuation plans immediately," the speaker repeated.

"How about I help you get your patients out for old time's sake?" I offered with a smile. I knew how irritating things like this were. It happened a lot in Las Vegas because the city was a breeding ground for crazies. It never amounted to anything more than an annoyance for hospital staff, and a fun trip outside for the patients.

"You're an angel. I'm supposed to clear the third floor, why don't you take that one and I'll get the rest?" she said, setting her stethoscope down on the desk.

"You got it." I smiled.

"I owe you!" she yelled over her shoulder as she headed off down the hall.

Many of the patients could walk out on their own, our job was just to assist and direct them to the evacuation route. I took the stairs to the third floor quickly and started scanning rooms quickly. The third floor was post-op recovery so it would be pretty empty at this time of day. I peeked my head into all of them but quickened my pace when I heard the sound of a little girl crying down the hall.

I got to the last room on the right and opened the door. "Is everything...."

My eyes widened as I processed what was going on. A little girl, about ten, sat in a wheelchair next to the window, tears dripping down her cheeks. Bauer stood behind her, holding onto a backpack that was ticking, a timer on the front reading 15:48 and getting lower by the second.

"Well, if this isn't just divine intervention." His face curled into a sickening smile. "I had no idea you were going to be here today but it just makes it all that much sweeter."

"Dr. Bauer, what are you doing?" I asked, slowly walking towards with my hands up.

"Don't come any closer, Daisy. One push of this button and the three of us and this entire building go out with a bang."

The little girl started to wail, terrified at what he had said.

"It's okay, sweetie." I reached out, trying to soothe her. "That's not going to happen. He's going to let you out of here, aren't you Bauer?"

My heart was beating out of my chest but I was trying as hard as I possibly could to remain calm.

"Now, why would I do that?" he snickered.

"Because this isn't about her. It's about you and me and this hospital. It has nothing to do with her."

"Shut up," he hissed. "It's your fault we're in this mess to begin with. If you had just let things play out as they should have, none of this would have ever happened. You would be on your way to St. Jude's and I would be well on my way to tenure. But you had to go and open your big mouth."

"Bauer, you need to let her go, and then you and I can have this conversation," I said quietly, not wanting to escalate this anymore.

"You chose that criminal over your career, your family. Everything!" he continued, ignoring anything that I had to say.

"I did what was right, Dr. Bauer. Talia's death was..."

"An unfortunate side effect, but it was a piece of something much bigger than you could ever imagine."

"What are you talking about?"

He threw his head back and cackled, the sound making me sick to my stomach. I used the opportunity to move a little bit closer to the little girl who was still looking at me in complete terror. "Oh Daisy, I really appreciate your naivety, but it's getting old. Alessandro started this war a long time ago, and it's high time I finish it. I thought I had shut him down with Talia, but then I found out that he was dating you... derailing everything I had worked so hard for."

"I don't understand..." I frowned, still completely confused.

"Of course you don't." He rolled his eyes. "Well let me spell it out for you. Before your boyfriend moved into town, I ran the top drug ring in the region. Not that hard to do when you're a respected doctor." He chuckled to himself. "I had the entire area cornered, and then came Alessandro Bosio, Mr. Holier-than-thou and his crusade to take the drugs off the streets. He thinks he's better than me because his group doesn't deal the drugs, but he's just as much at fault. What does he think his clients do with the guns they buy from him? Target shooting? Alessandro came in here and my business plummeted. Everyone was too scared to cross him with his Italian Mafia ties. I thought if I could just force him out, we'd be back on track. I nearly did it too, when his kid got shot. But then Alessandro met you and of course, the stone-cold mafia leader gets heart eyes for a resident in my program. It's almost laughable."

"It was you all along," I said breathlessly. Everything was slowly starting to click for me. Bauer was the guy who had been after us all along in his attempt to force Alessandro out.

"Of course it was, Daisy." He narrowed his eyes at me. "My last ditch effort was to get you to go to Tennessee. I saw him with you that day, and I knew he was falling for you. That this was my chance and he might follow you out there. So you can imagine how surprised I was to hear you turn down the job."

"You're disgusting." I glared, tears stinging my eyes. "You're going to rot in jail for all of this."

He rolled his eyes. "I'd have to be alive in order for them to throw me in jail Daisy." He smirked. "And neither of us are walking out of here alive."

CHAPTER 32

A LESSANDRO

I studied Ty carefully as he shoveled bites of waffles into his mouth. I had woken up with a new lease on life, determined that I was going to fix things. With Daisy, with Ty, with everything. Starting today I was turning over a new leaf, and going to focus on the future instead of being stuck in the past, surrounded by things I couldn't change. I had woken up early to work out and then showered and shaved, pulling out all the stops to get on Daisy's good side.

I was prepared to do all the pleading and begging I had to do to get her back—hell, I was almost looking forward to it. I had never groveled at a woman's feet like this before, but I wanted her to know exactly how much she meant to me. I had bought her an engagement ring, but hadn't gotten the opportunity to give it to her, and now it was safely stashed in my pocket, just in case. I wanted to be able to talk to Daisy and get her to come home so we could sort things out, and then propose to her the right way, but I was prepared to pull it out to prove to her just how serious I was.

After I got ready, I whipped out a cookbook and tried my hand at waffles. Ty had a killer poker face, but at the rate he was eating, I was pretty sure they had turned out good.

"So?" I asked, arching an eyebrow at him.

Ty finished chewing, eyeing me carefully. "They're alright. Not like Daisy's, but you're making progress."

I let out a sharp laugh. I would take that, especially on my first attempt. So far, things were looking up today and I was hoping to carry that luck to the hospital when I went to meet Daisy. I didn't have much of a plan, but I was going to stay there the entire day until she agreed to see me. I'd give her no other choice but to hear me out, and then, if she still wanted to, she could leave. I hoped she wouldn't, but at that point, at least I let her know how I truly felt. At least I didn't let her go thinking I blamed her, or that what happened changed my feelings towards her at all.

"I'll take it." I grinned, ruffling Ty's hair. "Are you going to be okay with Joe and Emily today?'

Ty nodded, wiggling out of my reach. "Are you going to make up with Daisy?"

"I'm sure going to try, bud." I smiled.

"Don't be an ass to her again." He narrowed his eyes at me.

I bit my lip to keep my laughter in. "Hey, watch your mouth."

"You say it all the time," he quipped, a smirk tugging at his lips.

"Well, I'm a grown up and that's a grown-up word. Don't let me hear you say that again," I warned.

Ty rolled his eyes, reaching for another waffle.

"Who's ready for some paintball?" Joe called from the foyer.

"Paintball?" Ty's face lit up as he abandoned his breakfast in front of him.

"Hell yeah!" Joe called. "Q is going to meet us with his nephew so your dad can get some work done today." He winked at me.

"So you're the one teaching him all the curse words." I chuckled, putting his plate into the sink. "Why don't you go get your shoes on, buddy?"

"First of all, I don't want to be blamed for him cursing, you have the mouth of a sailor." Joe grinned. "Second of all, I have some information you might find interesting."

I arched my eyebrow at him, taking the piece of paper he was handing me. I read it carefully, and the farther I got, the more it sucked the wind right out of me. "Doc is Bauer."

Joe nodded. "It's been him all along. Apparently he wasn't thrilled when we came to town and started monopolizing the turf."

My stomach turned at the idea of all of this. How had I not known from the beginning? It all made sense, and I had been so wrapped up in my other shit that I didn't connect the dots.

"And Daisy's job offer?"

Joe's face fell. "He called in a favor with the hospital thinking you'd go with her and he'd get the area back."

She'd be crushed if she ever found out that the offer hadn't been real, that it had just been part of an elaborate scheme. "Jesus Christ."

"Yeah. I'm thinking we keep that part to ourselves," Joe said. "So what do you want to do now?"

I clenched my jaw, thinking for a second. If I went after Bauer for this ridiculous scheme of his, I would be dragged right back into the past. The guy deserved to die a slow and painful death, not just for what he had done to my family, but for what he had been doing for years, but it would have to be at someone else's hands. I couldn't let it consume me anymore, and I was confident he would get exactly what was coming to him in jail.

"Nothing." I let out a heavy sigh. "It doesn't change anything really. You know he won't last long in jail, and I'm ready to move on."

Joe digested my words carefully and a smile crept onto his face. "Wow, look at you! Acting like a grown up."

"Yeah, yeah. Don't make me regret it." I chuckled. "By the way, if all goes well with Daisy today, I think I am going to step away from all of this for a while. I want to be able to focus on her and Ty and fix things."

"I think that's the best idea you've had in a long time." Joe smiled, crumpling the papers up in his hand. It didn't matter anymore.

Joe looked over my shoulder for a second at the TV and his face scrunched in confusion.

"What?" I asked, turning around and seeing a picture of the hospital on the news. "What is that?"

I pointed the remote at the TV, turning it up.

"Breaking news, out of Las Vegas now. A bomb threat has been called in to the local hospital and staff and patients are being evacuated now. Police are asking the public to avoid the area and proceed to the evacuation site to reunite with their loved ones who are at the hospital."

"Is that..."

"Daisy's there," I said flatly, staring at the screen. It took me a few seconds to gain my bearings but when I did, I grabbed my keys and took off towards the door, not even bothering to tell Joe what I was doing. I had tunnel vision, all that mattered was getting to her.

I drove there in record time, throwing my car into park and racing toward the building. They had everything blocked off with police tape, but I ran full steam ahead, with no regard to where police were trying to direct me.

"Sir, you can't go in there." An officer tried to block me.

I jerked away from him. "My girlfriend is in there..."

"Sir, I understand, but we're working on getting everyone out of the building right now. You can meet your girlfriend over at the reunification site."

I glanced at where she was pointing, but there was no sight of Daisy. I knew if there were still patients inside, that's where she would be. I made a split-second decision to go in after her. I brushed past the officer, entering the hospital quickly. I had to find Daisy and had to get her out of there.

"You can't just go in there! Sir!" the officer yelled after me, but no one could stop me.

By the time I got inside, most of the first floor was empty, but I ran into Peyton who was wheeling a bed outside.

"Peyton!" I jogged towards her. "Have you seen Daisy?"

"She's helping me evacuate patients on the third floor." Peyton's tone was tight. "Alessandro, I think there might really be a bomb. This isn't like the other times that we had the threats. Daisy thinks it's a prank."

"I'll find her, I promise," I said, squeezing Peyton's shoulder and heading towards the stairwell. I took them three at a time until I got to the third floor.

"Daisy?" I called down the empty hallway. There was no response, so I made my way from room to room as quickly as possible.

"Daisy, are you up here?" I called again.

Still no response.

"Come on, Daisy," I whispered to myself. I was almost to the last room, and at that point I had no idea what I would do if I hadn't found her. I was starting to panic a little bit. If this really was a bomb...

My heart nearly stopped as I looked into the last room. Daisy was standing in the center of the room, between a little girl in a wheelchair and Dr. Bauer who was holding a backpack with wires sticking out of it.

Son of a bitch.

"Well, it looks like the gang's all here." Bauer cackled. "This just keeps getting better."

Daisy gave me a desperate look as we locked eyes. "Are you okay?" I asked.

She nodded gently. All I wanted was to reach out for her and hold her in my arms, to comfort her and to protect her, but Bauer had all the power here and he knew it. The little girl behind Daisy was bawling, terrified for what was about to happen.

"Look, I'm sure we can work all of this out..." I turned back towards Bauer cautiously.

"There is no working anything out here, Alessandro. I was just explaining to your sweet little girlfriend here that no one is walking out of here alive. We're way past that. But if it makes you feel any better, you'll both die here together."

"Dr. Bauer, please," Daisy begged, biting her lip. The look in her eyes was shattering my fucking heart. "This is between us. You and me and Alessandro. Please let Chloe go."

Bauer started chuckling to himself. "I'm not a completely unreasonable man. The girl can go. I'll happily take Alessandro in her place."

"Okay." Daisy sucked in a sharp breath of relief, kneeling down in front of the little girl. "Okay, Chloe. Do you think you can get outside by yourself?" Daisy's maternal instinct kicked in and she wiped away at the girl's tears.

"Not without you." The girl continued to cry, clutching Daisy's hand.

"Chloe, sweetie, I can't go with you right now, but I promise, when all this is over, I'll come meet you outside and everything will be okay."

"Don't make promises you can't keep." Bauer chuckled. "Get her out of here before I change my mind." I assessed Bauer quickly, trying to figure out my next move. I could see the bomb slowly ticking down in his arms, and if I didn't move soon, he was right, no one would be leaving here alive. I inched my way towards him while he was distracted by Daisy and the girl.

His hand was on a trigger, and if I tackled him, it would come off. More than likely, that would blow the entire place up. I had to avoid that at all costs, but I had no idea how I was going to get it out of his hands without detonating the device.

"Go ahead, Chloe. I'll see you soon." Daisy mustered up as big a smile as she possibly could, biting back tears.

Chloe took one last look at Daisy and wheeled herself down the hallway as quickly as possible. We were all silent until we heard the doors of the elevator close. It was just the three of us.

"Bauer, I'm the one you really want, right? It's my fault you lost business, it's my fault Daisy didn't follow your plan, this whole thing is my fault. Now why don't you let Daisy out of here and you and I can settle this like men?"

Bauer eyed me carefully. "What you said is true Alessandro, this is about you. But I know I can cause you the greatest pain in your life by taking Daisy's right in front of you, knowing there is nothing you can do about it."

Bauer was crazed and there was no reasoning with him right now. I was going to have to take this by force if we had any hope of making it out alive. I turned slowly to Daisy, determined to let her know exactly how I felt, just in case this went south.

"Daisy," I said softly. "I'm sorry, baby."

Tears sprang to her eyes again.

"I don't blame you for what happened, I was angry and I said some things I shouldn't have, but I love you. I love you more than anything and I came here today to tell you that." My voice broke with emotion.

"I know." She nodded, a gentle smile on her face. "I love you, too."

"This is all very touching, but you're running out of time." Bauer snickered.

He was right, there were only three minutes left before the whole thing exploded. It was now or never.

"Run, Daisy," I said.

"What?" Her brow furrowed.

"Now, Daisy. Run!"

She glanced at me for a second, trying to decide what to do. I gave her a pleading look, and seconds later, she took off out of the room.

"Shouldn't have done that..." Bauer was halfway through his sentence when I lunged at him.

I gripped his shoulders, wrestling with him violently for a few seconds before shoving him backwards. It seemed like everything was moving in slow motion and then it all happened at once. I wasn't sure which came first, but as I shoved Bauer backwards, his finger came off the trigger and the bag fell to the ground as the two of us went crashing through the window.

Glass shattered all around us as we fell to the rooftop below, both reeling from the fall.

I looked up at the window we had just fallen out of, helpless as the entire hospital went up in a cloud of smoke.

CHAPTER 33

A LESSANDRO
    I had experienced pain in my life. There was the time my
brother Emmett dared me to jump off a swing in our backyard when
I was seven and I splintered the bone in my leg so badly that shards
of it were poking through the skin. There was the time an enemy had
captured me for twenty-eight hours and beat me with a pillowcase
full of bars of soap until I was absolutely senseless. And once when I
was a teenager, my dad took me ice fishing in Northern Canada. I fell
through the ice and the brutal frigidness of the water felt like one
thousand knives stabbing me on every inch of my skin. Those had all
been painful experiences, but nothing compared to the feeling of
watching someone you love and care about hurting and not being
able to do a damn thing about it.

    I had been in Denver next to Daisy's bedside for the last three
days, helplessly watching the machines she was hooked up to, as if
I could will her to wake up. She was airlifted here to University
hospital immediately after they pulled her body from the rubble,
and I came as soon as I had been cleared. After she ran out of the
room, Daisy must've known she wouldn't have time to make it out,
so instead of heading for the stairwell, she ducked under a desk at
the nurses' station, preparing for the explosion. I don't know how she
could've had that much sense in that moment, but I was thankful she
did, because it saved her life. The stairwell had completely collapsed,
burying anyone on it in thousands of pounds of cement. I couldn't

even bring myself to think about what would've happened if that's where she had been.

After Bauer and I crashed through the window, things started to happen in slow motion. There are parts that I remember so vividly that it's like I'm playing back a movie, but other parts that I can't remember at all. I don't know how I got down to the triage area, but after the explosion, the first thing I could remember was sitting in the tent being checked out by one of the nurses. I remember asking for Daisy about a dozen times, but no one would tell me what was going on. I wasn't sure how much time had passed but eventually, Peyton came to find me. She told me that they had found Daisy, but they were taking her to a different hospital because she had extensive injuries and the remaining local hospitals were already overwhelmed with patients. I remember thinking how bad could it be? If they're transporting her to another hospital, they must think she's going to be okay, right? Otherwise they would treat her right away.

When they required me to stay for observation, I was irritated, but optimistic about Daisy, but a majority of that faded away when I arrived in Denver thirty-six hours after the bombing. She was in bad shape, and hadn't improved much since. I had to lie to the nurses and tell them we were engaged to get any kind of information about Daisy, but I hadn't had much choice. They couldn't release medical information to me because we weren't technically family, so I hadn't thought twice.

Daisy had several fractured ribs, a collapsed lung, internal bleeding, and her left leg was broken in three places. The worst of her injuries though, and what was causing her to remain unconscious, was the small bleed in her brain. Right now, they couldn't tell how extensive it was because of the swelling, but from their imaging and tests, it looked like it was contained at least. Contained was good. As good as anything could be right now. It meant that her body was starting to try to heal it, and we would find out more soon. Her doctor warned me about all the possibilities. That she might not remember anything when she woke up. That she might need months of rehab and therapy to regain simple skills and movements. That she might not wake up at all. And many more.

I couldn't let my mind go there, though. I knew in my heart that she was going to wake up and she was going to be okay. That I would see her beautiful eyes again, and hear that sweet voice. I had faith that soon I'd be taking her back to Las Vegas and she and Ty and I would be a family. I hadn't given Ty all the details, but he knew something was wrong. My brother had flown in to stay with Ty after the explosion and he was ecstatic to see his uncle, and so far, buying my business trip excuse. It had temporarily taken his mind off of things, but I knew it was just a matter of time before he started asking questions. Hopefully by then I would have the answers.

Bauer had survived the explosion but had been taken into custody immediately. I would have preferred him to have been blown to bits in the explosion, but I was looking forward to the day that I could sit in the courtroom listening as they threw away the key on the guy. Or gave him the death penalty. Maybe they'd let me be a guest on the firing squad that day. That bastard wouldn't stop until he had taken everything from me.

I rubbed my forehead, leaning back into the recliner and settling in for another long night in ICU. Daisy was hooked up to so many machines and every twenty minutes or so, an alarm would go off and a nurse would have to come in and check it. I had gotten to know them quite well since I hadn't left this chair for longer than it took me to get a cup of coffee and use the restroom. I felt like my body was morphing into it by now, but there wasn't a chance in hell I was leaving.

"Mr. Bosio?" One of Daisy's nurses peeked her head in the door. This one was here a lot but I couldn't remember her name. All I knew her by was her rainbow stethoscope.

"Hello." I gave her a small smile, watching as a blush came to her cheeks.

"I just wanted to let you know, someone delivered breakfast burritos this morning, and there are a few left over at the nurses' station. They're cold and possibly stale by now, but if you'd like one, you're welcome to them."

I ran my fingers through my hair, shaking my head. "Thank you, but I'm okay. I'll go get something from the cafeteria in a little while."

She narrowed her eyes at me. "You said that last night but I have it on good authority that you didn't leave the floor." She smiled, letting herself inside the room. Fantastic. Company was the last thing I wanted right now. "You know, you sitting here is not going to make her wake up any faster. She needs time. Let her body work its magic."

"I know," I assured her. "But I want to be here when she wakes up. She'll be confused and I want to be the one to explain it to her."

"That's very sweet of you. But you should take care of yourself as well." She moved closer, flashing me a big grin. I fought the urge to roll my eyes. Yeah, I'm sure she'd be happy to take care of me if I just said the word.

"I am taking care of myself, but I appreciate the concern. If you want to be helpful, you could find out for me if anyone has contacted her parents."

She giggled, shaking her head. "You know I'm not supposed to give you that information, but I'll see what I can do."

"Thank you." I smiled, thankful that she was leaving. I knew she couldn't tell me, they'd been telling me that since I got here, but at least it got rid of her.

I'd been anxious about Daisy's family showing up here since the moment I got here. I would assume the hospital had been in contact with them, but as time went on and they hadn't shown up, I was starting to second guess that. I knew their relationship was strained, and that they hadn't been on the best terms when she last saw them, but this would trump everything right? I wouldn't pretend to understand family dynamics, but right now, I was glad they weren't here. I wasn't sure what I would say to them.

I stood up for a second to stretch my legs when the heart monitor on Daisy started to beep quicker. I snapped my neck in her direction, watching for any sign of movement. Was that... No, it was just wishful thinking.

Wait. Slowly, her fingers started to wiggle and I raced to the side of the bed, taking her hand in mine. The nurses had heard the beeping also, and were now in the room.

"Is everything..." Rainbow stethoscope trailed off, fixing her eyes on Daisy as her eyes started to flutter.

After a few seconds, they opened slowly, and Daisy moaned.

I put my hand to her cheek, tears pooling in my eyes. "Hi baby," I whispered, completely overcome with relief. She was awake. After all of the unknown and worry. She was awake, and whatever came after this, we would deal with, but the most important thing was that she was awake.

Daisy moaned again, unable to speak with the tube in her throat.

"Sir, I am going to need you to step outside for a second," a doctor said, stepping in front of me and adjusting something on Daisy.

"Can't I just..."

"Mr. Bosio, the doctor is going to take the breathing tube out and then you can come right back in." Rainbow Stethoscope smiled.

Unsure, I stepped back, letting them do their jobs as Daisy locked eyes on me. All the possibilities the doctor had told me started to flood my mind. Did she even recognize me? Was she trying to figure out who I was?

"Daisy, my name is Dr. Talbert. Can you hear me?"

Daisy nodded her head.

"Wonderful, I am going to get this tube out of your throat but I'm going to need your help." He checked several of her vitals as he spoke.

Daisy nodded again.

"Alright, I want you to take a deep breath and then when I count to three I want you to cough. Can you do that?" He started unscrewing things on her breathing mask.

"Okay, Daisy, here we go. One, two, three..."

Daisy coughed and right as she did, the doctor pulled the tube out. She winced, coughing a few more times before opening her mouth to speak.

"I need water," she said softly.

"Of course." Dr Talbert handed her a glass of water with a straw as I watched from the door. "Do you know why you're here Daisy?"

"I... I think..." She glanced back at me as if looking for reassurance. "There was an explosion."

I blinked my eyes in sheer surprise that she had remembered. Her doctor had me prepared for her to wake up and not be able to speak or remember anything, but so far, she was doing great.

"That's right." He smiled, nodding. "I am going to let you rest a little bit and when I come back, I'll explain your injuries to you. For now, I want you to just focus on resting and feeling better. Sound okay?"

"Thank you." She nodded with a small smile on her lips.

Dr. Talbert and the nurses left the room and Daisy and I were alone.

There were ten thousand things I wanted to say but when I opened my mouth to speak, nothing came out. Instead, Daisy spoke first.

"You're okay." She smiled, gently adjusting her weight in the bed.

I let out a sharp laugh. "I'm okay? You're the one in a hospital bed right now."

"When I left the room, I didn't think I was ever going to see you again."

"Here I am." I walked over and sat next to her on the bed, taking her hand in mine gently. "You're not going to get rid of me that easily."

Daisy frowned. "Alessandro, I never really got to tell you how sorry I am for what..."

I pressed my finger to her lips to silence her. "I don't want to talk about it. You have nothing to be sorry for, I am the one who should be sorry. I acted like a complete fool and I almost lost you because of it. I'm the one that fucked up, and I hope you'll forgive me and give me another chance."

"You were kind of an asshole." Daisy giggled. Jesus that sound was music to my ears.

"I swear to God I'll spend the rest of my life making it up to you if you'll let me." I grinned, kissing her forehead.

"I think I'll enjoy watching you try." Even lying in a hospital bed she was feisty. "Where is Ty?"

"He's back in Las Vegas with my brother. They airlifted you to Denver after the explosion and I came as soon as I could," I said, putting my arm behind her and pulling her towards me so that her head was on my chest. We fit together like a puzzle piece and I was in absolute heaven.

"Your brother?" She arched her eyebrows at me.

I nodded. "He came when he got word of the explosion. He's looking forward to meeting you."

"And Bauer?" She stiffened.

"He survived the blast, but he was arrested immediately. You don't need to worry about him anymore."

"I just can't believe he would do something like that. He dedicated his entire career to that hospital." She shook her head in disbelief.

"He's a sick man, Daisy. Nothing he did makes sense," I assured her. "This has been going on for years, and there's no way you could have known."

"How many people were killed?" she asked.

I hesitated before telling her, knowing it certainly wouldn't make her feel any better. She'd find out eventually though, and it was better that it came from me. "Ten. A doctor, two nurses, and seven patients."

Daisy closed her eyes tightly, biting her lip.

I pressed a kiss to the top of her head. "Daisy, I want you to put Bauer out of your mind. He's not going to be a problem for us anymore, I swear."

"I'll do my best." She sighed. "You know what would help?"

"I like where your head is at, but I don't think we can get away with having sex in here. Trust me the nurses are in here all the time." I chuckled, gently rubbing her shoulder. She was like one giant bruise and I was nervous to even touch her.

"Hmm, that does sound good, but I was actually thinking something more along the lines of ice cream. Cookies and cream to be exact." She smiled up at me, snuggling down deeper into my chest.

I burst out laughing. Of course that's what she was going for.

"I'll tell you what. I'll go down to the cafeteria and try to sneak some up here if you promise to stop thinking about Bauer," I tried to negotiate.

"Deal." She smiled.

"I'll be back in a few minutes. Do you need anything else while I'm gone?" I asked, prying myself away from her. I really didn't want to leave, but I'd do just about anything for her.

"Nope. Just the ice cream."

"Easy enough." I gave her one last kiss. "I love you Daisy."

"I love you too."

I slipped out the door, shutting it behind me and nearly running into a man as I did.

"Oh, I'm so sorry," he said, somewhat startled. "I didn't see you there."

"It's fine." I frowned, trying to figure out who he was and why he was trying to get into Daisy's room. He wasn't dressed like a doctor. "Are you going to see Daisy?"

"Uh, yes, I am." He frowned, looking back at me inquisitively. "I'm her father."

CHAPTER 34

ALESSANDRO

"You're Daisy's dad?" I stared back at him wide eyed, completely frozen. Seeing him here had completely blindsided me, and although I had a hundred things I wished I could say to the guy, words were failing me.

He nodded, eyeing me suspiciously. "Yes, and you are...?"

"I'm Alessandro...Alessandro Bosio. I'm..." I stuttered, trying to figure out the best way to approach this. I was pissed off that he was even here, showing up almost a week after the explosion, acting like he was concerned. I hated guys like him, those who thought they were better than others just because they were born into a certain set of circumstances. He had treated her like shit only a few weeks ago, and now here he was, ready to swoop in and be the supportive dad. It made me sick. I didn't need to know specifics, all I needed to know was that he was incredibly hurtful and disrespectful to Daisy, and that was enough. I had hated the guy before I even met him for the way he treated her, but I knew now wasn't the time or the place to approach that. Out of respect for Daisy, I would bite my tongue. On that matter at least.

"Mr. Bosio?" The nurse from earlier came towards us. "Someone will be down to take your fiancée in about thirty minutes. Dr. Talbert wants to do a scan just to be sure everything looks okay."

Fuck.

"Oh... Okay. I'll let her know." I nodded, noticing how Daisy's dad's ears perked up at the word fiancée.

The nurse smiled, turning on her heels and heading back towards the nurses' station.

"Fiancée?" He arched his eyebrow at me. "You're Daisy's fiancée?"

Now what the hell was I supposed to do? I just had to go with it. "I am," I said with a sharp breath.

"Wow." He sighed heavily, running his fingers through his hair and sliding down into one of the chairs in the hallway. "I didn't even... I had no idea she was engaged."

"It was fairly new," I said, sitting down gingerly in the seat next to him. How did I manage to get myself into these situations?

"She mentioned that she was dating someone when she was back home but I had no idea... I'm... I'm so sorry we had to meet this way." He held his hand out to me. "I'm Mark Taylor."

"It's nice to meet you, sir." I gritted my teeth, shaking his hand. "I've heard a lot about you."

He let out a sharp laugh. "Then I'm willing to bet you don't think very highly of me. I'm afraid I haven't really been there for Daisy the last few years. That's why it took me so long to come. I wasn't sure she would even want to see me. Is she..."

"She's awake," I assured him. "She was pretty badly injured though, so she's been unconscious since the bombing. The doctors think she'll be just fine but she's got a long road to go."

"Thank God." He shook his head. "Alessandro, you and I have quite a bit to talk about I think, but I'd like to go see my daughter if that's okay."

"It's fine by me," I said begrudgingly. If I had my way, he'd be booted out of the hospital right now but if Daisy wanted to see him, I certainly wasn't going to deny her that. "But I think she's the one you need to ask."

He nodded. "Thank you. I won't be long."

We stood up and I knocked gently on the door. "Daisy?"

"You're back with ice cream already? You're my hero!" She smiled, glancing over towards the door.

"Uh, actually. I ran into someone in the hallway. You have a visitor." I moved to the side, revealing her father standing behind me.

Daisy's eyes widened and she glanced back and forth between the two of us. "Wow. Hi dad," she said breathlessly.

"Hi sweetheart." Mark smiled sheepishly. Inside, I was thrilled that he felt ashamed. He absolutely should for the way he had treated her. I didn't even know the extent and it was enough to make my skin crawl.

"Alessandro, this is my..." Daisy started to introduce us.

"We met outside. He wants to talk to you for a few minutes, are you okay with that?" I asked, hoping she'd tell me to kick him out. That was something I would gladly take pleasure in.

She nodded. "Of course."

"Okay." I bent down and pressed a gentle kiss to her forehead. "I'll be right outside if you need me."

"Thank you." She smiled, squeezing my hand. I walked towards the door, reluctant to leave her alone. I knew Daisy could handle herself, but I still wanted to be there to support her. If I couldn't do that, I'd use the time to check in with Emmett and Ty and see how things were going. Hopefully it would take my mind off of the asshole at her bedside.

DAISY

When Alessandro walked out, I halfway considered calling him back into the room. I didn't have the strength to fight with my father right now, and despite the concern on his face, I had my suspicions about his reasons for being here. I wanted to think he was here because he was concerned, and deep down in my heart, I was actually glad to see him. It was amazing what a near death experience could do to someone.

We hadn't spoken since the night we had had the explosive fight after his party, and as angry as I was, something deep inside of me still wanted his approval. Or maybe more love than approval. Maybe that was all I ever really wanted. I wanted to know my dad cared about me, that I was important to him, and that was something I had battled with my entire life.

"How are you feeling sweetheart?" he asked, approaching me cautiously. He sat on the edge of the chair next to me, looking as uncomfortable as I was.

"Better than ever." I sighed, fighting the urge to roll my eyes.

He started chuckling. "You're right, that's a stupid question. I spent the entire time on the airplane trying to decide what I wanted to say."

"And that's the best that you came up with? Asking me how I'm feeling five days after I was nearly blown up?" I arched my eyebrow, cracking him a smile and cutting him a little slack. He didn't deserve it, but he was my father after all.

He smiled gently, appreciative of my peace offering. "Believe it or not, that was the best out of all the opening lines I was considering... But I agree, it sucks. So why don't I just say this?"

He paused, composing himself.

"Daisy, I am so sorry," he blurted out, tears pooling in his eyes. "Before you say anything, you need to know that. I am so sorry for the way I have treated you lately. I only ever wanted what was best for you, and I had a different idea of what that was than you did. I should have just let you follow your heart but instead, I tried to force my own ideals on you and now I've caused us to spend the last several years at each other's throats instead of connecting. And it was entirely my fault. I'm sorry, and I will never be able to tell you just how much."

I opened my mouth to speak, but I was too shell shocked to form words. I hadn't expected much from my dad, let alone an apology. Maybe me nearly dying had had an effect on him as well.

"Dad, I..."

"No." He held up his hand, shaking his head. "Please don't say anything. All of this is my fault. If I hadn't sent you to work with Dr. Bauer..."

My heart stopped at the very mention of his name, and I realized I didn't even know what had happened to him after the blast. I couldn't fathom the idea that my father knew what Bauer was up to all these years. He had his faults, but there was no way he was involved in anything like that. It still made me sick to think about all the people Bauer had hurt over the years, Talia just being one of them.

"There's no way you could have known what Dr. Bauer was up to, dad," I said, hoping that that was the case.

"I know, but if we hadn't insisted you come to Las Vegas to work with him, none of this would have happened. He was my friend, I thought... I thought... I never imagined he was abusing his position to do such terrible things. I mean, my God, Daisy. He killed a woman, did you know that?"

I bit my lip, nodding gently. A sense of relief washed over me that he hadn't known about it, and that he was so disgusted by Bauer's actions. My father took my hand in his, holding it gently.

"I wish I had something more to say to you besides I'm sorry, but that's all that seems to matter to me right now. I'm sorry for everything. For not believing in you, or supporting your dreams, and for putting you in this position, and for not being the parent you deserved all these years. If you give me another chance, I swear, I will do whatever it takes to make things right with you. All I want is to fix our relationship." I had hardly ever seen my dad cry before, but a few errant tears were starting to drip down his cheeks and I could see how torn up by all of this he was. It was such a welcome change that I nearly burst into tears myself. It didn't change the past between us, but it was a start and it gave me hope for our future relationship.

"I appreciate that dad, but it's going to take some time. Maybe we could start with dinner? I'd like to come see everyone when I get out of here."

He smiled widely. "I would love that. And you know, if you'd like to come back home to recover for a few weeks, your mom and I would love to have you."

"I know you would." I smiled. "But I think I'm going to go back to Las Vegas with Alessandro as soon as they release me. I promise I'll visit as soon as I'm feeling up to it though."

"Ah yes." He grinned. "Your fiancé seems like a wonderful guy. I'm looking forward to getting to know him. Why don't you bring him with you when you come to visit?"

I frowned. Fiancé? Had Alessandro told him we were engaged? Or had I seriously hit my head so hard that I didn't remember him proposing? Either way, I had to stop myself from laughing. He sure was something.

"Yes." I smiled. "He is. I think you guys will love him."

My dad stood up and kissed my cheek. "I won't keep you much longer. It's so good to see you sweetheart, and I'm so glad to know you're okay."

"I'll see you soon dad." I smiled as he walked out.

A nurse came in after a few minutes and checked my vitals, making all kinds of notes in my file before rushing out again. She let me know that they'd be in to take me for more testing in a few minutes. I was starting to get restless, and was about to stand up, right as Alessandro came back into the room.

"Hey!" he scolded, rushing towards my side. "You're not supposed to get up without someone to support you."

"I just wanted to take a little walk." I pouted, hoping my frown would make him cave and help me out of the bed.

"No way. Your leg is broken, you're not going anywhere until the doctor says it's okay. Now, climb back in bed like a good little girl and I'll give you your ice cream," he teased, winking as he pulled the covers back up around me.

"I'm fine, Alessandro. It would probably do my body some good to get up and move around. I'm sure we could find some crutches." I propped myself up, not willing to accept staying put just yet.

Alessandro shook his head. "The doctor said to stay put. You better keep your cute little ass in this bed until I say otherwise, or there will be serious consequences."

"You're hilarious." I rolled my eyes, sulking.

"And I can already tell you're going to be a terrible patient." He chuckled, sitting down on the bed next to me. "Seriously Daisy, I know you're feeling better, but you're not out of the woods. You're always preaching to me that I need to take care of myself, now it's your turn."

"Thank goodness I have a fiancé to take care of me," I teased, taking his hand.

Alessandro immediately froze. "I panicked. I told the nurses I was your fiancé so that they would give me information on you, and then one of them called me that in front of your dad," he rambled, looking completely terrified of how I was going to react. "Don't be mad at me, I was just worried about you and I..."

I leaned forward, kissing him gently. "Would you relax? It's okay. I kind of like being called your fiancé."

Alessandro broke out into a smile. "You do?"

I nodded, giggling softly.

"In that case..." Alessandro's smile was so bright it was nearly blinding. He reached into his jacket pocket and pulled out a small red box. He dropped down to his knees in front of me, slowly opening it.

I covered my mouth with my hands, both nervous and ecstatic. Was this actually happening?

"Marry me, Daisy." He grinned. "I love you more than I could ever describe. I love the way you are with my son, and the way you love him like he was your own. And I love the way you leave your dirty clothes right next to the hamper instead of putting them inside, and the way my drain gets clogged with your hair. And I love the sound of you playing the piano in my house and the way the entire house smells delicious when I come home to you cooking. I love how you hold me accountable, you have from the moment I met you, and I love how you push me to be a better person. I've never had someone that challenges me the way you do, and even though it's annoying as hell sometimes, I can't tell you how much it means to me. I love how passionate you are, and how you're not afraid to follow your dreams, even if it means completely changing your plan. I want to spend the rest of my life getting to know you, and showing you just how much I love you. I want to give you the life you deserve. Please, Daisy. Please say you'll marry me."

By the time Alessandro was done with his speech, I was trying so hard to listen but I didn't hear anything. I was overcome with happiness, unable to concentrate on what he was saying at all. I could feel tears start to well in my eyes as I leaned down and took his face in my hands. "Of course I will."

Alessandro smiled even wider, if possible, and took the ring out of the box. He slipped it gently on my finger, both of us staring at the sparkler on my hand. It was beautiful, so spectacular that it nearly took my breath away. I had no idea how Alessandro had pulled this off, or how long he had been planning it, but my heart felt like it could burst with happiness.

The last few weeks of my life had been such an emotional rollercoaster and now here we were. There was nothing in the world that could make me happier than the idea of spending the rest of my life with Ty and Alessandro, my own perfect little family. I hated to think about everything we all had to go through to get to this point, but at the end of the day, our love was the only thing that mattered.

I couldn't wait to get home to tell Ty the good news, but right now, all I wanted to do was enjoy my time with Alessandro, and relish in this moment. We may have been cooped up in a stuffy hospital room, but right now, I was on top of the world.

CHAPTER 35

D AISY
"Okay, easy does it," Alessandro coached, holding on tightly to my arm and guiding me into the house. It had been a few weeks since the explosion and I had finally been cleared to fly home. Despite weeks of rehab and most of my wounds healing up, Alessandro insisted on treating me like I was made of glass. It annoyed me at first, but it was kind of cute and I knew there was no arguing with him. He hadn't left my side the entire time we were in Denver, refusing to even get a hotel and sleeping on that awful pull-out couch in the hospital. It was nice to finally be home and be in our own space.

Alessandro fumbled with the keypad and let us both into the house. I hobbled in on my crutches. I was definitely counting down the days until I could get out of this cast and my leg would heal.

"Let me just get the lights..." Alessandro flipped the switch and as the foyer lit up, I saw the group of people with balloons and posters and flowers and all kinds of things staring back at me. Ty, Peyton, Q, Joe, even a few people I didn't recognize.

"Surprise!" they all yelled.

"Welcome home Daisy!" Ty grinned ear to ear, bouncing towards me. He wrapped his arms around my waist as tightly as he could.

"Not so hard, buddy." Alessandro chuckled, rustling his hair. "She's still recovering."

"I missed you!" I kissed the top of his head and gave him a tight squeeze back. "Did you plan all of this?"

"For weeks." Joe smiled. "It's been all he could talk about. How are you feeling?"

"Not too bad actually. It's been a long day of traveling but I'm happy to be home."

"And we're so happy to have you." Peyton gave me a big hug. "You look great! No one would even know you were nearly blown apart a few weeks ago." She winked.

"Okay." Alessandro let out a sharp laugh, shaking his head. "Not in front of the kid."

"Ah, come on dad." Ty rolled his eyes. "All the kids at school are talking about it. My teacher thinks it's so adorable how you saved Daisy."

"The kid's right. The phones have been ringing off the hook here." Q laughed. "You guys are celebrities."

My cheeks flushed with embarrassment. In preparation for Dr. Bauer's trial, small details of the incident had started to leak out. One of the biggest stories the media was focusing on was Alessandro and how his heroics saved so many lives. And what's a good story without a romantic twist? Somehow they had gotten details about the only reason he had been there was to save me, the woman he loved and wanted to spend the rest of his life with. I had to admit, it was a pretty amazing story and I was over-the-moon proud of Alessandro, but we had both been hounded by reporters and the media who were hungry for a comment. Now that we were back in Las Vegas, I was sure it would only get worse.

"Daisy, you and I haven't had a chance to meet yet." A man came forward who looked just like Alessandro, though a little more gray in his beard. He handed me a bouquet of flowers. "I'm Emmett, Alessandro's older and better-looking brother."

"You wish!" Alessandro laughed, slinging his arm around his brother's neck. "Good to see you, man. I thought you'd have to be back by now."

"Well, sometimes it takes an explosion to remind you how much your family matters to you." He smiled. "Turns out I can do a lot of the day-to-day stuff I need to from just about anywhere."

I felt a small pang of frustration that my own family wasn't here, but that was something we were working on. It would take time, but someday I was confident things could be repaired between us and in the meantime, I had a lot of people who loved and supported me. "I hope that means you'll be around more often."

"Absolutely. I'm looking forward to getting to know my new sister-in-law."

"We're not married yet," Alessandro reminded them. "We're going to take it slow." We had been discussing this quite a bit and even though Alessandro would have done it in that hospital room, we decided to give ourselves a little bit of time to settle in.

"Well, we live in a city where there are about four hundred places you could do it at any second if you change your mind," Peyton suggested.

"She's right, you can even have Elvis do it in a drive-through!" Joe added.

"I think the only thing we're thinking of doing right now is getting Daisy laid down so she can rest." Alessandro arched his eyebrow.

"Good point. We'll get out of your hair and let you guys settle in," Emmett said. "Who's up for some pizza? I'm buying." The group headed out the front door and we were finally left alone.

"I'm sorry." Alessandro kissed me softly. "I had no idea they were all going to be here."

"It's okay, that was really sweet. It was good to see everyone."

"Why don't you get settled upstairs in our room and I'll clean up down here and bring you something to eat?" he suggested.

"Are you sure you want me back in your room? I'm happy to sleep down the hall while I'm recovering. I'll be up a lot and it's kind of noisy..."

"Not a shot." Alessandro cut me off. "Go get comfortable and I'll be right up."

I got myself up the stairs and changed into some sweats before climbing on top of the bed. It felt like absolute heaven after the last few weeks of sleeping on the hospital cot and I knew Alessandro would feel the same. It was nice to just have a few minutes to myself, something that was hard to come by right now. Everything had been a whirlwind and it was hard to process all of it. So much had changed in such a short amount of time but I felt more settled than I had in a long time. Dr. Bauer was behind bars where he couldn't hurt anyone anymore, things were moving in the right direction with my family, and most importantly, my life here with Ty and Alessandro was like a dream. It was a dream I didn't know I had, but I was realizing it was something I could absolutely not live without. I wasn't exactly sure what the future held, but I wasn't nearly as focused on it as I used to be. I was able to be happy and content right here where I was. Well, with everything except for my itchy cast... I was ready for that thing to go.

"Okay." Alessandro came into the room carrying an array of food and setting it next to me on the bed. "Does something look good to you? Otherwise I can order take out."

"This is perfect." I smiled, eyeing the grilled cheese he had made. "Your chef skills are getting better."

"I wish I could say I made this but Joe's wife left enough food to feed a small army. This is just a small sample."

"That was really sweet of her. And for them to take Ty for a few days while we get settled again."

Alessandro nodded. "We're lucky to have friends like them. Even if you haven't officially met her yet."

"I'm sure I'll love her. Anyone who puts up with Joe has got to be a saint."

"Very true. Although the same could be said for me."

"You're not so bad." I grinned, propping myself up in bed. "Just a little hot tempered."

"More like hot and bothered." He chuckled. "How many weeks did the doctor want you to wait before we could have sex again?" Alessandro had been patient but both of us were desperate for each other. We hadn't gotten to properly make up yet and we were both champing at the bit.

"He said 3 more weeks for rigorous activity... but if you could be gentle..."

Alessandro's eyes got big and a temptatious smile tugged at his lips. "Oh I can be gentle. In fact, I don't think I've ever shown you just how gentle I can be. Why don't you lie back and let me take care of you like you deserve?"

"How can I refuse an offer like that?" Alessandro brushed his lips softly against mine and I set my sandwich to the side. Food could wait. I was hungry for something else.

6 weeks later

Alessandro held my hand tightly as we walked out of the courtroom. It was a blazing hot day in Las Vegas, but it didn't stop the crowds of reporters gathering at the sentencing for Dr. Bauer.

"Mr. Bosio, do you think the sentence was fair?"

"How are you feeling, Daisy?"

They shouted questions but Alessandro led us through the crowd confidently until we got to the car. Once we were inside, I felt like I could finally breathe. Moments ago, Bauer had been sentenced to life in prison without the possibility of parole. It was the highest-level sentence he could receive and it immediately was like a weight lifted off of my chest. He really was going away forever and would never be able to hurt anyone ever again.

It was tough to stomach at first. The man had been my mentor. I'd looked up to him and learned nearly everything I knew about being a doctor from him. Little did I know what was happening behind the scenes though. It made me nauseous that I was a part of any of it, but I knew there was no way I could have known what he was really up to, and Alessandro reminded me of that all the time.

Things between us were better and stronger than ever before, and we'd even made progress with wedding planning. We were both excited for it, but were also enjoying just being a family right now. We'd settled into a routine and life with Ty that felt so right and so seamless that I hardly remembered what my life was like before. My parents had been out to visit a few times and things were looking better than ever with them as well. I knew it would take time and we never had the relationship I wanted, but we were getting there, and they were thrilled with the opportunity to be grandparents to Ty. Maybe they were looking at this as some sort of second chance, but they doted on him and he loved them just as much.

Alessandro set his hand on my knee as we started to drive away, swerving through the mass of people. "You doing okay?"

I nodded. "I finally feel a sense of closure with him. He's really not going to be able to hurt us anymore."

"That's right, babe. And I'm pretty confident that he'll get exactly what's coming to him in prison."

"How are you so sure of that?" I eyed him suspiciously. Alessandro had done an incredible job of trying to stay out of everything to do with Dr. Bauer but I knew he had his limits. Bauer had gone after nearly everyone that Alessandro loved all because he was jealous of his success, and if I was being honest, I could understand where Alessandro was coming from. I craved a little retribution of my own.

Alessandro chuckled, refusing to look at me. "On the record, just a feeling. But off the record, I have friends in some pretty low places with nothing to lose. Bauer won't last long on the inside."

"Is it wrong that I'm glad to hear that?"

"Not at all." He shook his head.

"Where are we going?" I noticed Alessandro had turned off the highway and we weren't headed in the direction of home anymore.

"I just wanted a second to clear our minds after court this morning. And I've got a surprise for you." He whipped into a parking spot quickly.

"What kind of surprise?" I questioned, not able to be patient. I knew he had something up his sleeve for weeks, and I was dying to finally find out.

"Relax." His grin told me he knew exactly what he was doing. "Come on."

I followed him down a pathway and into the park to where a small bench was. When we got up close, I could see it was a bench that had been put there in memory of Talia.

"This city holds a lot of memories for my family, and most of them are bad. I lost my wife, I almost lost my son, and I almost lost the love of my life," Alessandro started. "I used to love Las Vegas, especially when we first moved here, it felt like the Wild West. But now it just kind of feels suffocating, you know?" He kept his eyes on the bench as he spoke. I grabbed his hand, stroking the back of it gently. Alessandro let out a heavy breath and reached into his pocket. "I have been doing a lot of thinking and with me taking a back seat with the organization for a while, I think it might be time for a move."

I arched my eyebrows at him in shock. This was the very last thing I was expecting. "A move?"

Alessandro nodded, handing me a piece of paper. There were three one-way tickets to San Diego printed on it. One for me, one for him, and one for Ty. "When we first met, you told me how much you wanted to be in LA. Something about the sunshine and the adventure." He chuckled. "I know San Diego isn't exactly LA, but I think it's the kind of place we could raise a family in. Smaller, less crowded, beautiful beaches. It still has a lot of the character, but much lower crime rates and I think we can both agree that's something we need right now." He grinned.

"You're serious about this?" I asked, trying to process all of it. He was right. The timing couldn't be better. Alessandro had spent the last few weeks tying up loose ends at work so that he could be less involved and I hadn't even found another job yet. Ty would be out of school for the summer soon. But this was a huge commitment. Alessandro had spent years building a life and a home here.

"I'm positive." He took my hand. "Like I said, I'm ready to move on from some of these memories and start making new ones with you. And our own family. So what do you say? How about it?"

I couldn't help but smile. "I think it sounds incredible."

"I was hoping you'd say that." Alessandro's smile was a mile wide. He swept me off of my feet, spinning me around as he kissed me.

This was perfect for us. It was a new start we all needed. A fresh start. A place where we could build our lives together, where we could raise our kids. A place that was full of adventure and opportunity and so many new things for us. It felt like we were closing the door on a really rough chapter in both of our lives and moving on together towards something much greater.

There was something kind of fun about the future being unknown. Neither of us had any idea what was to come, but we knew we had each other and we had Ty. And we were ready for our next big adventure.

THE END

EPILOGUE

A LESSANDRO
"Here?" I asked, nearly out of breath.

Daisy frowned from her spot on the recliner, tilting her head slightly to the left. "A little bit higher."

I moved the mirror up the wall about an inch, my muscles literally shaking; I had been holding it so long trying to find the perfect spot for it. "Better?"

"Too far." She grinned, clearly getting a kick out of all of this.

I fought the urge to roll my eyes and indulged her, slightly sliding it back the other direction. "Now?"

"That's perfect babe," Daisy said, finally satisfied.

"Great." I grimaced, setting the mirror on the floor and hammering the nail into the wall so we could finally be done with this project. We'd been at it all morning and I was dying to be done. Interior decorating wasn't exactly my forte and Daisy, who was usually a reasonable person, had gone completely over the top with this nursery. I indulged every bit of it though, and even though I acted like I was irritated, I was over the moon that we even had this opportunity.

In just a few short weeks, our baby girl would be born and our family would be complete. Daisy was 37 weeks pregnant and getting bigger by the second. It was incredible to watch her go through all of these changes and only made me fall deeper in love with her. I had been through this before, when Talia was pregnant with Ty, but

266

it was all new for Daisy. Every kick and movement and new craving were magical. And it was even more magical to watch Ty get ready to be a big brother. We had gotten married in a small ceremony on the beach when we moved out here, and hadn't even been trying when Daisy got pregnant. We'd been apprehensive at first to tell Ty since he'd dealt with so many changes lately, but he couldn't have been more excited. All he could talk about was what he was going to teach his baby sister and what they were going to do together. He had a long list of potential names picked out and told every single person we met that he was getting a little sister. Ty's big mouth had even been how Daisy's parents found out we were expecting. They had come to visit for the weekend and the very first thing Ty said to them was that she was pregnant. It was adorable how excited he was about the whole thing, I just hoped that excitement would continue when she was here and he wasn't the center of attention anymore. We'd been trying to prepare him as best we could.

The last few months had meant major changes for all of us, but the longer we were out here, the more I was sure that this was the right move for us. We had found the perfect house on the beach that was just north of San Diego. I spent most mornings running along the shore or teaching Ty how to surf in the waves while Daisy watched from our balcony. I hadn't decided exactly what I wanted to do yet, but Daisy had been hired at a children's hospital close to where we lived and was working as a Child Life Specialist. She was getting to work with and help kids just like she always wanted, and the best part was that she was only working a few days a week. It was the perfect situation, especially with the baby coming.

"You know, now that I'm looking at it..." Daisy teased, tapping her finger on her chin. "It maybe could be an inch or two higher."

"That's it." I tossed the hammer to the floor and made my way over towards her. "I'm cutting you off." I scooped her up into my arms and carried her out of the room.

"Alessandro stop!" She giggled as I carted her down the hallway towards our bedroom. When I got inside, I gently tossed her onto the bed and then pinned her down.

"You are officially... banned from that room... until the baby comes," I said, peppering her with kisses.

"But it's not done yet! It has to be perfect!" She pretended to pout.

"And it will be. I'll make sure of it." I lay down next to her. "But you are going to make yourself crazy obsessing over the details. She's not even going to be in there for the first few months of her life, everything will be fine."

Daisy sighed. "I know. You're right."

"Of course I'm right, I'm always right." I chuckled. "Now how about we work on getting you to relax." I started rubbing her shoulders, hoping to ease her tension.

"That sounds perfect." She smiled, melting into my touch.

"Mom! Dad!" Ty yelled from down the hallway.

"Ugh." I groaned. "Maybe if we're really quiet he won't know we're in here."

Daisy laughed. "You're terrible. We're about to have another one of those you know."

"I know. Which is why we should be taking advantage of any alone time we can get." I was only half kidding.

"Dad!" Ty yelled again, throwing the door open and coming right into the bedroom. "You promised we could go surfing."

"I did." I let out a heavy sigh, officially giving up on getting any alone time with my wife this morning. "I'll change and then we can go."

"Don't you think you could take one day off?" Daisy arched her eyebrow at both of us.

"Champions don't take days off, babe." I kissed her cheek and grabbed my suit to change into.

"He's six, Alessandro." She rolled her eyes.

"Seven in three weeks!" Ty gave her a giant grin. "Besides, if I want to compete in the competition next month I have to be perfect."

"Well, I think you're already good," she countered, propping herself up on the bed.

"You have to say that, you're my mom." Ty rolled his eyes and headed back to the living room to wait for me.

It still took my breath away every time I heard him call her mom, and I wasn't sure I would ever be fully used to it. It was both beautiful and heart breaking. The bond that Daisy and Ty had was like nothing I had ever seen before, and every single day I thanked God for bringing her into our lives. But it still stung that he was never really able to know his biological mother. There were so many parts of Talia that I saw in him and I wished more than anything he had been able to know her. One thing Daisy and I made sure of though was that he would never forget her. We had pictures of her around the house, and we made it a point to talk about her often. Ty deserved to know how many he had in his life that loved him, and Talia was included in that. I wasn't a particularly religious person, but I liked to think that she was up above us, smiling on the life we'd made and how far he and I had come. I liked to think that she handpicked Daisy for us and made our paths cross.

So much had changed in the last few years, and there was still so much to come. I never pictured myself being happy laying low like this in a California beach town, but this place and this family were everything I had ever dreamed of.

And for the first time in my life, I felt at peace. That I didn't have to chase after anything because I had everything I ever wanted right in front of me.

Don't miss out!

Visit the website below and you can sign up to receive emails whenever Alice Knight publishes a new book. There's no charge and no obligation.

https://books2read.com/r/B-A-JXIAB-OENTC

BOOKS 2 READ

Connecting independent readers to independent writers.

Also by Alice Knight